D0923460

SING
ME
TO
SLEEP

Burton, Gabi, author.
Sing me to sleep

2023
33305257529358
ca   06/27/23

Sing Me to Sleep

Gabi Burton

BLOOMSBURY

NEW YORK   LONDON   OXFORD   NEW DELHI   SYDNEY

BLOOMSBURY YA
Bloomsbury Publishing Inc., part of Bloomsbury Publishing Plc
1385 Broadway, New York, NY 10018

BLOOMSBURY and the Diana logo are trademarks of Bloomsbury Publishing Plc

First published in the United States of America in June 2023 by Bloomsbury YA

Text copyright © 2023 by Gabi Burton
Illustrations copyright © 2023 by Kaitlin June
Map copyright © 2023 by Sara Corbett

All rights reserved. No part of this publication may be reproduced or transmitted in any form
or by any means, electronic or mechanical, including photocopying, recording, or any information
storage or retrieval system, without prior permission in writing from the publisher.

Bloomsbury books may be purchased for business or promotional use. For information on
bulk purchases please contact Macmillan Corporate and Premium Sales Department at
specialmarkets@macmillan.com

Library of Congress Cataloging-in-Publication Data
Names: Burton, Gabi, author.
Title: Sing me to sleep / Gabi Burton.
Description: New York: Bloomsbury, 2023.
Summary: Saoirse Sorkova, a murderous siren whose very existence is illegal,
is forced to work with the prince she hates to hunt a deadly killer—herself.
Identifiers: LCCN 2022048118 (print) | LCCN 2022048119 (e-book)
ISBN 978-1-5476-1037-2 (hardcover) • ISBN 978-1-5476-1038-9 (e-book)
Subjects: CYAC: Sirens (Mythology)—Fiction. | Assassins—Fiction. | Fantasy. |
LCGFT: Fantasy fiction. | Novels.
Classification: LCC PZ7.1.B8873 Si 2023 (print) | LCC PZ7.1.B8873 (e-book) |
DDC [Fic]—dc23
LC record available at https://lccn.loc.gov/2022048118

Book design by Yelena Safronova
Typeset by Westchester Publishing Services
Printed and bound in the U.S.A.
2 4 6 8 10 9 7 5 3 1

To find out more about our authors and books visit www.bloomsbury.com
and sign up for our newsletters.

For Black girls everywhere who feel like they're not enough.
You are. I promise.

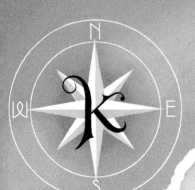

ENEMY
THE BARRIER

KETZAL
WITCHES

KEI

SINU
HUMANS

IDRIS
AIR FAE

JEUNE RIVER

GREYSN RIVER

SAOIRSE'S HOME

VANIHAIL
WATER FAE

PALACE

HARAYA HALL

BARRACKS

BHAIRI SEA

TERRITORY

KRILL
WITCHES

RDRE

KURR VALLEY
EARTH FAE

LAKE RY'ANNEN

PHYDAN
FIRE FAE

SERINGTON
MIXED FAE

BLIDDON
EARTH FAE

SING
ME
TO
SLEEP

CHAPTER ONE

Poisoned Lullaby

My mark has a death wish. Which, I suppose, is convenient for me.

It's two ticks since I stepped into the pub, I've yet to give any indication of my intent to seduce him, and he's already palming my ass like it's a tankard of cheap ale.

He hasn't even offered me a sodding drink.

My first instinct: snatch his wrist and twist until I feel the satisfying snap of cracking bone.

I know better than to trust my first instinct.

Instead, I turn swiftly, smile sweetly, and gaze into his eyes like they're a map to someplace less seedy with someone less slimy.

At the sight of my face, his jaw—scratch that, his entire face—goes slack, and his hand slides off my ass like it's slicked with oil.

It's typical.

I'm beautiful. Not arrogant, just honest. My birthright is coiling men so tightly around my finger, they'll willingly follow me to an early, watery grave—beauty is a given.

The eyes of the entire pub trail my every move, drinking me in, savoring me like a glass of the disgustingly sweet wine the fae like to drink. They watch my mark, too, with dark scowls instead of salacious leers. Not because of what he is but because he's drawn my attention in a room full of men who'd welcome me with open arms and silk sheets.

I drown out the feel of their eyes and focus on my mark. He was brazen enough to touch me on sight, but now he can't work up the nerve to speak.

Some marks require more effort. A few drinks to loosen up or a few minutes of idle conversation. This one won't need it. The cinnamon spice of his lust sits on my tongue and burns my throat, giving him away. I might not even have to sing to convince him to drink the poison stashed in my dress.

As a siren, I've always been able to feel emotions. Some are basic: sadness feels heavy and cold; happiness is light and warm. Some are more complex: bitterness is sharp like a sting, hot like a flame, and persistent like a bad cold. I can block out the way emotions feel against my skin, but when they're strong, I can't turn off the way they taste.

Without a word, I sink into a wooden chair at a pub table and cross one leg over the other. The hem of my inky-black dress slithers up my thighs.

I flash my mark an inviting smile and pat the empty chair next to me. He tumbles into it, eyes wide. The flavor of his lust mixes with something stale and bitter like rank alcohol— nerves.

As I lean forward, I have the satisfaction of watching his gaze slide from my luminescent honey-colored eyes to the dip in the front of my dress. The heat of his desire spikes, wrapping around me like a blanket of fire. I place a hand on his lower thigh, close enough to his knee to be benign yet far enough up his leg that his body tenses.

He swallows.

Biting back a smirk, I lean farther, pressing my full lips to the curve of his ear. He reeks of nerves, sweat, and freshly baked bread. "Follow me." I don't sing—not yet—but I slip a musical lilt into my voice.

He clenches the table so tightly, his nails leave indents in the wood. "Uhhh . . ."

I take it as a yes.

Standing, I grin, slow and seductive, before walking away, making sure the ass he seems so taken with sways with each step.

I don't need to hear the thunk of his boots behind me to know he's following.

The enraptured pub crowd parts for me like a pair of gossiping lips in a schoolyard. Their unbridled lust nearly sears a hole through my tongue, but no one tries to speak to me as I make my way through the side door of the pub and into the alley, breathing in the crisp Keirdren air.

It's a perfect night. The only light comes from the stars and the white light of the slivered moon. Mist hangs in the air, engulfing me in its cool, damp familiarity. The alley is still. The dark cobblestones are neatly paved and speckled with shades of brown and gray—a sharp contrast to the navy-brick exterior of the surrounding buildings.

My mark enters the alley.

I suck in another misty breath before turning to face him. His green eyes are still dazed as the pub door slams shut. We make quite the pair: me, armed with my face and vocal cords, and him, a dreamy expression and lovelorn eyes.

"What's your name?" he sighs out.

I smile and step closer. The toes of my shoes kiss those of his leather boots. "Saoirse." It comes out a breathy whisper.

My mark makes a noise that isn't a word.

I inhale, taking in fog through my nose, my mouth, my pores. The water tingles where it touches me, calling out. Urging me to act quickly. I tamp the feeling down like leaves at harvest. I want to take my time. Savor my kill.

The mist condenses around me, forming a sheet of water that curls into a long tendril.

He stares as I twirl the ribbon of water in my hands, around and around.

The water calls me to sing, but instead, I speak. "You touched me when you saw me. Why?"

His eyes follow the swirling water. "Y-you're beautiful."

I tilt my head to one side. The water speeds up, as do his eyes. "That means you can touch me?"

"Y-you're—"

"Beautiful," I finish with a roll of my eyes. "Yes, you said that. Do you make a habit of touching beautiful women without permission?" My eyes flash silver with my words.

His heartbeat quickens. He opens his mouth but doesn't speak.

Irritated, I release the water, and it splatters against the cobblestones, splashing his boots and my bare ankles. It sends a surge of power pulsing through me, and I can no longer stall my craving.

Kill.

My instincts tug at my heart, my lips part, and a song pours out. Soft, soulful, wordless.

What little expression remains on my mark's face melts like chocolate in the sun, leaving those bright green eyes vacant.

I am no longer smiling.

I bend toward him, still singing. He mirrors my movements, a puppet on a taut string, poised to snap.

Silver eyes holding his, I slide a hand down the front of my dress and slip out the vial of *shikazhe*. The midnight-blue color of the liquid gives away the vial's contents on sight. Still, when I hold it out, he takes it without question.

"Two drops on your tongue," I whisper.

Never, not once, does he look away from my eyes as he pops out the cork and tilts the vial, dropping two beads of blue onto his tongue.

I gently extricate the vial from his hands, tuck it back in my dress, and turn to leave.

There's a *thud* as his body hits the cobblestone. I don't pause.

The fun part is over.

My fingers plunge into the leather pouch tied around my neck for the small clay bead etched with golden runes. I set the gray bead on my tongue and click it into place, embedding it behind my false wooden tooth.

The transformation of the *keil* bead ripples across my face like a raindrop in still water.

My hair—dark and thick and wild—loses its shine, and the silken-smooth skin of my face—deep brown, like the bark of a samsam tree—withers into a burn that stretches from eyebrow line to chin across the right side of my face.

My steps echo against the cobblestones as I leave the alley. This part of South Vanihail is littered with shops, pubs, and restaurants in neat rows. Torches hang from light posts at each block, but their flickering does little to illuminate the quiet streets.

I plod to an alley a few storefronts away where I've stashed my leather satchel and extra set of clothes. It's a comfort to arm myself with loose pants, a thick wool cloak, and my usual worn leather boots.

I toss my pub clothes in my bag and shoulder it. The mist wisps against the exposed skin of my face as I leave the alley. It beckons to me, *sings* to me, but I tug up my hood and lower my head.

Only one kill tonight.

Most everything is closed this time of night, so aside from the whistling wind and occasional wandering water fae drunk on berry wine, the streets are quiet.

I trudge out of the clustered center to the sprawling outskirts of the capital sector of Vanihail. My already aching feet whine with the knowledge that I have another long walk ahead of me after this. It doesn't help that the paved cobblestones fade into dusty dirt roads as I cross from South Vanihail into North Vanihail. Time spent maintaining the sector decreases the farther you get from the coast—the farther you move from the Palace.

As I drag myself up the final hill, I spit out my *keil* bead and tuck it away. I sense my Employer's presence before I see him leaned up against the trunk of the samsam tree we've designated as our meeting point.

His silhouette mirrors the tree's: lofty, dark, and skinny, with spindly limbs that stretch longer than looks natural. As always, my Employer's face is hidden by nightfall and the shield of his cloak.

I stop a half-dozen paces away.

For a few ticks, we're silent, observing each other.

He speaks first. "It's done?" His voice is deep, gravelly, and no doubt disguised by a *keil* bead.

"Yes, sir," I say.

I know little about my Employer, he knows little about me, and we both know better than to ask questions. Still, I've gleaned the essentials. He's a right-leaning ambidex (most Keirdren soldiers are), he pays on time, and he's an assassin for the Raze—an infamous group of powerful fae who slaughters other powerful fae for a hefty fee at the request of still other powerful fae.

Usually, the Raze doesn't employ women, but five lunes ago, I became the first. Unofficially.

Everything about my Employer is calm. I run my tongue along the roof of my mouth, searching for an emotion other than the earthy flavor of his apathy.

As always, there's nothing.

A soft jingle of coins precedes my Employer dropping a burlap bag of gold ranis at my feet. "The Raze and Spektryl thank you for your service."

I've never met Spektryl and I doubt I ever will. As the Raze assassin credited with the highest number of kills, he's likely busy. At least, he used to be.

Five lunes ago, Spektryl stopped killing, and when the Raze hired me, all my kills for them were credited to him. My Employer has never told me why and, as long as he continues to pay on time, I don't ask.

I swoop forward and snatch the bag of ranis. "Thank you, sir."

With a nod, my Employer moves away from the samsam tree and melts into the night as though consumed by fog. An air fae trick.

I met him after I curled my fist around a sleazy water fae's throat behind a pub and squeezed until he stopped breathing. My Employer slinked up behind me with an alluring proposition: How would I like to get paid to kill?

It was an easy yes.

With my satchel weighted by gold and shoulders weighted by exhaustion, I descend the hill, headed home.

By the time I've made it into North Vanihail's residential area, my body aches. The houses are smaller here. Short, squat, and mostly made of rotting wooden slats coated in chipped paint, with thatched roofs that leak year-round. There was once a trail of dirt we called a street, but it's been overgrown by weeds that have since died, leaving a sad brown path in its wake.

My time in the Vanihailian Barracks means I'm in excellent physical condition, but I'm still half-asleep as I stumble up the rose-lined pathway to the tiny white mill house I call home.

I raise a hand to knock on the blue wooden door when it's yanked open, and I'm accosted by a nimble pair of brown arms twining around my waist and a flop of dark hair against my chest.

"Pinecone!" the creature attached to the arms cheers.

My exhaustion goes up in flames. With a wide smile, I return the hug, lifting her and spinning her around. "Hey, Beansprout!"

As a sprig, Rain had nicknamed the family after objects that snatched her attention. I was dubbed "Pinecone" and she "Beansprout."

I'm still carrying her as I march through the front door and kick it closed behind me. "Mom! Dad!" I screech, voice muffled from Rain's big hair. "It's me!"

"Is that my Pinecone?" Running footsteps thunk against the steps, and a breath later, my mother rushes into the main room. She wears a long white nightgown and forest-green slippers, and her hair is wrapped in olive leaves for the night. She claims it softens her coarse head of dark curls, but I think it reminds her of the home she left behind in the earth fae sector, Kurr Valley.

None of us is related by blood—hell, we're not even the same species—but they're my family just the same. Scratch that, they're my whole damned world.

I taste the fruity zing of Mom's excitement as she catches sight of me and charges.

I don't have time to set Rain down before she sweeps both of us into a hug. "Did the Barracks let you out before graduation?"

Her hug jostles the ranis in my bag, and the coins clink together. I jerk away. "Not exactly . . ."

My mom's excitement flickers away, replaced with something that stinks of disappointment, tinged with rotting fear.

Without missing a beat, she scoops Rain into her arms, taking her from me. She disguises the action as affection, but I see it for what it is. She's protecting Rain from me.

It stings.

More than stings.

I pretend not to notice.

"Saoirse." This is a different voice. Deeper.

I surreptitiously adjust the strap of my bag, slinging it against my back, out of sight and, hopefully, out of his mind. "Hey, Dad."

My father is a large man. Tall, hulking, bulky from hours tossing around heavy sacks of flour in the mill, with black hair and skin like burnt umber. He looks like he hasn't smiled in lunes. Or slept in lunes, for that matter.

I try to hug him, but he gives a sharp nod to the bag strapped across my chest. "What's in the bag, Saoirse?"

I fold my arms, sensing an impending spat. "Money."

Dad's expression doesn't change, but his stance stiffens. "Rain."

"Yes?" Rain sidles around Mom and hugs me from the side.

"Go wait in your room. Your sister will come see you in a moment."

"But—"

"*Now*, Rain."

She pouts but scurries away, shooting me one last look before darting to her bedroom or, more likely, to the top of the stairs to eavesdrop.

Twisting the bag around to my front, I drop the sack of coins on the floor. "You didn't have to do that." I nudge the bag closer to him with my foot. "This is for you. It should keep Rain safe for another few lunes."

My father ignores the gold in favor of scowling at me. "You know how I feel about how you made this money."

"You have any better ideas? The mill doesn't bring in enough for what Rain needs."

"And how would you know what she needs? You're never here."

It would've hurt less if he struck me across the face. Punch me in the gut, slash me with a blade, but *never* tell me I don't provide for Rain.

"Because I'm *working*," I say.

"You call what you do work?"

My nostrils flare. "I was talking about training at the Barracks. *That's* where I spend most of my time. Sometimes I go out for a job. And yes, Dad, it's all work."

A spot at the Vanihailian Barracks is one of the most coveted positions in Keirdre. To anyone but my father, having a kid in the Barracks—training for a ranked position in Keirdre's military—would be a damned high honor.

"You wouldn't need extra work if you hadn't insisted on joining the Ranks," he says.

"We're having this spat again? My graduation's tomorrow."

"Exactly why we're having this discussion. Do you think attending graduation is a good idea?"

"It's a necessity," I say. "When I place first at the Ranking, I'll get a highly paid assignment and we can finally stop worrying about missing payments."

"There's going to be water in the arena, Saoirse." His expression softens with his words. "If you lose control—even for a moment—everyone watching will know what you are. And they'll kill you."

My mother flinches, and I taste both of their fear again. Only this time, it's not directed at me but *for* me.

My anger flees. "I won't." I will myself to believe it. "I'll be careful. I promise."

Dad still looks unconvinced. "Saoirse—"

"Dad." I cut him off with a teasing grin. "Can't you just be happy to see me?"

He rolls his eyes but pairs it with a rueful smile as he tugs me into a hug. "Of course I'm happy to see you, Pinecone. I just worry about you. You take so many risks."

"I know." I pull back to allow my mom to join the hug. "But after I graduate, I can take better care of Rain. And in the meantime, my Employer ensures we're not in debt. I know it's a risk, but it's for Rain, and she's worth everything."

And there it is. The inevitable twinge of guilt.

The words are true. Mostly.

I like to think my work for the Raze is for Rain's sake. But it's a lie to suggest there isn't a part of me that can't resist the pull of a kill.

Sirens were made to kill. Our purpose is to lure, seduce, and destroy. It's wrong, and I know it's wrong, but that knowledge does nothing to ease the feeling of euphoria—of complete and utter *bliss*—when I lead a man astray.

The horrifying truth: I'm as drawn to water as men are to me. When I near it, it speaks to me. Urges me to act. *Kill*. The call of the water is as fierce as it is deadly. My own personal Siren Song.

CHAPTER TWO

Rainfall

When Rain's arms coil around me again, all the tension from my conversation with my parents drains like the sea receding from shore at low tide.

She attacks me from behind in the main room of our house. It's wide and open, with the soft blue of the kitchen bleeding into the muddled green of the sitting room. Mom's an earth fae, so the sitting area resembles a garden. A rug of multicolored rose petals stretches across the floor, resting at the foot of the green sofa that smells like grass after a rainstorm.

Rain's hands lock together on my stomach, anchoring me in place, and her face digs into my shoulder blades.

"Hey, Beansprout." I place my hands over hers. "It's harder to hug you when I can't turn around."

Her arms tighten. "It's also harder for you to leave."

A pang. Like something sharp and jagged pierces my gut.

I whirl. Her hands fumble before interlocking again, now at the dip in my back. I bury my face in her thick, dark hair, inhaling. She smells like oranges and tree sap. Like home. "I'm sorry I'm not around as much as I'd like," I mumble.

"Can't you stay the night, Saoirse? *Please?*"

Another pang, more painful than the last. She never calls me Saoirse.

"I'm sorry," I say. "But I have graduation in the morning."

"We could go together."

I pull away, enough to meet her eyes—a brilliant ice-blue thanks to the *keil* bead disguising her features—and my face twists into a frown. "You know that's not an option." I sound harsh. Harsher than she deserves, but she should've known better than to ask.

"But—"

"*No*. You're not going anywhere near the Ranking."

Rancid disappointment floods my senses, as if I've bitten into a juicy, rotten apple.

Since Vanihail is the capital of Keirdre's nine sectors, its Barracks are the most cutthroat, and our Ranking is the most brutal. It starts with all the Deltas in a massive arena. Each Delta begins with a single weapon ranging from something as basic as a slingshot to as lethal as a battle-ax. Killing is staunchly against the rules, but maiming is only slightly discouraged. Our task is to disarm our peers and cross the finish line with three weapons before the others.

Our place in the Ranking determines our assignment after graduation. First place gets the most sought-after and highly paid assignment in Keirdre. The losers—those who fail to disarm three people—will inevitably make a cow-cud salary in the human sector of Sinu, forced to spend the rest of their lives keeping humans in line: making sure they get to work on time, adhere to ridiculous species separation laws, pay their absurdly high taxes, and never defy an order from a "higher" species.

But none of that is why I don't want Rain at graduation. It's not the Deltas in the arena tomorrow I'm worried about—it's the audience.

I try to explain. "There are going to be a lot of powerful fae at graduation. Maybe even fae who advise the Royals."

The Royals. The reason we wear *keil* beads to hide. The reason our mill barely breaks even. The reason I'm terrified for Rain's safety. I don't know what they look like, but I've always imagined they have red eyes and permanent sneers.

All fae have bright, near-luminescent eyes. I've never seen a fae with red eyes, but considering the Royal bloodline is all but immortal—King Larster and Queen Ikenna have ruled the Kingdom of Keirdre for centuries longer than the eldest witch—I imagine they're as haunting as the legends surrounding them.

Some claim King Larster sold his soul to live forever, but I don't believe it. You can't sell what you never had.

"I'll be quiet," says Rain. "I won't even cheer for you. I'll—"

"I said no, Rain."

She pouts in a way that would be adorable if we weren't arguing over her life. Still, her emotions threaten to clog my throat, so I try the last tool in my arsenal: "I got you something."

Her expression shifts. Not exactly happy, but interested. "For me?"

Yes, for you. Anything for you.

"Of course." I dig through my satchel. "Here." I set a silver-dyed leather pouch on a beaded string into her palm.

She smiles, soft and warm like the rising sun. "It's like yours!"

"But better. It's your favorite color. And the string is prettier. I figured you could keep extra *keil* beads in here." I hold out part two of her gift—a *keil* bead.

She doesn't take it. "Isn't this your last one?"

I shrug. "I'll get more from Auntie Drina after graduation."

Still, she doesn't take the bead. "What if yours wears off during the Ranking?"

"It won't. It still has a few days left." *Keil* beads are hand-runed by witches. Rune magic is powerful, but not permanent.

"But—" Rain tries to object more, but I slice through her protests as though wielding a scythe.

"*Please?* I want to give this to you." And I do. I'd give Rain the world if I had it.

Reluctantly, she takes the bead and tucks it into her pouch. "Pinecone . . ." There's a question in her tone as she loops the string around her neck. "What if, tomorrow when you get your assignment, they place you somewhere far away?"

My stomach sinks. I know I should be excited for graduation—it's when I officially rise from a lowly Delta in the Vanihailian Barracks to a soldier in the Keirdren Ranks and receive my first official assignment in any of Keirdre's nine sectors.

Deltas are allowed to join their sector's Barracks and begin training as early as seven years old. Against my dad's wishes, I joined at nine. It's eight years later, and I'm graduating earlier than anyone thought I could.

I'm told the payoff is worth the grueling hours of training, barrels of sweat, and mountainside-steep cost of tuition. As I stare at Rain clutching that leather pouch like a talisman and watching me as if I'll sprout wings and fly away, I wonder if anything is worth it.

I drop into a squat in front of her. When she was younger, this would put our eyes on the same level. Now, I'm below her, looking up.

"Beansprout, I'll write you. No matter where I end up."

"But what if you end up outside of Keirdre?"

I will my face to stay impassive, but I can't help a few confused blinks. "What?"

"I heard that sometimes they assign Deltas to places outside of Keirdre."

I resist a frown.

Keirdre is surrounded by an invisible and impenetrable force that separates us from the outside world. Hundreds of years ago, Keirdre was under constant attack from neighboring kingdoms. Our former King, King Elrian, spent years fighting off invading forces attempting to overthrow him and destroy us. When those forces became too powerful, he gave his life to protect us.

According to legend, his life transferred to the barrier. He persists around us, protecting us, making the barrier as permanent and immutable as death. We're protected from the outside and our kingdom can flourish—at least, that's the narrative spun by King Larster.

The grim reality: only the fae are allowed to thrive.

There were only supposed to be three kinds of creatures in Keirdre: fae, witches, and humans. Despite the King's best efforts, a handful of sirens slipped through. They lived in Keirdre when the barrier was created, and each generation, their slim numbers dwindled. The rest of the kingdom assumes they've died out, but I'm living proof that they're wrong.

I don't know why the Royals despise other creatures, but they've never made their disdain a secret. Witches have been all but banished to the outskirts of the kingdom, and humans are barely paid servants. No matter what King Larster claims, the truth is clear—fae are the only creatures who matter in Keirdre.

"Don't listen to those rumors," I say. "It's just gossip. No one's going outside the barrier, and no one's taking me away from you."

Rain traps her bottom lip between her teeth for a count of three before nodding. "You're going to come see me before you leave on assignment, right?"

"Of course. A . . ." I pause with a grin. "What creature are we on today?" When Rain was a sprig, I used to read her endless stories of the creatures who live outside the barrier. Dryads with skin like bark, sprites small enough to fit in a pocket, impundulu who can transform into birds and take flight . . . We'd stay up late, poring over descriptions, staring at illustrations, and folding down the corners of her favorites. We folded over every other page.

Rain smiles and—*finally*—I taste the citrusy tang of her happiness. "Ogres."

"Perfect," I say. "I'll see you tomorrow after graduation. An angry horde of ogres couldn't keep me away."

The rough tree bark digs into my back. It would be painful if I wasn't used to it.

I twist to peer around the tree into the darkness. A guard stands leaned up against the high bronze gate that surrounds the plain gray of the Barracks.

There are guards posted at even intervals along the perimeter fence, but this one is my favorite entry point.

As I creep from behind the tree, my foot snaps a twig. For half an instant, the sound of cracking wood mingles with the chirping crickets.

The guard's head whips up from its resting place against the gate's metal bars. He's tall with cheekbones like glass, eyes like jade, and skin like warm hickory. He wears his guard's uniform: a navy shirt with close-textured black chain mail draped over his torso, paired with dark pants tucked into old boots. "Who's there?" His right hand reaches for the blade strapped to his waist.

I take another step. Crack another branch.

Dropping his hand from the blade, he throws out his arms, seizing water droplets from the air. He draws his hands together, and the mist clusters into pellets of water—dozens of them—frozen in the air and aimed at me.

"Relax." I grin and creep forward until my face is illuminated by the chaeliss torches atop the gate posts. "It's me."

Carrik sighs in relief. With his exhalation, the water drops from the air, and he sags against the gate with a mock-stern glare. "By the lune, Saoirse. I thought you were a trespasser. I didn't hear you leave this time."

I smirk. "Because I didn't want you to."

He laughs. "Cocky as ever, I see. I suppose this means you wanted me to hear you just now?"

"Of course. Graduation's tomorrow. I might not see you again."

"Ah." Carrik's tone darkens, and his bitterness settles on my tongue like ground sage. "You mean unless you get stuck on nursemaid's duty like me."

Carrik Solwey's time in the Barracks was legendary. He ricocheted to the top of his year faster than the recoil on a crossbow, but his fall was just as fast and significantly more painful.

When word spread that his mother was human and not a water fae like his father, as he'd led the Barracks to believe, his mother was sentenced to death. Her crime: procreating with a fae.

In comparison, Carrik's punishment was light. A fae less gifted would've been imprisoned—maybe exiled to Sinu—but Carrik's water affinity and skill with a blade are their own art form.

His revised sentence: a lifetime of nursemaid's duty. Watching over Deltas in the Barracks as they live out his dream.

I step closer to him. "You know that's not what I meant."

"Doesn't matter. You won't get stuck here. You're an ikatus and you're still number one."

Fae are born with an innate grasp of one of the four elements. Offspring of different elementals can have the affinity of either parent, but never both. Sometimes, children of fae are born with the bright eyes and sharp features of a fae but without an affinity. The ikatus.

As a siren, my power over water is equal to—*superior* to—the water fae. But my power over water is rivaled only by the water's power over me, so I joined the Ranks not under the guise of a fully fledged water fae but an ikatus who can't go near water without being ill.

That last part is at least close to the truth.

"I could still be a nursemaid." I try for levity. "I heard last year there were ten Deltas assigned guard duty of a spoiled Vanihailian."

The rising threat of the Raze has brought an increased need for wealthy fae to invest in security. Now, each class of Deltas has to fear wasting years of training to spend their lives guarding fae too weak, too lazy, or too rich to protect themselves.

"We both know that won't be you," says Carrik. "You're going to win the Ranking, and ten years from now, you're going to be Vanihail's Enforcer."

I lower my head. It isn't fair. Carrik can't help being half-human any more than I can help being a siren, but he's stuck on nursemaid's duty while I graduate tomorrow. "They won't make an ikatus an Enforcer."

"They will if they have to. And as long as you're better than everyone else, they'll have to." His face darkens. "It's different for me. They hate humans more than ikatus."

That's true. But what I don't say—*can't* say—is that the Royals hate sirens more than all of the above.

Not everyone supported the barrier's construction. Especially the few sirens trapped in Keirdre after its creation. They joined with a small number of fae, witches, and humans who wanted *out*. They called themselves the Resistance. In those early years, they were a force to be reckoned with—especially to the wealthy fae and Royals they targeted—but as the scattered few sirens died off, they weakened. As time passed and fewer people remembered the outside world, they've become mostly irrelevant.

Still, every few years, rumors float around that they've made another attack—broken into the Palace, stolen magicked items from a witch—in a vain attempt to escape the barrier.

I'm not sure what face I make, but whatever it is, it sobers Carrik's anger. "Sorry." His green eyes soften. "It's not your fault I'm stuck here."

"It's not yours either."

He offers a soft smile.

I stand next to him and rest my back against the gate, closing my eyes, enjoying the sound of the wind rustling the leaves and the coos of the night falcon, the smoky scent of samsam trees and the stale ocean air in the distance, and best of all—the tingling sensation of mist on my face.

The water pulls but, having been sated earlier, its call is weaker. Instead, it's rejuvenating. Like taking a nap after a long day.

"So." Carrik's tone is conversational, his anger dissipated. "Where'd you sneak off to this time?"

"Where do you think?" I don't open my eyes. "To see Rain before graduation."

"Ah, yes. Rain. How's my favorite Sorkova doing?"

My eyes snap open and I whack his arm. "Excuse you."

He chuckles. "Just telling the truth."

"She asks about you," I tell him. "I think she may have a crush."

"I have that effect on women."

I shove his arm again, laughing. "Dream on, Solwey."

"Why'd you have to see her tonight? Isn't she coming to graduation?"

My laughter shrivels up and dies. "No."

Carrik's eyebrows shoot up. "You seem . . . adamant."

"Rain has no business at graduation. *I* don't even like to associate with the higher-ups in the Keirdren ranks. I'm not putting her through that."

"What's the plan when you're one of them?"

I fold my arms. "I'll visit her."

He's watching me from the corner of his eye, gaze narrowed, trying to figure me out. "Rain won't like that."

"I don't care what she likes. I care that she's safe."

"Nothing's going to happen to her." He smirks. "If anyone wishes her ill, all they need to do is take one look at your face right now—I promise they'll change their minds."

I chuckle, allowing his words to lighten the fear weighing on my mind.

My good humor wilts at the hint of pale pink on the horizon. Morning is approaching, faster than I'd like.

"I should get going," I say. "Squeeze in a few hours of sleep before the Ranking. I'll—I guess I'll see you." A lie. This is goodbye, and we both know it.

"I hope not," Carrik fires back. "You're bigger than this place, Sorkova. Lune above, you're bigger than all of Keirdre. You're getting far out of these Barracks. No question." He glances at my feet and laughs. "But please, do me a favor and leave those boots behind."

I grin. I've had the same admittedly worn boots for as long as I can remember. I refuse to waste the ranis to buy new ones. Every scrap of spare money goes toward Rain. My boots will last, but Rain's safety is more fleeting. "They still work, don't they?"

"Not for much longer. Certainly not without me patching them up every lune."

His own boots don't fare much better. They're made of brown leather with a hand-stitched sheath that houses his mother's old dagger. It has a dark-green handle stamped with a faded black X. According to Carrik, she used to keep it on her at all times. For protection. It didn't work for her, but Carrik loves it just the same.

"You should get off that throne of yours," I say. "Your boots have seen better days."

"Mine still have the soles attached," he teases. "Yours . . . Throw them away. *Burn* them."

I smile at him. "You know I won't."

"Yeah. I do." He sighs. "What am I supposed to do without Saoirse Sorkova sneaking in and out at all hours and kicking my ass at sparring?"

I don't have many friends—my back is due to give any day now from the weight of my secrets—but Carrik is as good as they come. Better, even. Unable to resist the urge, I hug him. It's brief, but for a few ticks, his arms envelop me, and all I hear is his even, steadying heartbeat. The tightness in my chest eases and I'm calm.

When I pull away, I take a step back, inhale the mist through my nose—my own form of liquid courage—and dart forward. When I reach the gate, I leap, grabbing hold of the bars and using my momentum to climb over.

I land on my feet on the other side. With a final wave at Carrik, I take off across the lawn, headed for the side door I kept cracked open when I snuck out earlier.

In the doorway, I pause. Carrik's facing away from me, guarding his post in silence once more.

My first instinct: call out to him. One last time.

Instead, I enter the Barracks and close the door behind me without another word.

CHAPTER THREE

Warring Instincts

My tongue toys with the *keil* bead lodged behind my false tooth. I will it to stop, but it ignores me.

Pierce Flynn, Training Soldier for this year's graduating Deltas, stands behind the podium on a wide platform floating above us in the arena—this year's finish line for the Ranking.

He's prattling on about dignity and honor and some "special prize" for this year's winner into an asterval, a stone rod runed to amplify voice, but I'm only half listening. I'm more focused on contemplating which face in the sea of the audience belongs to my future employer.

We Deltas stand in the middle of the arena in lines as rigid as our spines. We're dressed the same: all black with a silver Keirdren crest pinned to our shirts. The fae soldiers in the audience wear the colors of their sectors: forest green and woodsy brown for the earth fae, dark blends of smoky gray and black for the fire fae, loose-fitting white and brown for the air fae, and navy and gold for the water fae. They sit above us in the stands, watching us shrewdly. Assessing.

Only fae attend Vanihailian graduation. Most witches aren't allowed in Vanihail, and the humans who live here are servants, not soldiers, so the only creatures here are fae and—

My body, already stiff, freezes over like a wintry stream.

A nervous pair of spelled-blue eyes peers at me from the crowd.

She's so tiny, I might've missed her, if not for my second traitor—Carrik. He's at her side, tall and instantly recognizable. Rain's hand is curled around his arm, and they watch me with matching trepidation.

My nostrils flare and my eyes are moments away from glowing silver and revealing myself as a siren to the arena.

She shouldn't be here. She shouldn't be anywhere near here.

"And now," Pierce Flynn is saying, "we will commence the Ranking!"

The stands erupt in cheers. I taste the tangy excitement of my fellow Deltas mingled with stale nerves. This is, after all, everything we've worked for. Years of training culminating in the Ranking, our final chance to prove we're the best. Disarm three Deltas. Make it to the finish line first. Two steps that moments ago felt simple.

I've been looking forward to this for as long as I can remember, but I'm too focused on not exploding in a shower of steam and expletives to enjoy it.

Control. I'm in total control.

I force air in through my nose and out through my mouth as Vanihail's Enforcer, Anarin Arkin, walks through the rows of Deltas, handing out weapons.

She's beautiful. Coppery brown skin, black hair chopped short, and bright violet eyes. She wears navy and gold, the colors of Keirdre and the colors of the water fae, with an Enforcer's pin fastened to her chest.

When she passes me, she presses my weapon for the Ranking into my palm: a dark-blue river stone.

My mind is still fixated on Rain, but the feel of the rock in my hands pulls me into the present. I take swift inventory of the wide field. Troughs of water are dotted throughout the arena, and chaeliss torches float overhead. With the grass beneath our feet and the air surrounding us, all four affinities are present. For everyone else, this is a comfort, but unlike the other Deltas, I can't use my affinity without exposing myself.

Finished doling out our weapons, Anarin joins Pierce Flynn on the levitating platform. "On my mark, let the Ranking— *begin*!"

The soldiers in the stands cheer their excitement, and the other Deltas sprint forward.

Blades clang together. An arrow streaks across my field of view.

I release a shuddering breath and tune it all out—Rain, Carrik, the audience. My fingers tighten around the stone as I form a plan.

Step one: win the Ranking.

Step two: get Rain out of here.

In order to achieve step one, I need to focus not on the girl sitting in the stands but on the Deltas swarming me like flies.

We're barely five ticks in and already, it's chaos. Shrieking Deltas slashing at one another, arcs of water flying about, fae tackling fae . . .

It calms me. Here, on the battlefield, I'm in my element. Fighting is as natural as breathing underwater.

A male Delta stands a few paces to my right, wielding a blade. His stance is strong, but his grip is clumsy. Self-assured, but mistakenly so. An easy target.

I dart toward him.

I swing my stone, aiming to hit his hand and knock away his sword.

Before I get a chance, he jerks the sword to his left, fending off an attack from a rival blade.

My eyes lock with his assailant's.

A female Delta with shorn hair and an amused snarl. Rienna Kasselton. She's hated me since I joined the Barracks and knocked her from first to second. In her mind, I'm her fiercest competition.

In my mind, she's dirt beneath my boots.

"Hello, Sorkova." She slices her blade at the light-brained boy between us as she greets me.

He barely manages a block.

"Nice to see you, Kasselton," I say back.

A hiss is my only warning before a wave of water drenches me from behind. Rienna's always made it a point to use her water affinity against me.

She smirks and hacks her blade at the boy again. "Feeling all right? Is the water making you sick?"

The water is cool as it soaks my skin and dribbles down my back. Each droplet stings, urging me to yield to my instincts.

Kill.

I can win this competition with my eyes closed. Obliterate the other Deltas with nothing but a song.

I shake myself of the feeling.

Control. I'm in control.

As Rienna rears the blade back again, I catch the wrist of the boy between us. Using his arm and blade, I parry her attack.

Rienna's face darkens.

I block her next swipe and use our crossed blades to shove her away.

As she stumbles, I jerk my leg up, kicking the boy in the back of the knees. He collapses, and his hold on the blade slips, making it easy—comically so—for me to pry it from his hands.

I face Rienna with his sword, my stone, and a smirk. "Actually, I'm feeling fine, Kasselton. How are you?"

Anger descends over her expression like a hawk.

Disarming her now would be easy. She's angry and thoughtless, and I've never engaged in a battle of blades I haven't won.

This must occur to her as well, because without warning, she swings her sword. It's easy enough to block, but the moment I move, she spins around and sprints away like a coward.

A Delta with a shield darts into my path. I shove my sword out as he passes, and he trips over it.

When he whirls to face me, he's off-balance.

I pivot so I stand alongside him, and with a swipe, I hit the hand holding the shield.

He hisses as blood trickles from the wound and I snatch his shield.

Two weapons taken.

I run, searching for my next target. Someone grabs my ankle.

With a grunt, I stumble but catch myself before my face slams into the ground.

My assailant squeezes harder.

I look down. It's not a person who's grabbed me but a clump of grass. It's stretched out like a hand and coiled around my ankle, holding me in place. The work of an earth fae.

Labored breathing behind me.

I whirl.

An earth fae jabs at me with a dagger.

With the grass tethering me, I bring up the shield and block.

The resulting clash of the knife against the shield sends reverberations through my arm.

I slam my free foot into my attacker's shin and jam the shield forward, hitting them across the face. They fall backward. I try to take the dagger, but they slash out, managing a thin slice on my palm.

I hack my blade at the grass knotted around my ankle, freeing myself. In the same motion, I swipe up, slamming the hilt of the blade into the earth fae's wrist. The dagger plummets to the ground.

I snatch it before running off.

Three weapons taken.

My final task: ascend to the platform floating overhead first.

A rope dangles beneath the platform, swaying in a breeze. I sprint toward it, shoving my stone in my pocket, my dagger in my boot, and securing my shield to my arm. I leap, catching the rope.

My sweating palms slip against the roughness, searing the pads of my hands. I ignore the burning and climb.

An instant later, there's a grunt beneath me and the rope tugs.

I'm unconcerned—until something jabs my heel.

With a hiss, I glance down. Rienna dangles beneath me. She uses one arm and both legs to climb. In her free hand, she holds the knife she just used to slice my foot. The blade has a trickle of red—my blood.

Rienna's mouth is twisted into a scowl. She draws back the blade a second time, preparing another strike, but I pull my burning arms faster.

She speeds up as well, but it doesn't matter. I'm faster than her. Stronger. And she was foolish enough to think she could outclimb me with one hand.

Rienna has looked down on me from the moment I announced myself as an ikatus to the rest of the Deltas in my year. She was the first to start up the chant of "runt" in the Barracks. She wasn't the last. Her fury sets my mouth on fire, but I don't swallow it. I savor it. For years, I tasted her misplaced disdain. Today, I bask in her anger. I've earned it. The crowd of Vanihail's military roars as I pull myself atop the floating platform. First.

There's something thrilling about standing on top of the world and soaking in the applause. It's as if, for a moment, I'm not a siren people fear or an ikatus people disdain but someone worthy. A soldier.

I savor the rush of my victory as the platform slowly fills with other Deltas.

We're once again standing in rigid lines, but this time, I'm in the front.

"Congratulations." Anarin Arkin shakes my hand. "Delta Sorkova, as the first-place champion of this year's Ranking, you have the honor of the most esteemed assignment in the Keirdren ranks."

The glares of the other Deltas burn. The tightness of their jealousy wraps around me like a patchwork quilt—subtle variations on the same underlying emotion. It's to be expected. With my ikatus title and stubborn refusal to sink below first place, I never grew on my fellow Deltas. I don't mind—they never grew on me either.

Anarin continues. "This year, His Highness Prince Hayes is recruiting."

I resist a scowl. Prince Hayes Finnean Vanihail. We all know of him. He's rumored to be the most beautiful boy in Keirdre. He's also rumored to be every bit as putrid and rotten as his father.

"His Highness is selecting a new guard from the graduating class of Deltas. As the highest performing Delta, this honor is yours."

The rush of my victory fizzles like a wet flame.

From the moment I joined the Ranks, I've wanted to be Vanihail's Enforcer. It's the highest position in Keirdre's military. Winning the Ranking guarantees a Delta an assignment shadowing a high-ranking soldier in Vanihail, which, usually, is the fastest road to becoming an Enforcer.

This year, the value of the prize has gone up—to everyone but me.

I'm a siren. I'm not even supposed to exist in this kingdom. The Royals hate anyone who's not fae. And, me aside, I don't want Rain within spitting distance of the Royals.

"Thank you for this honor, Enforcer Arkin," I say. "But I'm afraid I must decline."

The arena catches a collective breath.

The jealousy of the Deltas warps into earthy confusion and zesty surprise. Stares bore into me from all around.

Anarin's eyes harden. "This is not a request. It is an honor—"

"For which I am incredibly grateful," I cut in.

Again, the arena gasps. Now I've interrupted one of the most powerful women in Keirdre.

My mind flails, trying to think of a plausible excuse for turning down such a prestigious honor.

My nervous tongue finds my *keil* bead, and I realize I already have the perfect excuse.

I swallow, hands clenching at my sides as I try—to no avail—to douse the flames of humiliation that threaten to engulf me.

"I'm an ikatus." I sound hollow. "I am not suited to being the Prince's guard."

If the crowd wasn't staring before, they are now. Their confusion gives way to amusement—the smug, self-satisfied kind that tastes like a salted lime. Their gazes aren't sympathetic; they're sharp and scathing like shattered glass as they relish in my shame. I'm no longer the triumphant fae, winner of the Ranking. I'm an ikatus. Weak. A runt.

After all the hours I've given, blood I've spilled, and sleep I've sacrificed, I always thought I'd be rewarded in the end. Finally be able to prove my competence. Instead, I stand before the most powerful members of Keirdre's military and plead weakness.

I hate it.

I hate the Royals for putting me in this situation, the Ranking for momentarily convincing me I ever stood a chance of escaping the title of ikatus, and myself for spending every moment of my life hiding.

"You will not get this offer a second time, Delta Sorkova," Anarin warns.

My instincts are at war. My fury wants me to sing away the smug, arrogant looks on my fellow Deltas' faces. My pride wants me to take the job and prove to the sea of Keirdre's finest that I am not, nor have I ever been, weak. My Rain instincts want me to decline and take a position far away from the Palace and the Royals.

I meet those runed-blue eyes in the crowd.

Anything for you.

I guess it's not a war. Or, if it is, it's over before it begins, because Rain wins. She always does.

"I apologize, Enforcer Arkin," I hear myself say, "but I stand by my decision."

CHAPTER FOUR

The Silver Envelope

I slam my shoulder into Carrik's as I stalk past him, snatch Rain's wrist, and march her toward the exit, without so much as a greeting to either of them.

As we scramble away, Rain pauses to loop her bag over her shoulder but wisely stays silent as she trots to keep up with my brisk, *furious* strides.

"Saoirse." Carrik is less wise. He trails behind, trying to slow me down. "She was going to come anyway. I wanted her to be with someone you trust."

"Trust?" I scoff as I sidestep a cluster of fae too slow to move out of my way. A few of them recognize me. My humiliation from announcing myself as an ikatus lingers, so I embrace the heat of my fury instead. I'd rather be angry than shamed. "There's no trust between us, Solwey. You *knew* I didn't want her here."

"She was going to come anyway."

Now on the stone steps leading from the raised arena seats to the outside, I turn to face him. My eyes threaten to flash silver.

I'm *fuming*, but I've already revealed enough about myself in this damned arena for one day.

Control. Sucking in a breath, I shove aside my urge to drown Carrik where he stands for endangering my sister.

"She's *twelve*," I say. "You're one of the most gifted soldiers in Keirdre. Next time a little girl asks you for something so utterly beyond the barrier, tell her no."

Carrik approaches me slowly, hands raised, palms open, as though afraid I'll take off if he moves too quickly. He doesn't need to fear me running away. He *should* fear me punching him in the face.

"What should I have done?" he says. "Lock her up?"

"If that's what it took." I try and cool my temper with thoughts of my alternative assignment: shadow to one of Keirdre's Commands. A high honor and the unofficial short track to an Enforcership. The assignment I was hoping for from the beginning.

It doesn't work. I still want to punch Carrik.

"I'm fine, Pinecone. I wanted to see you in action," Rain speaks up.

I give her a look. "That was foolish. You know that."

We're the only three standing in the stairwell. I take advantage of the solitude to look Rain over. I know she's fine—Carrik would never let any physical harm come to her—but still, it calms me to inspect her myself.

Her dark hair is twisted into two tight braids against her scalp, she wears a loose-fitting dashiki dress, the hand not in mine is folded behind her back, her blue eyes are a little too wide, and she tastes like sour grapes and rancid wine. Guilt mingled with fear.

I frown. "What's behind your back?"

"What do you mean?" Her hidden arm doesn't move.

"Carrik, give us a moment." I don't look away from my sister.

"Are you still mad?" he asks.

"Do you really think the best path back to my good graces is challenging me?"

"Point taken." Carrik gives Rain a comforting grin before heading down the steps to wait outside the arena.

I squat in front of Rain. "What's behind your back?"

"Noth—"

I yank her arm into view before she can finish the lie.

A silver envelope with my name scripted across the front in metallic blue ink winks at me. Judging by the broken seal, Rain's already opened it.

My stomach drops.

"Wait!" Rain tries to grab it back, but I pivot, giving her my back as I wrench out the parchment crumpled inside.

I know what she is. Deliver 500 ranis to the Kivren Waterfront tomorrow at midnight or someone else will too.

Breath flees my lungs and my silver-flashing eyes illuminate the darkened stairwell.

"Saoirse?" Rain's voice.

It doesn't sound real. Nothing does.

The envelope slips. I think Rain catches it, but I can't be sure of anything through the haze of my mind.

Someone knows.

It echoes, over and over, drowning out anything else.

"Rain?" I'm speaking, but I don't recognize my voice. "Where did you get this?"

"I found it in my bag. Someone must've put it there during the ceremony."

Someone knows.

My parents fear someone finding out about me, but I can take care of myself. My biggest fear has always been Rain. Someone discovering she's not fae and taking her away.

My eyes threaten to leak angry, terrified tears. I thought I was being careful, if not with my own secret, at least with Rain's. This note is proof I was wrong.

I rip the envelope from her a second time, but it's pointless. My vision is clouded and I can't breathe.

Deep breath in. Deep breath out.

I need to be in control. For Rain.

The gears in my brain start to churn.

The stands were flooded with high-ranking soldiers in Keirdre's army. Any one of them could have left this note.

Deep breath in. Deep breath out.

Step one: narrow down the suspect pool by inspecting the only evidence I have.

My eyes clear and the envelope comes back into focus. The handwriting is unfamiliar—left-handed, judging by the smears—and there's a red-wax seal pressed to the back inlaid with an insignia I recognize. A wide samsam tree with the exterior branches reaching out and the interior branches twisting into the letter *K*. One of the outer branches stretches out farther than the others with a single dangling apple. The Royal insignia.

Those who work directly under the Royals wear pins with this symbol fastened to their chests. But the insignia itself—the official seal of the Royal family—is rare. Only the King and the King's heir have one.

Whoever wrote this note has access to the Royals. Worse, whoever wrote this note went out of their way to make sure I *knew* they had access to the Royals.

"Saoirse?" Rain's timid voice drags me from my thoughts.

I slip my arms around her, hugging her so tightly, I'm sure she can't breathe.

I inhale. Tree sap, oranges, and Rain. "We're getting you out of here," I say into her hair. "Right now."

"What are you going to do?"

"Don't worry, Beansprout." I don't answer her question. "I'm going to take care of this. Of you." Taking her hand, I start down the stairs and we exit the arena.

Carrik paces outside. His eyes jump to us as we step out. "Everything all right? Do you need me to—"

"You've done enough." I curl my hand tighter around Rain's. "I'm taking her home."

"How many times do I need to apologize for you to forgive me?"

Someone knows. It's all I can think. All that matters.

"I don't care what you do," I say. "Clearly, you don't care what I want, so what does it matter to you?" I march away, crushing Rain's hand in mine.

This time, Carrik chooses wisdom. He doesn't follow.

CHAPTER FIVE

Dreamweaver

My thumb traces the wax seal. Rain is home safe, but I'm back at the Barracks, analyzing this sodding letter for the thousandth time.

What I've gleaned so far:

First, whoever wrote this note wanted me to know they have access to the Royal seal.

Second, the writer of this note is left-handed.

Third, when I find them—and I will—I'm going to kill them.

My bedsprings squeak as I rummage beneath my mattress, feeling until I find the wood of my *lairic* bracelet—thirteen beads strung on silver wire. Twelve of the beads are crafted from the wood of a samsam tree, polished to a shine, and etched with five silver runes. The thirteenth is a deep-red bloodstone spotted with a green so dark, it appears black.

I slip the bracelet over my wrist and twist the wooden bead to the right of the bloodstone until the correct rune faces outward. I twist each bead, working from left to right, until the bracelet displays a familiar *lairic* configuration.

Drawing my knees to my chest, I prepare myself to plunge into the world of Dreamweaving.

I push the bloodstone. The bracelet runes glow, casting silver light over my wrist.

My room dissolves into droplets of colors that drizzle down my field of vision like rain on a windowpane. The raindrops swirl together, mixing with other shades like a paint palette, melting into a new world.

I close my eyes, waiting as the whir of my shifting consciousness fades into the dull roar of the ocean.

I peel my eyes open to all-consuming brightness.

My lids flutter shut, warding off the brilliant white. I wait five ticks before opening them again.

I'm ankle-deep in white sand, facing the clear blue sea, not a cloud in the sky. A gull caws overhead and a warm breeze sends a fine, salty spray of seawater into the air. I cup a hand over my eyes as I peer around.

Lying in the sand a couple dozen paces down the otherwise empty stretch of beach is a figure I'd know anywhere.

The woman has long, long legs; tawny-hued skin; and waist-length hair the color of freshly fallen snow. Her eyes are closed and her hands are folded beneath her head, but I know she's awake.

I trudge through the sand to stand at her head. "Auntie Drina."

Her eyes snap open.

Y'ddrina's eyes remind me of the night sky—velvety midnight blue spattered with gold. She's undeniably beautiful and, like all witches, appears young. While most fae live around 150 years, witches live three times longer. I've known Y'ddrina my entire life, and she's never revealed her age.

My family and I know nothing of my birth parents. I was found toddling around Drina's backyard when I was two and raised by my aunties in the witch sector of Ketzal until I was five. That was the same year the orphaned Rain came to live with us, and my mother discovered she couldn't conceive a child of her own.

A perfect match, Mom likes to say. An instant family.

This last part is always said in love, but I know it's not true.

When my parents took me in, they assumed I was an ikatus. My brilliant honey eyes give me the look of a fae, and my refusal to speak in my early years gave me the air of incompetence associated with the ikatus.

The first time I spoke, I was seven. Except I didn't speak.

I sang.

Which, of course, sent all of our worlds spiraling. Neither of my parents will ever admit it, but I know they must resent it. The little orphan fae turned out to be a supposedly extinct siren, making their lives infinitely more complicated.

They love me. I know they do. But that doesn't erase the fact that their lives would be easier if they didn't.

Drina tosses her head back dramatically and groans. "Dammit, Saoirse, of all nights to Dreamweave . . ." She sweeps an arm around the serenity. "This kind of dream only comes along once or twice in a lifetime."

As always when I'm near a large body of water, I have the urge to dive in, letting the water wash over me and soothe away my problems. From here, within Drina's dream, it's easy to pretend the ocean stretches out forever. There's no Keirdre, no barrier, no hiding. Since this water isn't real, the second addiction that typically accompanies my proximity to water—the insatiable hunger to drag someone into the murky depths with me—is nonexistent.

"If good dreams happened every day, they wouldn't be good. Just dreams," I say to appease her.

She scowls, unmoved. "Fine. I'm letting you in. But know that it's under duress."

Instinctively, I close my eyes—I hate this part.

My *lairic* beads allow me to Dreamweave into the consciousness of anyone with a *lairic* configuration, as long as I know their sequence. But only witches can pull a Dreamweaver from their consciousness and into their physical world. Even though my body remains in the Barracks, when Drina lets me in, I can physically interact with her world. My beads were a gift from Drina. Like most things spelled by witches, they're illegal. And rare.

I grit my teeth as my mind jerks from my auntie's dream and into her reality with a splintering pain that makes my eyes water. The jolt is always jarring and leaves my head spinning.

The surrounding warmth of the beach dims into a concentrated heat in front of me. The sound of the waves fades into clinking dishes and crackling fire.

I open my eyes.

I sit in Drina's tiny living room on an old sofa, huddled around the hearth. The room is cramped, cluttered, and scattered with colorful plants. Red roses and blue larkspurs on the ceiling, green ivy up the wooden walls, and a blanket of woven water lily pads around my shoulders.

Drawing the blanket tighter, I make my way to the kitchen. My steps are wobbly like a newborn calf after Dreamweaving, so I lean against the doorway, watching Auntie Drina as she putters around.

She sets a rusty copper kettle on the stove. "You could've stayed seated, love. I'm just boiling some water."

The kitchen is small. There's barely enough room for three people, and every last lick of counter space is covered with stacks of cracked plates and metal pans.

"Drina?" a raspy voice calls. "You awake?"

Footsteps patter down the hallway and stop outside the kitchen. Auntie Aiya, Drina's would-be wife if marriage between witches and fae were legal.

"Hi, Auntie," I say.

Legally, Drina and Aiya aren't allowed to live together. Sectors are divided by species. Drina and Aiya's home is in Ketzal, a sector for witches and warlocks. The Enforcers in the fae sectors are strict about adherence to separation laws, but the witch Enforcer of Ketzal is less archaic.

Aiya blinks her lilac-colored eyes at me and adjusts her turquoise headscarf. "Saoirse?" She tugs me in for a hug. "Is everything all right?"

"I'm fine. But I need to talk to you."

Aiya pulls back to give me a rueful smile. "On one condition?"

I can't help returning her smile. "What?"

"Promise me that one day, you're going to visit when you *don't* need something."

I laugh. "Deal."

It's been years since I traveled to visit my aunties in person. Vanihail is at least a four day's journey from Ketzal. The distance alone is far enough, but much of the trip is lengthened by how treacherous the roads become the farther you travel from the Palace.

She glides across the floor to Drina, pecking her cheek. "I think I'll need tea for this."

Drina grins. "I just put on a kettle."

This time, Aiya kisses her on the mouth. "This is why I love you."

"And I love *you* because you're good with plants," says Drina pointedly.

Aiya rolls her eyes, still grinning. "Is that your way of asking me to check the luneweed?"

"Since you're awake."

With another laugh, Aiya slips out the back door to the yard. My aunties' house rests on a large plot of land, most of it filled by their expansive herb garden. Aiya's earth affinity means she can grow specialty herbs no matter the weather, and Y'ddrina's magic means she can brew potions, poisons, and poultices with the garden's spoils.

Together, they have one of the most successful—and illegal— potions businesses in Keirdre.

I give Drina a look as the door thuds behind Aiya. "You're growing luneweed?"

"Yes." She pulls out a set of chipped teacups from a high cabinet. "Don't look at me like that. The King keeps raising the cost of potion supplies. We can't afford to turn down the business."

"But it's luneweed."

Luneweed can be watered and harvested only at night, and the liquid extracted from the root is deadly—but only to fae. With no antidote, it's no wonder it's highest on the King's list of outlawed substances.

Poisons are one of the many reasons witches are banned from fae sectors, with the very rare exception of witch graduates from the Ketzalite Barracks who receive assignments in Vanihail.

"It's worth the risk. We can sell it for nearly twice as much as other potions," says Drina.

"Who are you selling to?"

She waves a hand, dismissing me. "You didn't come here in the middle of the night to ask about my herb business."

It's clearly an evasion, but I let it go. "I'm sorry it's late, Auntie."

She wraps an arm around my shoulders and guides me back to the sofa. "Sit, love, and tell me what ails you; *then* I'll decide how sorry you should be." She sits next to me and holds out her hands, warming them in the fire.

"I graduated today," I say.

Feather-soft smile. "I know. Kiernynn keeps me apprised of you and Rain. Is your assignment far?"

The back door creaks as Aiya returns from the garden.

I take a breath, tensing for the blow I'm about to deliver. "I was selected as a member of the Prince's personal guard."

Crash from the kitchen—Aiya's dropped something.

I stand to help her, but Drina's hand on my arm stops me. *"Sit."*

I sink back into the sofa.

Flickering firelight dances across Drina's skin. Her expression gives nothing away.

"Drina?" I start cautiously. "Can you say something?"

She continues to gaze into the fire. "You . . . declined this offer. Didn't you?" Her words are careful, as though lining up the perfect shot with a crossbow.

"Of course," I say.

She's a witch, so I can't sense or taste Drina's emotions. Still, her relief is palpable as she places a hand over her heart and exhales heavily. "Lune above, Saoirse, you scared me half to death."

Aiya treads into the room holding a cracked porcelain tray with three steaming cups of tea. She sets the tray on the table between the sofa and the hearth and hands out cups.

Aiya doesn't speak. She situates herself on the sofa, leans into Drina's side, and takes a long sip of tea. Herbal, from the smell of it. She, too, looks near weary with relief.

I frown between the two of them. They're *too* relieved. "What aren't you telling me?"

Drina's cup rattles as she sets it on the table—she's trembling. "The Palace is a dangerous place for you." Neither of them will meet my eyes.

"I know," I say. "But that's not all of it."

My aunties stare at each other with some deep meaning I can't catch. Drina looks to me again. "I'm not sure what you're talking about, love, but I'm glad you said no."

It's so clearly a lie that I'm offended they expect me to accept this, but I know my aunties. If they don't want to do something, no amount of prodding will change their minds. "Fine. Don't tell me." My tone is clipped.

"Is this what you came here to tell us?" asks Aiya.

No. "Part of the reason." I pick up my tea and huddle it, both for warmth and to steel my resolve lest I meet Auntie Drina's all-knowing gaze and crack. I can't tell them about the note. Not until I know how I'm going to find the bastard responsible and kill them.

Lying is practically second nature to me, but Drina's midnight eyes see through me like polished glass, and she can read my moods like pages in a book. I will my face to stay calm.

"Who all lives in the Palace?" I set down my teacup and try for casual. "Aside from the Royals?"

"King Larster has his advisers," says Drina. "Some who live in the Palace, some who don't but visit often. They're all wealthy Vanihailian water fae. Aside from that, Palace guards and human servants."

"And soldiers?" I say.

"Only Palace guards. Soldiers haven't been allowed in the

Palace for lunes. There was a string of robberies in Vanihail, and the Palace went on lockdown. Essential Palace workers only."

Which means with my new position as a soldier shadow, I'll have no reason to go near the Palace. With just two Royal seals in existence, the only way someone used one for the note was if they had access to the Palace and close ties with the Royal family.

"Love?" Drina is still watching my face warily. "Why do you ask?"

"No reason." I clear my throat and feign a smile. "Just curious. The other reason I'm here is we need more *keil* beads. I gave Rain the last one yesterday."

"I'll get those." Drina stands. "Be right back."

Aiya sips her tea as we wait. "We worry about you, Saoirse."

"I know." But I'm only half listening. My thoughts are with Rain, the red wax seal, and the silver envelope. The use of the seal is too obvious to not be intentional. With only two in existence, someone *wanted* me to know they have access to the Royals. Access I rejected when I declined a job as the Prince's guard.

"Be careful," says Aiya, as though reading my mind.

I frown. "What do you mean?"

"We can't give you as many *keil* beads as we normally do. Drina needs umbian clay, but it's getting more expensive. Part of the King's plan to put an end to witch businesses like ours."

"Why? Rich fae use *keil* beads all the time." Wealthy fae women use *keil* beads to obscure unseemly marks. They wear them on jewelry pieces, often strung with fancier gems.

"Rich fae buy from Palace-approved witches in Vanihail," says Aiya. "Not lowly witches who operate outside Vanihail and outside the law. If the King had his way, we'd all go out of business.

Besides, it takes time for clay to form, and we're working with a very limited supply in the barrier."

"Are you saying we're running out?"

"There's no need to worry."

"Yet." I say what's hanging unspoken between us.

Drina sweeps back into the sitting room before Aiya can respond. She hands me a sack of beads. "Here you are, love."

"Thank you."

"We should check the one you have now," says Aiya.

I pop the *keil* bead out of my mouth and hand it to Drina for inspection. The gold etching of the rune is still there but fading. "You've got some time left with this one. Switch it out in three days."

"I will." I slip the bead back behind my tooth and feel the change rain down my face. It was Drina who crafted the disguise of my *keil* bead. As a sprig, I asked her why she chose a burn and she said, "People only ever see one thing at a time. That burn is the first and last thing they notice about you. Which is what we need to keep you hidden."

At the time, I didn't understand. But now every day proves that she was right.

"Thank you. Both of you." I twist the *lairic* beads of my bracelet to the correct configuration. With one last smile, I press the bloodstone.

I'm jolted into my body with enough force to make my head pound like beating drums.

I open my eyes. I'm back in my room at the Barracks, body cold from the loss of the blanket and fire, with a bag of *keil* beads in my lap.

I'm drained from Dreamweaving, exhausted from this day,

and tired from lack of sleep, but I tuck the bag under my mattress and shove on my boots.

My parents would kill me. Drina would kill me. Lune above—*I* would kill me if I were in their shoes, but I don't see any other choice.

If I want to find whoever is blackmailing my sister, I need to work in the Palace.

CHAPTER SIX

Dotted Lines

My knuckles are poised over the wood of the door to Anarin Arkin's office. My steps here were sure, but now my feet falter.

Am I being rash?

Maybe. Probably.

But it's for Rain. And if it's for Rain . . .

I knock.

"Come in."

I push open the door. Like everything in the Barracks, the walls of Anarin's office are gray. The only splashes of color are the Keirdren flag hanging behind her desk and a dark-blue basin resting on a cabinet. Water fae always keep a supply of water on hand.

Anarin sits behind her desk, foreboding and stiff, even at this hour. Someone sits in the cushioned seat across from her, facing away from me.

The hairs on the back of my neck prickle. The air quivers with an unknown energy. Eager. *Intense.*

"Delta Sorkova." A frown slashes across Anarin's face. "What are you doing here?"

"I've changed my mind, Enforcer Arkin. I would like to accept the position as the Prince's guard."

Anarin's eyebrow jumps. "You cannot simply change your mind, Delta. I warned you I would not extend the offer a second time. You—"

"Wait." The voice that speaks up is low, commanding, and lune above if it isn't sensual as hell.

The figure sitting across from Anarin stands and turns toward me.

My tongue toys with the *keil* bead in my tooth as my face struggles to remain still.

I've heard stories of Prince Hayes's otherworldly beauty. Still, I admit to being struck stunned at the sight of him.

Skin dark and sable, hair short and coily, jaw strong and firm, lips sensuous and relaxed, and eyes—his *eyes*—the color of the ocean and swirling like waves. They call to me, as if drops of the actual sea reside in his face.

One look at him confirms every rumor I've ever heard. How a single smile can send the most stoic person melting into a puddle. How fae, witches, and humans alike are drawn to him. How the barrier itself weakened when he was born, not built to contain such beauty.

It's not that he's beautiful—which he is—it's his *presence*. His entire being commands attention and respect. It fills the room like water, drowning me in his potency. He makes his way across Anarin's office and stands in front of me. Close. Too close. But I make no move to get away.

"Y-Your Highness?" Anarin's on her feet. "What did you say?"

"I said 'wait.'" The Prince's ocean eyes sweep my face, lingering on my burn, before meeting my own. His face lights with boyish curiosity, and my tongue lights with his smoky-sweet interest.

Anarin glances from him to me and back again. "Wait for what, Your Highness?"

"For my approval." The Prince's gaze never leaves mine. "You want this job after all, Delta Sorkova?"

It takes me a few ticks to find my voice. "Yes, sir."

"You previously refused?"

"Yes, sir."

"Why?"

I take a breath before repeating the lie that burns like acid. "I'm an ikatus, sir. I did not feel . . . worthy to hold such an auspicious title."

Those eyes rake me up and down. For a tick, they narrow before widening again. "And since then you've stopped being an ikatus?"

"Since then I've had a chance to think. I'm better than the other Deltas. I've proven it. In training and in the Ranking. If you allow me, sir, I'll keep proving it."

"Hmm." He continues to stare at me, and I continue to stare back, struggling to stay afloat in the ocean of his eyes. I'm not sure how long we stand in grueling silence. Finally, "Delta Sorkova, the position is yours."

"I—" Anarin's jaw unhinges. "Sir, are you sure?"

"Absolutely." He relieves me of the intensity of his gaze and gives Anarin a perfect smile that fills the stale office with warmth—except warmth is too subtle. *Heat.* His smile transforms the room into a sauna.

"I want the best," he says. "If the best is willing, I want *her.*" He's looking at me again. "Please take a seat, Delta Sorkova."

I clumsily settle into the chair that the Prince just vacated, feeling oddly off-kilter. There are only two chairs in the room, but the Prince wastes no time in situating himself in Anarin's desk chair as if he owns it.

The smoothness of his movements makes my skin crawl—as

do his clothes. He wears a loose white dashiki swirled with blue and gold, a pendant fashioned into the Royal insignia, dark pants, and leather hunting boots. His boots are so pristine, it's clear they've yet to actually go on a hunting excursion, and the rest of his appearance is so regal, it's clear they never will.

The thought loosens my shoulders, and I take my first normal breath since entering the room. When I look at him—*really* look at him—I see him for what he is. It doesn't matter how uncannily perfect he is. He's a Royal. The Royals are shrouded in beauty, but it's all to mask the fact that they're the reason behind everything I hate.

The clarity calms me.

Prince Hayes slides a sheet of parchment across the desk to me. "I was preparing this for the second-place Delta. Now that you're here, you can sign."

I don't take it. "What is it?"

The corners of his eyes crinkle with amusement, but he doesn't smile. "It's a contract." He hands me a dark-inked pen. "For your first year of employ."

Briefly, I scan the document, pausing at the salary amount. It's almost double my annual tuition at the Barracks. Any lingering doubts that this is the right choice vanish. With this much gold, I'll be able to pay for Rain's school, her added expenses, and have enough to replace the blackmail money in a few lunes.

I sign on the Prince's dotted line.

The Prince grins as he takes the parchment back. His eyes dance over my signature. "I can't read this. What's your name?"

"Saoirse."

"Then congratulations, Guard Saoirse Sorkova." He extends a hand. "It's a pleasure to meet you."

The combination of his smile and his eyes and his presence

overwhelms my senses. I fear touching him will cause me to disintegrate into a pile of ash.

So I give an awkward seated bow. "Thank you, Your Highness."

His brow furrows in bemusement, but he doesn't comment. "Tonight is your final night in the Barracks. Tomorrow, a carriage will deliver you from here to the Palace."

"I can find my own transport, sir. I'm going home tomorrow first."

"Is your home here in Vanihail?"

"Yes, sir."

"Then I'll arrange for a carriage to deliver you to the Palace from your home. Around midday."

Alarm bells sound in my mind. I don't want a Royal carriage coming to my home or near my family. "I can manage."

"I insist." His tone is jovial, but his Princely title and the set of his chin make it clear: it's not a request.

My eyes narrow but I keep my tone level. "Thank you, sir."

The Prince nods to the door, eyes not leaving my face. "Anarin, you're dismissed. Saoirse, a moment, please."

He's just commandeered her desk and casually dismissed her from her own office, but Anarin makes no objection.

My tongue works away at my *keil* bead again. This must be about graduation. I rejected a job from a Royal in front of Keirdre's most influential soldiers—I'd be a fool to assume there would be no consequences.

The instant the door closes behind Anarin, I'm on my feet, bowing again. "Your Highness, I apologize if I—"

"None of that," he interrupts with a wave of his hand. "I've never understood bowing."

Confused, I straighten. "Sir—"

"And I hate being called 'sir.' "

"Your Highness—"

He chuckles. It's deep like the ocean and smooth like chocolate. "I'm not being clear. You don't need to bow and you don't need to address me by title. We are—" He breaks off, assessing me. "How old are you?"

I'm still recovering from his laugh. "Excuse me, sir?"

"How old are you?"

"Seventeen."

His response smile is devastating. "See? We're the same age. You've graduated from the Vanihailian Barracks, so I can't imagine I'm even half as accomplished as you. Besides, we've only just met—I hardly think I've earned your respect yet."

"Of course you have, Your Highness." In my mind, the words are wry, but aloud, they drip sincerity.

"Hayes," he says firmly. "Please. What was the point of my parents giving me a sodding name if all anyone is ever going to call me is Your Highness?"

His smile is charming. *He* is charming. And apparently, he doesn't want to punish me for initially declining his offer.

Taken at face value, it makes for a lovely portrait. But I know better. Prince Hayes is a Royal. More important, he's a means to an end—a mark. And one of my most important rules: never call a mark by name.

So I say, "If you are not in search of an apology, Your Highness, why have you requested a private word?"

"You're ignoring my request to call me Hayes?"

I feign confusion. "Was it an order, sir?"

He tilts his head, considering. "I suppose not."

"Then surely that means I reserve the right to respect His Highness as I see fit?"

For a tick, he blinks those eyes at me, stroking something on a black chain around his neck in thoughtful contemplation. Then he tosses his head back and laughs. "Fine. Call me 'Your Highness' if you wish. And to answer your question, I want to ask you something: How does an ikatus manage to surpass fae with affinities?"

There's no judgment in his tone, but my spine stiffens just the same. "I'm a hard worker, sir."

"And that's enough?"

"Evidently."

"Hmm . . ." He continues to run his fingertips over the necklace. "Another question: Do you mind if I ask how you got that burn?"

Whatever subtle expression I've allowed to creep across my face slithers away like a snake in the sun. "Is that an order, sir?"

He frowns. "No."

"Then yes, sir."

His frown grows more pronounced. "Sorry?"

"Yes, sir," I say again, "I do mind."

CHAPTER SEVEN

Reflections

Our house borders the Jeune River, one of two rivers in Keirdre. The large wooden mill wheel turns in the flow of the river, connected to the white stone building where we pound and store flour.

Rain and Mom sit in the space of greenery between the house and river. Rain wears a white shirt with billowy sleeves and a loose-fitting dark-green skirt. Mom wears a golden-yellow dress with emerald-green stitching at the seams. They lie on a blanket surrounded by tiny blue and red flowers—Mom always makes things bloom when she's happy.

Dad stands along the river. He uses his affinity to *push* the water through the wheel, faster than the current.

Rain perks as I approach. In an instant, she's at my side, pulling me close, hiding her face in the folds of my shirt.

I breathe her in, fingers knotting in her kinky hair.

Safe. She's safe.

"Pinecone!" Mom's voice is smiling. "How was graduation? Rain said your assignment isn't too far away?"

I give her a sharp look. "You knew she was coming?"

"She wanted to support you. And Carrik went—"

"Why the hell didn't you stop her?" My arms constrict around

Rain in my anger. She squirms, but I don't let go. "You *know* it's dangerous. What were you thinking?"

The flowers blooming around my mom wither to a crumbling gray.

"Calm down," my father says.

"I'll calm down when you stop sending my sister into danger!" My eyes flash silver with my words.

Mom and Dad shrink back. The mill wheel creaks as Dad steps away, and it slows without his added speed. Something sharp and rotting blossoms in my mouth. Dad's fear. Mom's fear. Of me.

I close my eyes. Breathe in, out. Slowly, deeply.

Control. I need to get my temper under control.

Eyes still squeezed shut, I let my skin soak up the warmth of the sun and the fine mist that sprays from the rushing river.

My heartbeat slows, my hold on Rain loosens, and my shoulders ease.

I peel my eyes open. They're honey-colored, and I'm me again.

"Sorry," I murmur. "I just want to make sure she stays safe."

"Rain's fine," says Mom gently. "Nothing happened at graduation, right?"

"Something *did* happen," I say.

Rain's eyes flick nervously to mine, and the silver envelope hangs unspoken between us.

"I was offered a job. As personal guard to the Prince," I say.

Four long ticks of silence.

"What?" Dad roars. "You can't be serious. You took a job working for the Royals? The ones who—"

"I'm well aware what the Royals have done, but it doesn't matter. We need the money."

"We can make more money," Dad says.

"We're millers. You know how this works. The Royals control the price of flour, and the King has made sure we always have less than we need. I've accepted the job, and I'm not changing my mind."

Before Mom or Dad can object further, I pull at Rain. "I'm going to talk to Beansprout. I'm not debating this anymore," I call over my shoulder as I tug her into the house.

She hugs me again once the door shuts behind us. "I thought you turned down the job?"

"I changed my mind."

"Because of me?"

I place my hands on her shoulders. "Doesn't matter. I'm going to find who left that note. To do that, I need you to tell me the truth: Is there anyone outside the family who knows about you?"

"No."

"Are you sure? You never mentioned it at school? I won't be mad—I promise. I just need to know."

Rain shakes her head. "I swear, I never told anyone."

I search her eyes for deceit. My tongue roots around my mouth for a hint of deception. Nothing. It's not definitive proof, but Rain's never been a good liar. Slowly, I nod. "I'm going to find who wrote the letter. In the meantime, don't tell anyone, especially not Mom or Dad. Promise me?"

"I promise."

"Good." I procure the sack of *keil* beads Drina gifted me from my pocket and pass it to Rain. "For you."

Her eyebrows scrunch. "There's only four."

"I already took half." A lie. I took two. But if I tell Rain, she'll insist on dividing the rest between us, and I'll sleep easier knowing she's safe in her disguise for the next few lunes.

As Rain pockets the *keil* beads, I glance outside. Our parents are still at the river's edge, not paying attention to us. I hurry into the living room and kick up the corner of the rose-petal rug. Crouching, I lift the loose floorboard where I know my parents hide the money I make from the Raze. We're between payments for Rain's . . . additional expenses, and we have a bit saved up. Not much but enough to at least hold us over until I get my first wages and return the money.

Rain watches as I dig through the burlap sack and snag handfuls of ranis—practically all of it. "What are you doing?"

"I need gold to pay whoever wrote the note. Tonight at the waterfront." I readjust the floorboard and straighten the rug.

"You're actually going to pay them?"

"I'm not taking any chances."

Rain wrings her hands together. "Five hundred is a lot. Don't we need that money?"

"Yes. But don't worry—when I find who's doing this, we're getting it back."

"What're you going to do to them?"

Kill them.

There's no doubt in my mind and no alternative. But I don't want to see the look of horror that would cross Rain's face or taste the fear that would dance across my tongue.

So I feed her a half-truth. "I'm going to make sure they never threaten you again."

Hoofbeats pound on the road that leads to our house, announcing the arriving carriage to all of North Vanihail.

I sit on my bed, examining my room, making sure I don't forget anything. The walls are lavender and rosemary with white lilies painted near the floorboards and ceiling, and ropes of honeysuckle twist around my headboard. I've never been good with plants, so Mom keeps them alive while I'm gone.

Three knocks on the front door.

"Pinecone!" Mom calls. "The carriage is here."

"I'll be down in a moment."

I take a last lap around my bedroom, soaking it all in. The scuffs on the floor from Rain always forgetting to take off her shoes in the house. The singed dresser from that time Mom made cookies and set down the still-hot pan. The window screen Dad made me so I could stare at the river when I longed to be near water.

My footsteps falter in front of the mirror hidden behind my cracked-open closet door. For a tick, I wrestle the desire to take a peek, and before I can fend off the feeling, I open the door.

As a sprig, I was enthralled by my own appearance. My aunties tell me I used to sit in front of any reflective surface I could find and stare. For as long as they'd let me.

When I learned what I am and started using *keil* beads to hide, I yearned for glimpses of my real face.

I joined the Barracks when I was nine. I spent my days pretending. Pretending I was weak. Pretending to be an ikatus. Pretending the scathing comments didn't sting.

My solace was night. I'd remove my *keil* bead, lock myself in a bathroom, and watch my reflection—my *real* reflection—stare back. In those moments, I felt like myself. And at the time, being myself didn't scare me.

As I grew older, I came to realize my face wasn't a harmless infatuation but a deadly weapon.

Like any girl, I remember my first time.

I was twelve years old. I'd snuck out that night to visit Rain, and I was walking back to the Barracks. The moon was half full and, like the fool I was, I walked along the beach.

My feet sank into the soft, wet sand, and the waves lapped against my ankles in the surf.

I felt each drop of water where it came into contact with my skin, the light sting of the salt, the grit of the sand.

There was a man on the beach. Skin pale like hay and reflective in the moonlight. He had the look of an earth fae, and he was alone. Temptingly so. Just staring at the ocean, peaceful.

I still remember the call of the waves that night. They sang to me, drawing me nearer to the man.

My whole life, I'd heard the call. But before, the water's missive was just to touch. To swim. That night, the call was *hungry*.

For the first time, I removed my *keil* bead, exposing myself to someone who wasn't my family. For the first time, my face was my own and there was no need to hide. No need to pretend.

The ocean sang to me, and I echoed its mournful tune. Beautifully soft, melodic. Dark.

I stared into the man's green eyes. That one look lasted a lifetime. I felt his mind, tangible as the sand beneath my feet.

There's something unspeakably beautiful about an empty mind, ready and waiting to be flooded with my will. I was powerless against the pull of the ocean, and the man—I never learned his name—was powerless against my Siren Song.

He followed me calmly, almost gleefully, into the sea. So desperate to appease me, he stepped farther and farther into the ocean until he was swallowed whole by the waves.

He never resurfaced.

I wish I could say it made me feel horrible. I wish I could say the sight of his eyes, open and vacant in the water, haunts my nightmares.

But that would be a lie.

The truth: the feeling—the rush of the water, the pulsing adrenaline, the *taste* of his blank-slated mind—was euphoric. Addicting. I had the best sleep of my life after my first kill.

To this day, *that* is what terrifies me. Not the act of killing but how refreshed I feel after. As much as I long to lose myself in the water's pull, the instant I return to shore, all I see is my mom's disappointment. Taste my aunties' fear. My father's anger.

And my bliss—beautifully fleeting—shrivels up like a scrap of parchment aflame.

So I avoid mirrors and anything that might reflect my eerily perfect face. Not because I feel guilty but because I know I should. And because I now know that the sight of my face enchants all who see it, myself included.

Looking at it now, I feel that familiar thrum of self-appreciation at my loose hair. It's long and full of springy, unkempt curls. As a siren, I love the feel of my hair whipping around me, but as a soldier—a newly minted Keirdren Guard—it isn't practical.

I knot my hair into a braid and twist it into a tight bun at the back of my head. A monster tamed.

Finished, I slam the closet door, sealing the mirror away.

Taking hold of my two traveling rucksacks, I lug them downstairs.

My parents stand in the main room with a tiny man decked in Keirdre's colors. My parents seem . . . awkward. Neither of them can stand still, and they stare at our scuffed wooden floors like pages in a good book.

At the sound of my footsteps, the man turns, and my parents' discomfort makes sense.

He's human.

Short, wiry, and as wide around his torso as my thigh is thick. His dark hair is shorn, and his brown eyes are tired.

"There you are." My mom's smile is wooden. "This young man is going to escort you to the Palace."

"Are these your bags, ma'am?" The human reaches for my rucksacks.

Instinctively, I yank them out of reach with a skeptical look at his twiglike arms. They look like they'd snap if I clutched them too tight, and I can't imagine what would happen if he tried to lift my heavy bags. "I can carry them."

"I insist, ma'am." The human's smile doesn't reach his eyes. "His Highness asked me personally to carry your things for you."

I want to object, but he'll never defy a direct order from a superior—certainly not a Royal. Gingerly, I hand him my bags, wincing when he slumps under their weight.

My hand twitches. I want to help, but I don't want to insult him or, worse, get him in trouble. It's standard for humans to receive public punishments for any indiscretions, real or imagined, against the fae. I've heard horror stories of disappearances, humans forced to continue working while stripped of pay, and lengthy imprisonments for minor infractions.

"I'll take your things to the carriage while you say your goodbyes." The human grunts, straining from the hefty bags.

I wait until he wobbles through the front door and is out of earshot to give my parents sharp looks. "Where's—"

"Upstairs. In her room," says Mom. She raises her voice. "Beansprout? Come say bye to your sister!"

I suspect she was listening at the top of the stairwell, because Rain immediately races down the steps and flies at me in a tawny-hued blur. "Be safe, Pinecone," she murmurs into my chest. "I love you."

"I love you more."

I hold on to her, soaking up my Rain. "I'm going to visit," I promise. "All the time. A herd of trolls couldn't keep me away."

I straighten from Rain and approach my parents. I hug my mom first, who cries into my shoulder. When I hug my dad, he's still.

"Stay safe, Saoirse," he says.

I hear what he doesn't say. "Don't take unnecessary risks. Don't get discovered."

"I'll be fine," I say.

"I know." Something like sadness sneaks onto his otherwise-impassive face, too faint for me to taste. "But I want you to be better than fine."

My gut tugs, telling me to promise to be careful, but I don't want to lie to him any more than I already have. Instead, I give my family one last wave and walk to the awaiting carriage.

The human is trying to shove my bags into a rack fitted beneath the carriage for luggage. He stops as my footsteps crunch behind him. His dark cheeks are flushed—from embarrassment or exertion, I can't tell. A tall and serene fae stands alongside him. Immobile, expressionless, and making no effort to help the struggling human.

The fae is very . . . neat. His black hair is shorn as close to his scalp as possible without broaching on balding, his clothes are ironed so crisply that I fear touching him will draw blood, and his boots are so perfectly polished that they could be mistaken for mirrors. The near-luminescence of his eyes marks him as a fae, but he wears a Palace guard's uniform, navy and black, giving no indication of what his affinity is.

He doesn't speak, just tugs the handle to the navy carriage, gesturing for me to enter.

I climb inside—and almost jump when I'm met with a beautiful fae sitting leaned up against the window on the opposite side.

Prince Hayes.

Fury roils my stomach like the storming sea. I hadn't thought to expect him. Hadn't realized my forced time with the Prince would start so soon. Still, I grit my teeth and dip into a bow. "Your Highness."

His expression doesn't change, but my tongue detects something light and sweet like a ripened pear. He's amused.

"You're a bad listener. I thought Deltas were trained to be obedient?"

I fight a scowl. Everything about him is smug. From his clothes, to his broad smile, to his perfect eyes that watch me. Daring me to do something.

What that something is, I have no idea. But it aggravates me all the same.

I take the bench across from him as close to the door as possible. Linking my fingers in my lap, I look forward, hoping he'll take the hint and let us travel in silence.

He sits at the edge of my periphery, knees bent outward, hands splayed on either side of him, eyes trained on me. "You live in a mill house?"

"Yes, sir." Outside, the human boy sighs in relief as he finally fits my bags beneath the carriage.

"Alongside a river," the Prince adds.

It's not a question, so I elect not to respond.

It takes him a few ticks to realize I'm not going to answer.

He tries again. "It's odd for an ikatus who apparently gets ill around water to live so close to a river."

It's still not a question, so I remain silent.

He huffs childishly. I assume he catches on at this point, because after a moment of quiet—serene on my part, frustrated on his—he asks, "Why?"

The carriage rocks gently as we start to move.

"My parents don't suffer my same affliction, sir. And I tend to avoid the river." Both true statements. To an extent.

"Hmm." He mulls over my answer. "Can you get on a ship?"

"No, sir."

"Hmm . . ." The low timbre of his hum sends a shiver down my spine. "Are you sure? My eighteenth birthday is in one lune, and my party is on a ship. You're invited. All of my guards are."

"Regrettably, I can't attend," I say coolly.

"You don't sound regretful. Which is odd. I don't make a habit of visiting guards at their homes. For you, I made an exception."

My eyes narrow. "Why?"

He slides down the bench to sit across from me. "I think you're interesting."

I once again note the swirling patterns in his ocean eyes before forcing my gaze to fall to the window, watching Vanihail. The houses we pass are short, narrow, and wooden. We're in North Vanihail—*my* side. The side of the millers, weavers, and masons. The side of those with blistered palms and fingers worked raw. "You don't know me," I say.

"I'd like to remedy that."

"Why?" I met him yesterday, and already he asks too many questions. Watches me too closely.

If this Prince is anything like his father, he's a snake. He'll slither up, silent and swift, before wrapping around me. Loosely at first, then coil so tightly, I wouldn't be able to remember when I drew my last breath.

"I've never met someone timid enough to reject a job at the Palace out of fear of incompetence but bold enough to barge into an Enforcer's office in the middle of the night."

"I knocked," I say. "And that was a onetime thing, Your Highness. Usually, I'm boring."

He grins, showing too many teeth. "I don't believe that for a moment."

I don't respond. I don't trust myself to speak.

The houses outside are steadily growing. The small wooden houses have warped into large navy-brick manors. I see the massive stone structure of Haraya Hall, Vanihail's sentencing chamber. Human punishments are usually doled out in Sinu, but once a lune, there's a massive sentencing in Vanihail.

"You know," the Prince says when I remain silent, "a typical conversation goes back and forth."

As if entertaining him is my job. I swallow a scoff, and it burns like too-hot tea the whole way down. "You are my Prince and superior." I should stop there, but I make the mistake of meeting his eyes again. The expectant look on his face makes my blood boil and tongue loosen. "It was never my intention to converse with you. I intend to take orders from you and guard you, as my job requires."

He crooks an eyebrow. "And if I ordered you to have a conversation with me?"

My hands twitch against the desire to cross my arms petulantly. "I would remark on the weather and hope you find the topic too dull to continue."

If I expected frustration, he disappoints. "This is unfortunate, Saoirse. I'd hate to have to order you to talk to me. Orders aren't really my style."

I respond before thinking. "Talking to you isn't really my style."

He throws his head back and laughs. It's the strangest blend of sinister and alluring. "If your feet are as quick as your tongue is sharp, I'm sure you'll be a welcome addition to my guards."

The amused flavor of his emotions tells me he's goading me, but I've learned my lesson. I ignore him and stare out the window.

We ride in silence until the Palace looms ahead. I've only ever seen it from a distance, under the cloak of darkness. In the daylight, the surface of the Palace is smooth and glassy. From a distance, it appears black. Up close, it's a murky midnight. The blue exterior swirls in constant motion like it's swaying. Or breathing. It's beautiful. In a dark, eerie kind of way.

"You've never seen the Palace before?" The Prince is watching me. I don't think he's looked away since I stepped into the carriage.

"Not from here." I follow the movements of the Palace exterior, transfixed.

"Looks like you caught Dad in a good mood. Well—not a bad mood."

I frown. "What do you mean?"

"The Palace reflects his moods. Today, he's calm."

"That's unusual?"

"It is when I'm here." His grim smile is accompanied by bitterness, like raw parsnip. "With any luck, you'll never have to meet my father. Something tells me he wouldn't like you very much."

CHAPTER EIGHT

A Dollhouse

Meeting new people isn't daunting—it's too familiar to be daunting—but it's inevitably draining.

Strangers have the same reaction to seeing me: first, they stare for a breath longer than they should, then they stop looking at my face altogether to overcompensate for initial rudeness.

Shaking hands is the same. People either look directly into my eyes to avoid letting their own wander to my burn or they stubbornly stare at my wrist, pretending my face doesn't exist.

So far, the head of the Prince's personal guard, Zensen, isn't rude and doesn't stare. As he leads me through the Palace corridors to the Prince's war room to meet the other guards, I hope they're the same, but my hopes are low. People have a way of living down to my expectations.

Zensen fits here, in the corridors of the Palace, like a character plucked from the portraits on the walls and brought to life. Stoic and calm. Not Royal but regal.

As much as I despise this place, it's beautiful. Velvet navy carpets line the floors and heavy tapestries drape the walls—the same deep-blue, glassy material as the outside. The handles of the mahogany doors are handcrafted from erstwyn—a metal so beautifully sheer that, when polished, it looks like blown glass.

But tied to each beautiful ornament is a seedy, ugly story. Dyes made by earth fae in Kurr Valley who get less than a fraction of the selling price, tapestries hand-stitched by over-worked, skin-and-bone humans in Sinu living on scraps and fear, and chaeliss lights magicked by witches in Ketzal not even allowed in the Palace. The beauty of the Palace is a veneer, shrouding the broken pieces that make it whole.

Still, everything about it draws me in. Up close, the surface of the walls churns like waves. The sound is music to my ears. Soothing like a stormy sea.

I've spent my life hating the Royals, yet here I stand, in their Palace, admiring their spoils, contracted to their Prince. Owned like a doll, obligated to do their bidding.

Zensen hasn't spoken since offering his name. Normally, I appreciate the silence, but I have questions that need answers.

"Did you attend graduation?" I ask.

Zensen gives a stiff nod. "I went with Hayes. And Erasmus. You'll meet him momentarily."

I make note of this. I'm compiling a list of everyone in the stands at the Ranking who frequents the Palace—anyone who could have slipped that note in Rain's bag.

Zensen pushes open the steel-reinforced door to the Prince's war room and allows me to walk in ahead of him.

The war room has no windows. Torches are bracketed to the walls around the perimeter, but the light isn't far-reaching. A table cuts through the center of the room surrounded by high-backed wooden chairs that look about as comfortable as the cold, gray floor.

Four people sit around the table. As expected, they all stare as I enter, but I only count three looks of surprise.

The woman sitting closest to the door is stoic. Her dusky

complexion is paired with tight silvery curls, her mouth is set in a flat line, and her eyes—one gray flecked with green, the other green flecked with gray—look unimpressed. Her speckled eyes and bright hair give her away: she's a witch.

I'm as taken aback by her as the rest of the guards are by me. Fae *hate* witches. How a witch came to work for the Prince—a member of his personal guard, no less—I can't fathom.

The heavy door slams shut behind me. The sound is a splash of ice-cold water to the dazed inhabitants of the room. The surprised stares glide away from me, but the taste of their burning curiosity lingers on my tongue.

"This is Saoirse." Zensen makes his way to the head of the table. "She is a recently graduated Delta and the newest addition to Hayes's guard."

They grumble a greeting, and I claim the empty chair next to the witch. She tilts her head and smiles, eyes glimmering with mischief. "Good to meet you, Saoirse. I'm Laa'el." The mischief spikes. "How old are you?"

"Seventeen."

"*Seventeen?*" The fae on Zensen's right echoes.

I almost cough on the bitter resentment that accompanies his indignation.

Laa'el smirks. Clearly, riling the fae was her intent.

The fae in question is older, tall, has a faint stoop, and his hair is graying. He makes no effort to hide his scowl. "I knew Hayes was hiring a graduate, but a child?"

"Our job is not to question the Prince, Erasmus," says Zensen sharply.

So this is Erasmus. The other member of the Prince's guard who attended graduation.

Erasmus glowers at me as if I hired myself. "If they're letting children graduate the Barracks, perhaps their standards have lowered since my graduation."

"Probably, E." A fae watches him in lazy amusement. She's exceptionally pretty. Dark russet-toned skin, a heart-shaped face, and big blue eyes. "Plenty of things are bound to have changed since you were a sprig—they've even invented the wheel."

"Thank you for the insight, Jeune," says Erasmus waspishly. "I truly appreciate your generation's contributions. What are they again?"

"My most crowning achievement is not needing my father to buy my way into a Palace job."

His face darkens. "I graduated the Barracks at the top of my year."

"You placed *thirteenth* in your Ranking. I was first in mine."

The torches lining the room *jump*. Flames arch over our heads, accompanied by a loud clap from Zensen. *"Enough."*

Silence.

The flames return to their original positions, and Zensen adjusts the cuffs of his shirt. "If you're all finished, we will do introductions for our newcomer. I implore you to allow me to finish before we commence bickering." He looks at me, expression calm. "I'm Zensen, fire fae and head guard for Hayes."

As we work around the table, I commit each name to memory. Erasmus is an air fae, Jeune is a water fae, Devlyn is an earth fae, and Laa'el is a witch.

It's an odd mix. The Royals are notorious for favoring water fae. Until today, I didn't even realize the Royals employed anyone else as Palace guards.

I assess them as I would a sparring opponent. There's a high likelihood one of them either delivered the silver envelope or knows more than they should, and I intend to find out who.

"We start each day here," Zensen explains over my roaring thoughts. "To review Hayes's schedule. Only senior guards—myself, Erasmus, or Jeune—can be alone with Hayes. Saoirse, you are a novice until I or Hayes says otherwise. Everyone else is a junior guard."

"You speak of rank as if it means something," Laa'el mutters. "I have been here longer than you, and I am still not a senior guard."

"A witch cannot be a senior guard," says Zensen.

"A ridiculous rule. Clearly"—Laa'el jerks her head at me—"fae cannot be trusted to protect other fae."

I raise an eyebrow. "What does this have to do with me?"

"Your face, girl. If the fae are so skilled at protection, what happened to your face?"

Of course my face. She remained impassive at the sight of me, but as promised, my burn is the first and last thing anyone sees when they look at me. "I fail to see how that's any of your concern."

She smiles. At least, it's supposed to be a smile. It looks more like she bares her teeth in semi-good humor. "How much ranis do you have on you, girl? I've a few *keil* beads I could sell you to fix your face."

"I'm not interested." My voice is ice. "And there's nothing about me I need you to fix."

Sharp, tangy surprise arises from the fae in the room but, like all witches, Laa'el's feelings remain a mystery to me.

The look Zensen gives Laa'el is biting, but he offers no verbal reprimand. "Rotation is determined by me." He keeps going as if she hasn't spoken. "Each day is divided into three shifts—morning, evening, and night. You will have one shift each day with the exception of mandatory Royal events. They are not common, but Hayes's birthday celebration is one lune away, and all guards are required to attend."

"Am I on the rotation tonight?" I'm already spinning through excuses for why I can't. Aside from having no desire to see the Prince again today, I have a previous engagement—delivering money to Rain's blackmailers at midnight.

"Not tonight." Zensen lays a wide sheet of parchment across the table. "Tonight's schedule is already set. You can use this day to unpack and rest. Tomorrow"—he picks up a pen and scrawls my name on the schedule—"you will join me for the night shift. We meet outside the Prince's room at midnight."

He writes my name in neat, loopy letters. Not the handwriting of the silver envelope. It doesn't mean he's innocent, but it's information I tuck away.

When we're dismissed, I hurry to my room to avoid getting sucked into a conversation. All of the guards' chambers are in the same corridor as the Prince's bedroom and war room for ease of access, so it's a short sprint down the hall to my new lodgings.

I turn the erstwyn door handle and enter. It's nicer than I anticipated. Large with a wide window framed with gold curtains, a bed double the size of mine at home, and a samsam wood desk.

A smooth, flat stone sits on my desk with a rune carved into the surface. I press a finger to the rune, and the overhead string of chaeliss lanterns ignite all at once, bathing my room in orange light.

First order of business: I yank the curtains closed, drowning out the light. The dimness brings a comforting sense of solitude

to the extravagant newness, and the seclusion makes it feel more
real. More like mine.

Second order: I yank the mirror from the wall where it hangs
above my desk, flip it over, and cram it under my bed before I
get lost in my reflection and my instincts guide me to something
I'll regret.

Six sets of my new uniform sit folded on my bed—long-sleeve
navy shirt with gold detail, black pants, and a gold pin with Keirdre's crest.

After changing, I sift through my rucksacks at the foot of my
bed, feeling for my pale-blue freya candle. I set it on the corner
of my desk.

When I light it, the wax melts quickly and the surrounding
surface of the desk pools with molten candle. It shrinks until it's
less than half of its original height—which means it's a smidge
past midday.

My freya candle is a gift from Auntie Drina. Unlike my *lairic*
beads, it's not illegal, but it's very rare for non-witches and very
expensive. Drina didn't give this to me out of necessity but, in
her words, "Just because."

It's my most prized possession.

Aside from telling time, it's useful.

I pass a hand over the candle, and the flame flares blue like
the sky on a crystal day—a letter.

The fire sputters and shoots ash into the air. It flickers faster
as the dark ash billows like a plume of smoke, hovering above
the candle as it shapes into a thin sheet. The flame brightens,
and the sheet of ash solidifies into a page of vellum covered in
familiar curling handwriting.

I snatch the vellum and greedily drink in the words of
my sister.

Pinecone,
Good luck on your first day! Please, please, please stay
safe and don't do anything rash. And don't forget to tell
me everything!
Love,
Your Beansprout
By the way, you should forgive Carrik!

My lips curve into a smile.

I have every intention of taking a self-guided tour of the rest
of the Royal Dollhouse, but for now, I sit at my desk and write
to Rain.

CHAPTER NINE

Wasted Potential

The Kivren Waterfront is abandoned this time of night. When I lived at the Barracks, I'd often escape here to jump into the sea away from prying eyes. I'd sink to the bottom, rest in the sand, and just . . . *breathe*.

Now I'm short of breath, and my nerves are strung sky-high.

The sand is coarse underfoot, and the vast ocean, pitch-black with the moon's reflection bouncing in the waves, stretches out before me. My serene memories sink in the brackish water. The waterfront is no longer a place of refuge but a grim reminder that even my best efforts weren't enough to keep my sister safe.

I turn from the sea and search the empty beach for a spot to stash the heavy bag of gold hidden in my cloak. There's a lone bench of rotting wood a couple dozen paces away. I trudge through the sand and slip the bag underneath it.

The exposed, flat beach is a perfect dropping location. There's nowhere for me to keep watch over the bench without being seen by anyone coming to retrieve the money.

I want to wait anyway, but I can't risk the blackmailer seeing me and exposing Rain as punishment. The threat in the silver envelope was clear: I upset the blackmailer, Rain gets punished.

My gut wrenches in protest, but I skulk away from the bench and head back to the Palace, contemplating all the ways I can find this blackmailer and sing him to his grave.

Zensen is rigid against the Prince's door when I arrive for my guard's shift the next evening.

He doesn't move as I approach, but he murmurs a lackluster, "Good evening."

"Good evening, sir," I say.

"Zensen," he corrects. "We use first names."

"Don't bother with her," someone behind me says. "You'd sooner convince the Palace to jump into the ocean than get Saoirse Sorkova to move a single pace to the right."

I force my eyes not to roll as I turn to the approaching Prince. Erasmus stands on his right, stoic, and Devlyn is on his left, grinning.

"Thanks, E, thanks, Dev." The Prince dismisses them. "Have a good night." Humming to himself, he slips into his room but leaves the door open. "Saoirse, I hope your first shift is uneventful. I plan on staying in, but if anything changes, I'll let you know. Good night."

He closes his door.

Zensen and I stand in stillness for all of ten beats before the door bursts open with enough force to make me jump.

The Prince has returned.

Worse—he's smirking and tastes of mischief.

In the brief moment he was in his room, he's changed into a dark dashiki and matching pants. The neck of his tunic dips to his navel, displaying his toned chest and clearly defined abdominal muscles.

I avert my eyes when I realize they've trailed lower than they should.

"Change of plans," the Prince announces. "Zen, contact the usual crowd. I'm hosting a party in celebration of the newest addition to my guard."

The suggestion is so nonsensically beyond the barrier, it takes me several moments to realize he means me.

"Sir, I don't need a party," I say.

He grins. "Think of it as an early birthday celebration for me, then."

Wonderful. A full lune to celebrate the birth of another sodding Royal.

As if sensing the direction of my thoughts, the Prince adds, "Have fun tonight. That's an order."

I swallow my protests and try to ignore the smirk on his face that I already know is going to crawl under my skin and stay there to rot.

His party reeks of garlicky overconfidence and the noxiously sweet berry wine he and his friends are gorging themselves on.

I'm doing my best to melt into the walls to avoid being noticed by either the Prince or the many, many fae milling about.

His room is massive enough to house two fiddlers, a drummer, and a dance floor. The fae not standing near the drinks tables, pouring wine down their throats, flail in the middle of the room.

Like the rest of the Palace, his room is—I begrudgingly admit—beautiful. Strands of chaeliss lanterns float overhead and meet in the middle of the ceiling around a flaming chandelier suspended from a midnight ceiling. His bed is big enough to have swallowed three of mine whole. Resting alongside it is a stone basin of water.

I stay on the opposite side of the room from the basin, but my eyes are drawn to it. Being surrounded by so many fae makes me edgy. Like they might see through the screen of my *keil* bead. In my discomfort, the water offers a false promise of solace. It would quiet the pounding in my head, but it would also make the urge to kill overwhelming.

My fingers twitch, eager to reach the water.

Control.

I'm in the Palace surrounded by the children of the most influential fae in the kingdom—I need to maintain total control of my instincts.

I fold my arms and draw myself closer to the wall.

"Saoirse." The Prince stands before me.

I tense. Lost in watery fantasies, I hadn't noticed him slinking toward me.

"Sir," I say.

"You haven't moved." He sounds disappointed. His alcohol-glazed eyes droop into a pout as he rests against the wall next to me. Even drunk, the motion is smooth and graceful. Not clunky like the rest of the fae stumbling around his room. I wonder if it's natural for him or if he taught himself to be beautiful.

"You could at least try to have fun," he says after a pause.

"I did, Your Highness. I asked to leave."

He chuckles dryly. "You think standing in an empty hallway is more fun than a party?"

"Yes, sir." I have no intention of talking to any of his so-called friends, and considering how focused they are on dancing and wine, they've hardly noticed me.

The Prince looks like he wants to argue, but the fight drains from his face and he sighs. "You're probably right." He flops to the floor. Scratch that—"flop" is too harsh a word. The movement is sudden, but it's still fluid and gentle. He pats the floor next to him. "Let's sit."

I wasn't expecting him to concede. And I don't like it when he surprises me. It makes it harder to figure him out. "I'd rather not, sir. I like to stay alert."

"Saoirse." He slurs my name so it comes out sounding like *Sasha*. "Nothing bad will happen if you sit and take a break for five minutes."

He hasn't given an order and I'm tempted to refuse—*but* the Prince is drunk, and nothing loosens a fae's tongue like too much drink or a too-pretty girl.

I lower myself to sit beside him.

He grins. "You even make sitting look stiff."

"I told you, sir. I'm always on alert." I press forward before he can respond with something inane. "I didn't see you at the Ranking, sir."

If he thinks the question is odd, he doesn't show it. "I wasn't there. I was trapped in Anarin's office in the Barracks."

"Why?"

"Too many people. My father doesn't like for me to go out in public places. But I made Zen and E let me sneak a peek. I saw you." His words are still slurred, but his stare is sharp. "You were worth the risk."

I stare at a spot on the wall over his shoulder to avoid his gaze. "What's the point of having guards if you can't go out in public?"

"My father doesn't trust my guards." Wry grin. "Probably because I hire witches and ikatus."

"Then why hire a witch?" *And me. Why hire me?*

I haven't asked the question aloud, but he hears it just the same. "I hired Laa'el to annoy him. And you . . ." His sentence trails with a smirk. "Because you're the best. And you don't like me."

He's surprised me again. "I . . ." Choose my words carefully. "I don't see why that would entice you to hire me."

The Prince smiles. It's more thoughtful than amused. "I thought you'd deny it. What about me don't you like?"

Spoiled, arrogant, bossy, and a Royal come to mind, but what I say: "I just met you, sir."

"So I must've made a strong impression," he says. "I like you."

"You don't know me."

"You make a strong impression." His head lolls against the wall. "Even if you pretend to be boring."

"I'm not pretending."

He chuckles. "Yes, you are. That's your thing, isn't it? Pretending."

My chest constricts, and the large room feels so tight, I can't breathe. Is he hinting what I think he is?

"What do you mean?"

"You know what I mean." He meets my eyes and, for a moment, the haze of alcohol fades and he's looking at me—*really* looking at me. Like I'm polished glass and he can see right through me. Then it fades, and his face slackens.

Before I decipher the shift, he leans away and retches.

I still want to ask him what he meant about pretending, but a group of concerned, equally drunk partygoers swarm us asking if he's all right. They're loud, they smell, and they're crowding me against a wall.

The water calls to me from the other side of the room.

Kill.

My head is pounding.

I take a breath and eye the Prince. Considering the fact that he's still half slumped over, I doubt he's up for answering more questions—or that he'll notice if I slip out.

The pressure in my chest grows, and my decision is made. Tuning out the water's cry, I shove my way out of the Prince's room.

I rest my back against the wall, chest heaving as I suck in the not-stale air. I only spent an hour in the heat of the Prince's room, but I'm more drained than if I ran to the edge of the barrier in Kurr Valley and back.

Zensen is across from me, expression unchanged, but I taste the sweetness of his amusement. "I take it you didn't enjoy the party in your honor?"

I hadn't thought him capable of humor. "Not particularly."

The door creaks open, and the Prince stumbles into the hallway. "Saoirse?" He's still saying my name wrong.

The lights in his room were dim. Here, in the corridor, I see him more clearly. His hand-spun clothes are rumpled, there's a stain on his collar from his vomit, his boots have lost their shine, and his eyes have a drunken emptiness to them.

He's the second-most powerful man in Keirdre, but all I see when I look at him is wasted potential.

"Sir, you should go back inside," I say. "Perhaps some water—"

"No." He sounds petulant. "Zen, give us a moment?"

"Er . . . I'm not sure I should—"

"Just wait around the corner."

"Of course." Zensen ducks around the corner without another objection.

The Prince slumps against the wall beside me. "I'm sorry for throwing up on you."

Is that why he stumbled out of the party after me?

"You didn't," I say.

He frowns. Looks me over once. Twice. Three times. His frown deepens. "Then why did you leave?"

"Sir, I spent the whole night waiting for an excuse to leave."

"Hayes," he corrects. "Call me Hayes."

"Is that an order?"

He groans. "Why do you always ask me that?"

"You're my Prince. I want to make sure I'm respecting your orders."

Something flickers in his eyes, but it's gone before I can identify it. "You never said why you don't like me."

"You never said why you think I'm pretending."

He flashes a humorless smile. "I keep expecting you to deny it. I don't know why." Pause while he picks at drying vomit on his collar. "I'm going to figure you out, Saoirse."

"Why do you care so much?"

He grins lazily. "Because we're kindred spirits."

I'm so startled, I clap a hand over my face to hide a laugh. "Sir, we are the furthest we could possibly be from kindred spirits."

"Not true," he objects. "When I met you, you looked like you had something to prove."

"What do you possibly have to prove, Your Highness?"

"My father despises me."

The audacity of the comparison sears me raw. A spoiled Prince free to throw lavish parties from the comfort of his house-sized bedchambers draws parallels between us because his father doesn't approve of the way he spends his time? It's more than maddening. It's absurd. Egotistical. *Infuriating.*

"And that makes us kindred spirits?" Somehow, I keep my voice level.

"You disagree?"

I've spent the past nine years working harder than anyone else, swallowing my own shame, battling off the disgust of my fellow Deltas, pushing myself harder than anyone else, to be the best.

The Prince has spent his life drinking himself sick and throwing parties from the safety of his oversized bedroom.

But I don't say any of that. "I can't imagine our spirits would have much to discuss, Your Highness."

He gives me a slow grin. "I knew it." He chuckles. "You're not boring at all."

Rustling from down the hall cuts off my response—it's coming from my room.

My first thought—the blackmailer. What if they followed me here? What if they want more money?

"Did you hear that?" I say.

"Hear what—"

I take off sprinting down the hall before he's finished the question.

I try the handle to my room—unlocked—even though I know I locked it when I left. My fear fuels me as I slam the door open and burst inside.

It's pitch-black save for a hint of hallway light spilling in.

Faint movement to my right, near the bed.

I pounce.

My right hand latches on to the shadowy figure's arm, holding them still.

They pull—a vain attempt to tug free—but my grip is stronger.

I swing my free hand to wrap around the stranger's neck, shoving them against the wall in a choke hold.

A hand flies up and encircles my wrist. It yanks, trying to pull my hand from their neck.

Light floods my room.

My hand stays wrapped around the intruder's throat as I look to the door.

Devlyn stands next to my desk, chaeliss stone in hand, eyes wide in a mix of surprise and guilt, strong enough to taste.

My gaze snaps to the person pinned to the wall.

The water fae in the Prince's guard. Jeune.

I drop my hand.

She tumbles forward, clutching her neck as she gasps for breath.

The image of her hunched over and struggling to breathe is pathetic enough that I should feel guilt or something like it, but I don't. I'm *furious.*

"What the hell are you doing?"

She sucks in a final breath and half rises. Her hands still support her upper half on her knees, but she brings her head up to assess me. "I wasn't expecting that from an ikatus."

"Seems like you weren't expecting me at all," I say back.

"Fair." She inclines her head toward me. "I assumed Hayes would keep you occupied a bit longer."

"Turns out, he can't handle his liquor." I speak through gritted teeth. "I'll ask again: What the hell are you doing here?"

Before she can respond, another voice speaks from behind me.

"Saoirse?" The sodding Prince. "You all right?"

Brilliant response time.

I walk away from Jeune to the door.

The Prince and Devlyn stand in the hallway, watching our spat. They eye me curiously as I come to the door.

They still look curious as I close it in their faces.

I pivot and crook a pointed brow at Jeune.

She sighs. "You're being dramatic. We do it to all the new guards. Think of it like . . . initiation."

"I prefer to think of it as trespassing. How did you get in here?"

"I just picked the lock; it wasn't hard. I think you're over-reacting. Look, for your first night shift, we swipe something and see how long it takes you to realize it's missing."

"Fun game," I deadpan.

"You didn't let me finish," she says. "When you realize it's gone, you follow a trail of clues to find it. It's supposed to test and sharpen your deductive skills."

"You said 'we,'" I comment. "Who else is involved?"

"Everyone."

"Even Erasmus?" I have difficulty picturing Erasmus, who can't go more than a few ticks without making some scathing comment about how young I am, engaged in a childish prank like this.

"He knows about it. He thinks it's a useful activity." Seeing my expression—I don't know what it is, but I'm sure it borders on disdain—she takes a breath. "It's not that serious. You weren't supposed to catch me, and you sure as hell weren't supposed to pin me to the wall. You got any more tricks hidden in your uniform?"

I scowl. "That's my business." I move aside and jerk my door open, motioning for her to leave. "The surest way to make it your business is to not get out of my room. *Now.*"

Jeune holds up her hands in surrender. "Point taken and lesson learned."

"Yet you're still here."

"I just want to say I'm sorry. Here, I'll take the rest of your night shift so you can get some sleep and cool down." She smiles and makes her way to the door. "You're good at this. Maybe we could spar sometime?" She opens the door. "I'll see you tomo—"

"Wait." I hold out a hand, palm up. "Give it back."

"Give what back?" Her eyes widen in fake innocence. "If you can't tell me what I took, then—"

"My freya candle."

With a long sigh, she slaps the candle into my hand. "You've got a good eye."

I think about saying thank you.

Instead, I shove her out the door, slam it shut, and turn the damned lock.

CHAPTER TEN

Blue

M_y desk rattles as I slam down my freya candle and fall into the chair, *seething*.

I don't believe that this was for some petty game. If she had an ulterior motive—as I suspect she did—she must know more about me than she let on. I already feel the Prince knows too much, and with Jeune's intrusion, I fear she either had something to do with the silver envelope or suspects I'm not what I say.

My blood pulses a roaring drumbeat in my ears, flooding my other thoughts.

I strike a match and hold it to the freya candle.

I inhale as the burning wax recedes. Watching it burn down, down, down, until only a fifth remains, is oddly soothing.

My stare shifts from wax to flame.

It's burning a brilliant blue.

The pressure in my head lessens, and the drums fade.

I pass a palm over the flame and wait as the ash forms a page. I expect a reply from Rain, but when the page is complete, the handwriting isn't hers.

My heart tugs. The penmanship is rough and blocky— Carrik.

I contemplate throwing the letter away unread, but I only have the strength to entertain the thought for an instant before I yank the vellum from the flame.

Saoirse,
I'm sorry.
Rain let me borrow her freya candle to write to you. Please. Let's talk.
Carrik

Short and to the point. Flowery language has never been us.

I set the letter on my desk, still unsure if I'm going to respond or not.

I figure that with Carrik's letter delivered, the flame will revert to its usual orange. Except it's still blue.

Reaching out again, I wave my hand over the candle. Ash shoots from the flame, molding itself into a second sheet of vellum.

It's blank.

My stomach drops—not in dread but in anticipation—and I can't help the eager stutter of my pulse.

It's from my Employer.

I leave the page suspended in the flame, mind whirring. I don't *need* this job. With my new Palace salary, I never need to take another job from the Raze again.

The problem—the horrible, ugly problem: I *want* to.

The Palace makes my body hum and blood burn. The Prince watches me too closely, the guards are too familiar, and Jeune's invasion is a fresh wound. The thought of a kill excites me.

But that's not fair. Even if Jeune hadn't crept into my room and the Prince were less intense, I'd thirst for a kill.

The blue flame fades to orange as I take the blank page from the candle, contemplating my choices.

The most logical course of action: ignore the note. *Don't* find my next mark.

Yet my first instinct: go. *Kill.*

Lune above, I'm sick of ignoring my instincts.

I try to rationalize what I know I'm going to do. The kill is as much a part of me as my dad's water affinity is a part of him. Or Mom's earth affinity. Or Y'ddrina's magic. If I deny myself a kill for too long, the end result is violent and tragic. This I know too well.

My feet lead me to my still-unpacked rucksack. I sift until I feel my *lairic* bracelet. My fingers twist the beads to the configuration I know by instinct. I run the stone bead over the page, and dark ink bleeds across the vellum in my Employer's slanted cursive.

Felix Fleming.

Underneath his name is a rune configuration.

Each mark is different. Sometimes, the note gives me an address. Other times, it's a time and a location. Rarely, I'm given a *lairic* configuration.

These are trickier. When I Dreamweave, I'm not physically with my mark. He can see me, and if I touch him, he perceives it as real, but others around him can't see or hear me and, since my touch isn't real, it can't inflict damage. Any poison I provide will leave him unscathed, and any blade I wield will leave him unmarked. I sit at my desk as I twist the beads into the configuration on the vellum. I place the page in my freya candle's flame.

With no intended destination, the fire licks it up, burning it to ash.

I press the bloodstone, closing my eyes as my surroundings melt away. It's late, so there's a chance that when I appear in my mark's consciousness, I'll find myself in a dream and need to find a way to wake him.

When I open my eyes, I'm in an office.

The walls are a rich red, covered with tapestries and gold-framed paintings. The ceiling is dotted with chaeliss torches, all lit, despite the late hour.

My eyes fall to the desk beneath a floor-to-ceiling stained glass window. Behind the desk is a young man bent over a sheet of parchment, scratching away. He's dressed in the colors of a fire fae: smoke-gray pants and a black tunic. His eyes are bright gray and lined with ash to make them appear larger. A Phydian beauty ritual. He taps a black coin against the desk's surface as he writes, the movement repetitive and absent.

He hasn't noticed me yet.

I push my tongue against the *keil* bead in my mouth, spitting it out.

My mark must hear me move, because he looks up. First, I sense his shock, but the sensation ebbs and flows seamlessly into the taste of spicy lust. His expression falters, and his brilliant gray eyes comb over my body.

He doesn't speak. I think he's forgotten how.

"Hello," I say, low and sultry.

The spice amplifies. "H-hi," he stammers. "Er . . . hi."

I never tire of this part. The first instant a mark lands eyes on me. The instant the mere sight of my face sends his mind flee-ing for cover and his jaw crashing to the floor. It's gratifying to watch a man settle himself so comfortably in the palm of my hand.

I can't tell if we're in a dream or his reality, so I circle the desk to stand next to his brown leather chair.

Gentle as a caress, I lay a hand on his shoulder, leaning forward to stare into his eyes.

He leans as well, perhaps thinking I mean to press my lips against his.

Instead, I give his shoulder a pinch.

My mark jumps, but our surroundings remain as they are.

Good. He's awake.

I feign a breathy laugh and remove my hand from his arm, holding it out for him to take. "Can I show you something?"

"I—I shouldn't—" He blinks, trying to clear the fog my presence swirls in his mind.

My lips part and I sing—just a few notes. The mild panic in his face wisps away. He's a blank slate once more.

"Let me show you something." My hand hovers over his, a breath of air separating our skin.

Silently, he closes the gap.

I step back, pulling my mark to stand. He's tall. I have to tilt my head back to look at him. His age is difficult to place. The lines around his eyes make him look older than me, but the plumpness of his cheeks makes him appear younger.

My eyes hold his captive as I guide him backward. Two men wait outside the office. They straighten to attention. "Sir," the taller of the two says. "Is there something we can get for you?"

It takes me a tick longer than it should to identify them: guards. Assigned to protect wealthy and influential fae. It's considered a shameful job, rivaled only by nursemaid's duty at the Barracks and a position in Sinu, but with the Raze more powerful than ever, many wealthy fae see no alternative.

"Er—" Clearly, my mark also forgot about his personal guards. I trail my hand up his back, drawing a shudder. "Dismiss them."

"You're both dismissed for the night," he echoes woodenly. In his haze, it doesn't occur to him to question why he can hear me but his guards can't.

The men exchange skeptical looks. "Your father—"

"I don't need a nursemaid," says my mark. "And I'm visiting Fin. I'll be on horseback, and when I arrive, he'll have enough security."

They look as if they intend to argue further, so I say, "Tell them you'll complain to Training Soldier Pierce Flynn if they stand in your way."

It's a cruel blow, but the moment my mark repeats it, the guards duck their heads and stand aside.

I'm better able to grasp my surroundings once my mark and I are outside. My consciousness has drifted out of Vanihail, into the neighboring sector Serington. This community is too expensive-looking to be familiar to me, but I know where we are in proximity to the Vanihailian border. More importantly, I know where we are in proximity to the Greysn River.

"What brings you to Serington?" I ask as we traipse through the streets. "You have the look of a Phydian."

"M-my father." His eyes drink in my face as he speaks. "I'm visiting him."

"How sweet."

He stumbles over loose gravel in the road. His eyes drop and he frowns. "Where—what am I doing?" he mumbles to himself. "I shouldn't—"

I cut him off with a song, the melody warm and smooth like a hot drink on a cold day.

His face slackens again. No one we pass can see or hear me, so I turn around, continuing my song and dropping his hand.

He reaches out to me. With each step I backtrack, he stumbles forward.

I guide my mark down as many narrow alleys as I can. It's late enough that the streets are deserted, but I don't want to risk him being seen or recognized. I almost sigh in relief when I pick up the sound of the Greysn rushing behind me.

My feet speed up until I'm sprinting backward. He runs as well, chasing me. I cease singing in favor of running and don't stop until I'm at the river.

There's no one around. Just me, my mark, and the Greysn.

A drop of water soars through the air from the river. It lands on the back of my hand. Then another. And another.

I stand, swaying like a willow in the wind, eyes closed, head thrown back, reveling in the chill of the water.

When I finally blink open my eyes, I feel them flashing, fierce and silver.

Kill.

The water whispers in my ear, my mind, and I give in.

I step back and sing again.

My mark follows.

Another step and I feel the water lap against my ankles. *Kill.*

Another step and the water is to my knees.

My mark's movements are clumsy as he wades through the shallows to get to me.

When I step back again, my foot hits nothing but water. I sink back, allowing the water to swallow me whole as I submerge myself in the roar, singing all the while.

The world is shades of blue. Turquoise near the surface, where the moonlight hits the water, gradually darkening to a deep midnight below. The river swirls with tree branches, silt, and leaves, but they swerve around me as I drift deeper and deeper into the water.

The current tugs, too strong for most fae to survive, but not strong enough to overpower me.

The tips of my mark's boots appear near the surface before he plunges, headfirst, into the river after me.

I keep singing. I love the sound of my voice underwater. It has a haunting echo that ripples through the water, intense enough to feel.

My mark's eyes are wide and desperate as he paddles down, fighting the current, yearning to reach me.

I take hold of his outstretched arms. A reward for his dedication.

I taste the tang of his gratitude and the sweet honey of his relief.

His mind is open to me, blank pages for my perusal. All I sense is me. His desire for me. His willingness to do whatever I want.

I revel in these moments. The moment before a mark becomes a success. I'm free from the weight of obligation, judgment, and pretending. I'm not a daughter, monster, or weakling. Just . . . me.

I keep my arms around him. The water surges as I sing softly into his ear, gently stroking his hair as if I'm singing him to sleep.

His body goes limp in my arms.

I loosen my hold and release.

The river sweeps him away in a blur of blues.

CHAPTER ELEVEN

Weapon of Choice

I'm a churning mess of exhaustion and exhilaration as I burst into my room after the morning briefing.

I'm tired—I only managed to squeeze in a few hours of sleep—but also brimming with restless energy from last night's kill.

My instincts are singing, already thirsting for the rush of another kill, while my body yearns to drown in my bedcovers until my next night shift.

Both sides—instinct and body—lose. As I enter my room, my steps falter.

A silver envelope taunts me from my unmade bed.

I slam my door shut and stumble forward, snatching the letter and ripping it open.

The handwriting is the same. Except it's crueler. The writer's smugness shines through the looping letters.

I'm glad to see you know how to follow directions.
Have you ever heard of King Larster's creature cullings?
I assume you haven't. For your next task, find someone who has and report to me what you learn.

I flip over the parchment, hoping for something written on the back. As before, the only identifiable feature is the Royal seal pressed into red wax.

They're toying with me. They want me to know they can enter my room whenever they please. I'm not safe from them, and neither is my sister.

I trace a thumb over the unfamiliar handwriting. *Creature culling.*

I've never heard of it, but it's sinister-sounding enough to make the hairs on the back of my neck rise.

Whoever left this note has access to the Palace and the Royal seal. Considering only the King and Prince have a seal, I have to assume it was someone working closely with either of them.

My top contender: Jeune.

Next on my list: Zensen and Erasmus. They were at the Barracks for graduation. And by the Prince's own admission, they were briefly at the Ranking.

A knock at my door cuts through the muck of my questions.

I shove the letter under my pillow before opening the door.

The Prince flashes his perfect smile from the other side. Zensen stands stoic over his shoulder.

"Your Highness." I dip into a bow.

He sighs. "Don't you ever tire of bowing?" Somehow, his voice is free of alcohol-induced grogginess.

"I could never tire of giving my Prince the respect he deserves, sir."

His eyes narrow, but his lips strain against a grin.

"Did you want something, sir?" I ask.

"It occurred to me that no one has shown you the training room, and I thought I would. Personally."

"I'm sure I can find it on my own, sir." I start to close the door, but he shoves a boot inside, stopping me.

"I was actually hoping for a weapons demonstration." As he speaks, he rests his body against the wood of the door, nudging it open farther and bringing our faces closer together. Part of me wants to step back; the other part fears it'll seem too much like a retreat.

I don't move.

"Do you have a weapon of choice?" His breath fans my cheeks. *My face. Or my voice. Depends what I'm wearing.*

I hold my tongue and pretend to contemplate. "A crossbow." I'm too aware of the narrow space between us. The energy he emits is packed with warmth. *Heat.*

"Really?" He tastes intrigued. "I've never used one."

A pointless statement. He's a Royal; there's no reason for him to do anything other than look pretty (check) and kill anything he doesn't like (another check).

When I don't respond, he continues. "I want to see you perform. I only caught a glimpse at the Ranking." His tone is casual, but the taste of his curiosity is too intense to be idle.

"Is this an order, sir?" I ask.

He groans. The sound is part amused, part frustrated, and loaded with enough heat to thaw winter. "Think of it as a skill assessment for a new hire."

It's not an unreasonable request for a new employer to make of an employee. Holding in a glower, I leave the Prince standing in the doorway to slip on my shoes.

"Are those your boots?" he asks. "They're ancient. When was the last time you got a new pair?"

I finish tying the laces and leave, taking care not to brush against him. "I'm not sure, sir."

"You're not sure or you don't want to tell me?" He falls into step beside me. Vaguely, I'm aware Zensen follows us, silent as ever.

"Both," I say.

"Fair enough. Perhaps with your new salary, you can buy yourself new boots. Or maybe a pair for your sister."

My hands curl at the mention of Rain. Of course he looked into me—and of *course* my sister appeared on a background check—but the thought of a Royal knowing anything about her sends my pulse thrumming.

"My sister doesn't need new boots," I say dismissively.

"Hmm. If you don't mind my asking, your sister goes to Caruston. It's a pricey school."

That's an understatement. Caruston Academy is the most expensive school for water fae in Vanihail. With Rain's added expenses, our bills are even more exorbitant than the wealthy fae who can actually afford tuition. If it wasn't absolutely necessary, we'd send her somewhere else. *Anywhere* else. But Caruston is the only school that suits Rain's needs.

"That's not a question," I point out.

"I'm wondering how a family of millers can afford to send a daughter to Caruston but not buy the other a decent pair of boots."

He knows.

The thought crashes into my mind like driftwood on a beach.

It would make sense that he knows. It would explain why he watches me too closely, constantly pesters me, and why that damned smile of his seems as sly as it is beautiful.

"Saoirse?" he presses when I don't say anything.

"Debt, sir." It's true. To an extent.

"Ah. Sorry." He sounds contrite, but I don't believe it. Not when he's once again wearing hunting boots crafted for tramping leaves and rough terrain but used instead for traipsing velvet rugs and rose petals.

"You could always raise the price of flour," I say. It's meant to sound flippant, but he slows as he churns my words.

"What do I have to do with the price of flour?"

"The Royal family sets a limit on how much we're allowed to charge, sir," I say slowly. "The limit makes it nearly impossible for millers to make a profit."

"For how long?"

My brow creases at the surprise in his tone. "Forever." I run my tongue along the roof of my mouth, searching for deception. Instead, I find vinegar—like wine gone bad mixed with a rancid lemon. Guilt and shock. He truly didn't know.

The Prince is still frowning. "I'm sorry if I—"

I walk faster. "There's no need to apologize, Your Highness."

He trots to keep up. "Perhaps I could speak with your family—"

"*No.*" An image enters my mind: his ocean eyes fixed on my sister and Rain—*my Rain*—in danger.

I duck my head to hide my flashing silver eyes.

The Palace fades away. Thoughts of witnesses and consequences drown, flooded by the sudden, insatiable urge to *kill*.

Kill the Prince. Kill the damned King while I'm at it. Anyone who can hurt Rain.

The Prince stills beside me. "Saoirse? Are you all right?"

The smoothness of his voice grates on my fraying nerves.

Kill.

Everything about him is perfect and I *hate* it.

But I need to calm myself.

I think of Rain. Killing the Prince won't keep her safe from everything else. The blackmailer. The ever-increasing cost of her school.

I take a calming breath. When I open my eyes, they're back to honey. "It was a statement made in jest, Your Highness. And I would prefer if we kept the conversation clear of my family."

"Understood." We walk in silence for a few paces but, of course, he can't let it stay. "I must admit, I had an ulterior motive for inviting you to the training room."

"Invite?" I force my tone to lighten. "Does that mean I can decline?"

He fights a grin. "I wanted to apologize. For last night."

I wasn't expecting that. "The party?"

"I should've let you leave sooner. You weren't having a good time. And perhaps I could have spared you from having vomit on your shoes."

"Sir, you didn't vomit on my shoes."

He glances at my worn boots. "You sure?"

He sounds so much like Carrik, I almost laugh.

We come upon a set of large double doors. Zensen pushes them open, stepping aside. The Prince gestures for me to enter first.

The Palace training room is a deep pit with rocky walls. Weapons to the right, targets to the left, and elevated sparring rings in the middle.

"I had the other guards clear away. Figured you'd prefer the privacy," says the Prince.

He's right, but I won't give him the satisfaction of thanking him. Instead, I cross to the wall of weapons. He stands behind me as I grab a crossbow. His front is a hairsbreadth from my back, and the warmth of his body wraps around me like an embrace. Or maybe a cage.

"They're kind of beautiful." He reaches around me and runs

a hand over the crossbow's frame. He doesn't touch me, but the hairs on my arm reach for him. "Can you show me how it works?" Hot breath brushes the side of my face and goose bumps trail up my arms.

I don't answer right away.

Instead, I sling a quiver of bolts around my back, forcing him to step away and giving me a chance to catch my breath.

Inhale. Exhale.

Crossbow in hand, quiver strapped to my back, I walk to the middle of the room, facing the row of targets.

I angle the crossbow at the floor and place my foot in the stirrup. Grabbing the string, I pull it back, hooking it in place. Reaching behind me, I snatch a wooden bolt from my quiver and set it on the rail. I slide it back until it sits in place before resting the crossbow on my shoulder, stock against the side of my face.

"Using a crossbow is easy, Your Highness," I tell him briskly. "Just aim." I point at the target. "And shoot." I pull the trigger, and the bolt slices through the air and hits its mark—dead center.

My mouth fills with the lemony zest of his amused surprise.

"I think you skipped a few steps in your lesson," he says.

My eyes stray to Zensen, watching the Prince from the side of the room. There's a letter hidden in my room demanding answers. As much as I want to take advantage of the Prince's pleasant mood and ask him about the "creature cullings," I can't with Zensen here.

I return to the weapons wall and find a bin of gray clay projectiles molded into nighthawks. I *will* get answers. If not now, then later, once I've managed to slip the Prince away from his other guards for a few stolen moments.

For now, I replace my quiver of wooden bolts with metal-tipped ones and thrust the bucket of birds into the Prince's hands.

He looks at the bucket, then back at me. "What am I supposed to do with these?"

"You said you wanted a demonstration of my skills, sir. You throw; I'll shoot." I take the stance, waiting.

Nothing happens.

I lower the crossbow. "Your—"

He chooses now to toss the first clay bird.

Instinct takes over. I raise the weapon to my shoulder, aim, and shoot. The bolt pierces the clay, and it bursts into pieces that rain on the floor.

He tosses the next one. I shoot again.

I lose myself in the rhythm. Training puts me at ease. I can be quick, strong, and fierce without the probing judgment of being an ikatus or the nagging fear of discovery.

The Prince's tossing speed increases with each bird I take down, but I never miss. I'm almost disappointed when he runs out.

He looks at me, both eyebrows raised. "I admit I'm impressed. Can you teach me?"

"I already did, Your Highness." I walk around the room, collecting my fallen bolts. "Aim and shoot."

There's a hand on my arm, stopping me.

I jerk away from his touch, eyes narrowed. I hate how warm he is. Like a blanket too close to a fire. It's distractingly comforting, but I feel I'll burst into flames at any moment.

He raises his hands in surrender. "Sorry. Just wanted to say that you don't have to pick these up. I'll get some servants in here."

My eyes stay slivered, hearing what he doesn't say: *human*

servants. Maybe even the twiglike boy who drove the carriage that brought me here.

I don't dignify his words with a response. Stooping, I pick up crossbow bolts and shattered birds. The Prince watches in silence for a tick before joining me. "So," he says as he cleans, "a crossbow is what helped you keep up with the other Deltas?"

"What do you mean?"

"I can't understand how an ikatus kept pace with fae with affinities. Did a crossbow help even it out?"

I shrug. "I worked harder than the other Deltas. I was in the training room hours before anyone else and hours after they left."

"Why?"

Why? "So I would be the best."

"Why did you want to be the best?"

I don't understand the question. "Should I have aspired for mediocrity?"

"No, I'm just wondering if there was a particular assignment you were hoping for?"

"Whichever paid the most."

"Right. You're here for the money—money you refuse to use to buy yourself a decent pair of boots."

I shove the bolts back in their respective quivers and don't answer. He hasn't asked a question.

The Prince frowns, sensing my sour mood. "Saoirse—"

"Hayes." Zensen approaches with his usual stiff back and matter-of-fact tone. "You have that meeting—with the King and his investigators."

Irritation takes refuge on the Prince's face, and the briny, picklely taste lodges on my tongue. "You know I don't want to go to that."

"And *you* know your father has given you no choice," says Zensen.

I follow their exchange with a frown. "The King's investigators, sir?"

The Prince is still scowling. "We received news this morning of a missing person. My father insisted we send Keirdre's best to investigate."

My half-wired, half-drained mood gives way to dread. "I wasn't aware the Royal investigators looked into missing persons." I try to sound casual. I'm not sure I pull it off.

"Usually, they don't, but when the missing person is an Enforcer's son . . ."

A memory from last night shoves into my brain.

"What brings you to Serington?"

"M-my father. I'm visiting him."

My mouth is dry.

The odds that my mark is the same as the Prince's missing person are slim—they have to be—but I don't believe in coincidence.

I'm still processing when the Prince gives me a farewell nod and follows Zensen to the doors.

I take a step after him, stumbling through racing thoughts. I've never had to deal with a Royal investigation headed by the King himself. If this meeting is about my kill from last night, I need to know. Which means I need to pilfer whatever information I can before the Prince disappears.

"I thought you were going to help me clean, sir?" I say.

He turns, expression guilty. "I would, but my father will kill me if we're late. If I'm not in the war room by—"

"The war room?" I interrupt. "Why would the King's investigators meet in the war room?"

"Not mine. My father's." He makes a face and casts his eyes about the training room. "I can come back," he offers. "And help you finish cleaning. After the meeting."

His earnestness is disconcerting. "It's all right, sir. I'll manage on my own." I start cleaning again, picking up pieces until the doors close behind the Prince and Zensen and I'm left alone with the burning question: Is my mark from last night the Enforcer's missing son?

I want to shake away the thought—slam it on its back like a sparring partner—but it lingers.

As I finish cleaning the training room, I know what I need to do.

Step one: find the King's war room.

Step two: sneak into the meeting.

CHAPTER TWELVE

Hidden Affections

Admittedly, neither step is well thought out. The Prince might be an overgrown sprig, but I can't traipse into a meeting with the King of Keirdre and expect a seat at the table—or even a space in the back of the room.

I slip out of the training room to search for the King's war room. Walking through the Palace without a plan feels dangerous. Like I'm a mouse sitting in a freshly tilled field with a hawk circling overhead.

The Palace walls are raucous today. The swirls are stormier, the once-soothing sound of sloshing waves has transformed into growling thunder, and the midnight surface ripples as though being continuously pelted with rain.

The King must be in a foul mood.

I'm still contemplating my limited options when my aimless wandering leads me to a human servant. She walks ahead of me, head ducked. Barely seen and rarely heard. A human's mantra.

"Excuse me!" I call out.

She doesn't react.

I frown. No human would ignore the call of a superior. Ignoring a fae is punishable by imprisonment, sometimes even death.

My confusion clears like smoke in the wind and I realize my

mistake: humans don't expect politeness from a fae. She likely doesn't realize I'm speaking to her.

Guilt churns my insides as I plant my feet. "Stop. Now."

She turns, averting her eyes to the floor and shuffling to me. I taste her fear from halfway down the hall. It's sour like vinegar and burns my throat like cheap whiskey.

My voice softens as she gets closer. "Do you know where the King's war room is?"

She nods.

I open my mouth to ask her to direct me, but she pivots and walks away, her slow movements making it clear I'm meant to follow.

As she directs me through the corridors, I keep track of the rooms we pass, memorizing the route.

We ascend a flight of stairs and stop at a set of steel doors inlaid with the Royal crest across the middle where the two doors meet.

The human grinds her hands together. "Would you like me to knock, ma'am? Announce your presence?"

Her body wracks with shivers as if to protect itself from a nonexistent chill. This close, she's younger than I thought. Not a woman at all, but a girl. Somewhere between my age and Rain's. And despite the smooth, youthful skin of her face, her eyes are older. The eyes of someone who's seen more than she should have to. Her fingernails are caked with dirt, her hair is short and oily, and her shoes manage a level of deterioration that rivals my ancient boots.

"No," I say, scrutinizing her. "You're free to leave. Er—this is a sensitive matter the Prince has entrusted to me. I ask that you be discreet." I should stop here. Speaking to a human with

kindness is frowned upon, but she's too young, she's clearly terrified, and when I look at her, all I see is Rain. I can't help myself
from adding, "Thank you."

Her head bobs nervously, and she scurries away.

I circle the perimeter of the war room. The walls here thrash
more violently than the rest of the Palace. Every few moments,
the murky blue flashes with lightning and rumbling thunder
sends reverberations through the air.

I find a closet diagonally across from the war room doors. Perfect for lying in wait for passing prey. Hidden inside, I tuck my
guard's pin away and turn my shirt inside out, obscuring the gold
detail. I spit out my *keil* bead and work my fingers through my
hair, loosening the braid until its weight unfurls around my head.

Satisfied, I crack open the closet, watching the war room
door. Waiting.

Minutes later, the door on the right opens and a man steps
out. He has the look of someone dignified, but not wealthy,
dressed in black with a few muted splashes of Keirdre's colors.

I'd know what he was even without the King's crest pinned
to the front of his shirt—an investigator.

He starts to walk in the opposite direction from me. I push
open the door. "Sir?" I call to him.

He pivots, only slightly at first, but then fully when he catches
sight of my face.

I never get tired of the burning taste of their craving for me.
Or that look: that dazed, *ravenous* look. It's not because of vanity—
at least, I like to think it's not—but because of the power that
courses through me like a river. The power they unwittingly or
unwillingly cede to my beauty.

"Sir?" I say when my new mark gawks rather than speaks.

"Er—yes. Sorry. Hello." He comes closer.

"Can I have a private word. *Please?*" The word "please" comes out with a musical lilt.

I know better than to sing. He'll live to tell the tale of this conversation. Talking with a beautiful woman in a closet is strange, but not newsworthy. Talking with a beautiful woman who uses song as persuasion would directly point to a siren. I'll have to be subtle with my gifts.

He practically floats over to me and stares into my eyes, lost. "Hi."

I close the closet door, trapping him in. "Hi, yourself." I lace my fingers around the back of his neck, tethering him to me. He's taller than me only by a hair, so I rest my forehead against his.

His breath falters against my cheeks.

I don't close my eyes, wanting to savor every look, every desirous expression, that passes over his face. His eyes stay open as well, too besotted to waste time staring at the inside of his eyelids.

My instincts hiss at me.

Kill.

It would be easy. We're alone, there are no witnesses, and he's completely under my spell.

My fingers are already around his neck. With a flick of my wrists, I can satisfy my cravings and quiet the Siren Song in my mind.

But—

That's not why I've brought him here. And killing him means forestalling answers.

Shoving aside my instincts, I let my fingers play with the knotted clumps of hair at the nape of his neck. "I have a few questions—"

"Yes." The word bursts out of him. "Whatever you want."

I smile. "What's your name?"

"Grisham Haverly."

"What do you do, *Grisham Haverly*?" I sneak a tune into his name.

He shudders. "I'm—er—an investigator. For the King."

"Really?" I lift a coy eyebrow. "Sounds important." I drag my hands from around his neck to rest on his chest. "Are you important?"

His heartbeat accelerates beneath my palms. His jugular moves as he gulps. "I'm whatever you want me to be."

It's a good answer. "What are you investigating for the King?"

"A disappearance."

I run my hands up and down his chest. "Who disappeared?"

"I'm—n-not supposed—"

"Please?" Another lilt.

He melts. "Felix Fleming. He's the son of the Enforcer of Serington, Wren Fleming."

I go still. Not panicked, not frantic—still. My heartbeat remains at the same even rhythm. My breathing doesn't change. But my mind is whirring a thousand paces an instant.

"How long has he been missing?"

"Just since last night. He's a fire fae from Phydan, visiting his father. He wasn't in his room this morning."

"Do you have any leads?"

"What's your name?"

"Answer my question first. Any leads?"

"None yet," he says. "What's your name?"

Rather than answer, I brush my lips against his cheek.

His body clenches.

My lips skim across his cheek and up his jaw until I reach his ear. I hum, just a few low notes. He shudders as my breath nuzzles his skin before I pull away. "It was nice meeting you, Grisham Haverly." I reach behind me and open the door, holding it for him.

He starts to walk out, steps lethargic, but he spins around just before I close the door. "Can I see you again?"

The word "no" sits on my tongue, but something gives me pause. The note that demanded I learn about the King's creature cullings is branded with the Royal seal, and Grisham works directly with the King.

"Do you know of the King's creature cullings?" I ask.

His eyes widen, and his glazed expression dulls with surprise. "Where did you hear that?"

I take it as a yes. I twine my arms around his torso, cradling my cheek against his chest and angling my head to stare into his eyes. "Tell me about it?"

"Yes," he says immediately. "Can I—can I see you again?"

I want answers now, but I fear he's been gone too long from the war room. I need to speak with him again when there's no one around and no King awaiting his return. "Tomorrow night," I promise. "Meet me here at midnight."

Wordlessly, he nods.

"And, Grisham?"

He makes a noise to confirm he's heard me, apparently having given up on words.

"Can you bring me something tomorrow?"

"Anything."

"A letter with the King's seal." I push him out of the closet before he has a chance to object. "I'll see you tomorrow," I whisper as I close the door behind him. I shove my ear against the wood, listening. For several ticks, I hear nothing as he stands, staring at the door, hoping for another glimpse.

Finally, with a heavy, wistful sigh, he plods away. What I just did was risky—maybe too risky—but now I know: last night, I killed an Enforcer's son, and today, the Royals are hunting me.

It's day three at the Palace, and I've already given the Royals another reason to want me dead.

CHAPTER THIRTEEN
Ulterior Motives

Convincing Grisham Haverly to meet me again was easy enough. Figuring out how to wiggle out of my night shift is more complicated.

I don't know anyone in the Prince's guard well enough to ask a favor. Which means, unfortunately, I'll need to make a friend.

With the exception of Carrik, I've warded off friendships like a curse for the past seventeen years. I've never wanted to expand my circle. Given Carrik's recent betrayal, the thought is less appealing than ever.

It's unfair to him. In and of itself, Carrik bringing Rain to graduation wasn't *that* dangerous.

Thoughtless? Yes.

Infuriating? Absolutely.

But if graduation had unfolded differently, I'd have forgiven him by now.

The problem isn't what he did before graduation, it's what happened after. Whenever Carrik so much as jogs through my mind, all I see is that damned silver envelope and I *blame* him. It's irrational, but that doesn't make it less real.

Still, I need friendly advice and, as it happens, he's my only friend.

I leave the Palace after the morning briefing and head for the Barracks. My intentions: find Carrik at his usual post, ask his advice, leave.

For the short walk from the Palace to the Barracks, I maintain that resolve.

I weave through the trees that surround my former residence. The same ones I used to sneak past on my way back to the gate. Back to Carrik.

Unbidden memories flicker in like firelight. Of nights spent camped outside, waiting for the sun to stretch its arms over the horizon. Pastel-lit mornings spent training. Beating him at sparring—always. Hours of goading each other. An eternity of talking.

Laughter.

Carrik could always make me laugh.

For all the secrets I keep from him, he knows me. As well as anyone can.

He comes into view through the tree line. Leaned up against the gate looking bored as ever, head against the metal bars, arms folded. Casual.

Except his shoulders are tight, his neck is tensed, and his eyes are wide. A stranger would mistake him for relaxed. I know he's poised, ready to strike.

"Solwey." I step from the trees.

"Saoirse?" Carrik's head falls forward in surprise. "What are you doing here?"

"I need advice," I say.

"You never answered my letter."

My eyebrow shoots up. "And that means I can't ask for advice?"

"No, I just didn't realize we were on speaking terms."

"I didn't say we are."

He stares at me. I stare back.

He blinks first, eyes lowering. His serious expression melts into something more amused. "Does that Prince not pay you enough to buy a decent pair of boots?"

It's so familiar, I almost laugh. I manage to resist, but he sees through me and sends a smirk my way. "Go ahead. Let it out. I won't get too beyond the barrier and start thinking we're on speaking terms yet."

My eyes roll as I chuckle. "I can't believe the first thing you do is insult me. I thought you were trying to get back on my good side?"

"We don't speak for three days and you went and got a good side?" He makes a show of looking me up and down. "When did that happen?"

I laugh full-out. "I hate you."

Smile. Soft as drizzling rain. "I missed you, Sorkova."

I missed you too. I take my place against the gate next to him. Same as always. "It's only been three days."

"It felt longer. I'm sorry about Rain."

I don't know how I ever thought I could stay mad at Carrik. The idea seems ludicrous now. "I know. She's the one who told me to forgive you."

"I knew there was a reason she's my favorite." He grins. "Seriously, Saoirse, how are you?"

"Fine." I shrug. "You'd hate the Palace. Everything is so . . . *much.* And the Prince is an overgrown sprig. Except worse, because he has authority."

"Have you met any other Royals?"

"No. But the Prince threw a party and invited all his rich friends."

"That doesn't sound too bad."

I give him a look. "He threw it *for* me."

Carrik tosses his head back with a laugh. "*You* were the guest of honor at a Royal party? I can't tell you how much ranis I'd pay to see that. How horrible was it?"

"Worse than you can imagine."

"If you ever feel like it's too much, write to me. I'll keep you sane."

I can't help a smile. "Don't think this means we're friends again. I'm just here for advice."

He laughs. "Whatever you say, Sorkova. What can I help you with?"

"I need to know how to make friends."

"Bond over something you're good at. Shouldn't be too hard—you're good at everything. Pick a skill that someone else can do too. Then make yourself a *little* worse to boost their confidence."

"That sounds ridiculous."

"It works." Carrik smirks. "I've been doing it to you for years."

I cackle, shoving him away. "You're such a lightbrain."

We fall into our usual pattern, talking as we always do. And laughing. Always laughing.

As we catch up, I spin through his advice. I already know who my first target will be and, assuming Carrik's right, I already know *exactly* how to get what I want.

Armed with an insincere smile and a plan, I rap on the door two down from mine.

With two hours before the morning briefing, most of the Palace is still asleep.

I'm about to knock a second time when a bleary-eyed, messy-haired Jeune opens the door.

"Sorkova?" Her voice is husky from sleep. "What're you doing here?"

The truth: everything about Jeune sets off my mental alarms.

Whatever her agenda—and I'm certain she has one—I'm going to uncover it. And if I play my cards right, I can squeeze out information *and* a favor. In one fell swoop.

I shield my suspicions behind a smile. "I'm going for a run. I was wondering if you wanted to join?"

She blinks, alert enough to be wary. "*You* want to go on a run with *me*?"

I expected hesitation. "I run better with someone to push me." I smirk and add, "And I like to win."

I could flood the barrier with all I don't know about Jeune, but one thing I *do* know from fighting her in my room—she's competitive.

As calculated, her eyes spark at my words and her chin tips in defiance. "And you're so sure you're going to beat me?"

"There's no reason to believe otherwise." I quirk an eyebrow. "Unless you want to prove me wrong?"

I'm clearly goading her. She knows it and I know it. But I also know she's going to rise to the bait.

A few ticks pass.

"Let me change." She closes the door and emerges minutes later, hair tied back, dressed, eyes like steel. "Where were you planning on running?"

"Palace field?" My room overlooks a wide green field that's within the Palace gates and perfect for running laps.

She shakes her head. "Boring. How about a more scenic route?"

"Where?"

"Somewhere better than a field. Trust me."

I don't. Not even a little. But as the one who extended this peace offering, I have to at least pretend otherwise. I motion her forward. "Lead the way."

We slip out the back exit of the Palace. For fifteen minutes, we run alongside each other through the cobblestoned streets of Vanihail without speaking. We're in the sector center, so we're surrounded by navy-brick shops and markets. This early, the only people outside are human servants doing chores for their employers.

"I asked around about you." Jeune pierces the silence.

"Oh?" She takes a right and I follow.

"Apparently, everyone at the Barracks thought you were an asshole."

It's unsurprising, but I wasn't expecting to hear it from Jeune.

She grins when I don't reply. "I understand. I'd rather be an exceptional asshole than average."

"Really?" I say. "And which are you?"

She laughs and pulls ahead of me. "If you manage to keep up, I'll tell you."

She guides me past the sector center and into the dense surrounding trees. There's no path, but we don't slow as we cross into the woods, and the even cobblestones transform into knotted tree roots and patchy weeds.

"I was surprised you wanted to run with me, given what happened with your room," says Jeune after a pause.

"You mean when you broke in and searched my things?"

She eyes me warily. "I'm sorry about that. I mean it. It's just something we do."

"Was there anything in particular you were looking for?"

"No." It comes out too quickly, and I taste something faint but stale. Guilt. She's lying.

My eyes narrow, but I don't call her on it. Pressing too hard will clue her in to my suspicions. "I don't like people poking around my things."

"I won't do it again. Promise."

We run deeper into the woods. "Why did you ask around about me?"

"I was curious. I asked some other Deltas about you after you turned down being Hayes's guard at the Ranking."

"I thought you weren't at graduation?" Zensen told me on my first day that he and Erasmus were the only guards who had attended the ceremony with the Prince.

"I was there. We all were. We watch every year."

I frown. "But Zensen said—"

"Oh," she cuts in, "Zen and Erasmus were with Hayes this year. They were shut in Enforcer Arkin's office during the Ranking, but the rest of us had front row seats."

Which means all of the Prince's guards were at graduation and any of them could have slipped that note into Rain's bag.

Oblivious to my thoughts, Jeune continues. "It was refreshing to see you in action. It's been a while since I met someone better than me."

This gets my attention. "You think I'm better?"

"I know you are." She sends her shoulder playfully into mine. "And you know it too. You're an ikatus, so I know no one's ever given you a break—which means you aren't just the best in your year, you're the best by a *lot*. I don't resent people who best me— that's for average assholes—but I'm exceptional. Like you."

The admiration in her tone is genuine. In another setting, I might feel pride, but now, it makes my stomach turn. Dealing with sincerity has never been a strength of mine. It makes me feel . . . uncomfortable. Out of control.

I pump my arms faster, picking up my pace. Not enough to seem intentional but enough that Jeune has to push *just* a bit harder to keep up. A small change, but it puts me back in control.

"Can I ask a favor?" I say.

"Really?"

Instead of answering, I run faster.

Her breathing shallows. "Well . . . can I ask you something in return?"

No.

"Depends on the question," I say.

"How did you get that burn?"

Instinctively, my face stills, but I catch myself—I *want* her to see a reaction from me. I want her to know to steer clear of this question forever and always. As much as it burns me from the inside, I want her pity to swallow her curiosity whole. As a sprig, I wanted a way to explain it. Drina cautioned me against it. Opening up makes it fair game for future conversations. Shutting down slams the door on the topic forever.

So my expression drops: my eyes darken, lips tighten, and nostrils flare. "No."

She soaks up my response like a sponge. "Consider it dropped. Permanently. What was your favor?"

"Could you switch shifts with me? I'm supposed to work the night shift tonight. You're working the morning, right?"

She hesitates. "I'm not sure if Hayes—"

"Let me worry about the Prince," I say. "Are you willing to switch?"

A battle wages briefly across her face before she nods. "If Hayes agrees, so do I. And, Sorkova?"

"Yes?"

"How would you feel about making this run a regular thing?"

How would I feel about regularly picking her brain to see which of the Prince's guards might be blackmailing me—even if that someone is Jeune herself?

I hide a smile.

CHAPTER FOURTEEN

Burned Gold

The dining hall is as richly decorated as the Palace corridors. Windows take up two corner walls, floor-to-ceiling. Streams of morning sunlight brighten the space, but the frosted glass shields the Royals from the outside.

To my relief, the head of the table, the King's seat, is empty. The Prince sits on the right-hand side and Queen Ikenna on the left. The Queen has the same bold beauty as her son. Dark skin, hair so black it's almost blue, pinned back in a pouf. Her dress is black as night and stamped with bloodred roses across the skirt. Her eyes are the color of the ocean, like her son's. Unlike her son's, they're completely vacant.

Including the two Royals, there are fourteen people at the breakfast table, all engaged in idle chitchat. Except the Queen. She doesn't speak at all.

Erasmus and I stand against the wall, across from the Prince. When I first entered the dining hall, the Prince was visibly surprised to see me, but if his smile was any indication, he was pleasantly so.

Erasmus, on the other hand—aside from briefly questioning if the Prince was aware of my switch with Jeune (I lied)—has

ignored my presence altogether. I think he means it to be a punishment, but I relish the silence.

At the end of breakfast, Erasmus and I follow the Prince out
of the dining hall.

The Prince slows to walk beside me, motioning for Erasmus to trail us. "I wasn't expecting to see you in the daylight,
Saoirse."

I taste Erasmus's fury at my lie and swallow it, resisting a grin.

"Jeune and I switched, sir," I say. "I'm visiting my family
tonight."

"Ah. Well, I don't mind the switch. You might be a bit bored,
though. No parties in the middle of the day." He grins. "All I've
got lined up is preparing for my birthday—" His sentence falters
as a tall man approaches.

The Prince steps forward to greet him, but I hover back. I recognize the approaching stranger. One of Felix Fleming's guards.
My tongue fiddles with my *keil* bead.

"Your Highness." The guard bows. "I'm sorry to interrupt
your morning, but I have questions about Mr. Fleming."

The Prince's eyebrows jump. "If you think I can be useful,
ask away."

"I was with Mr. Fleming the night he disappeared, sir. He said
he was coming here."

"He told you he was coming to the Palace?"

"Yes, sir. Did you see him?"

I shuffle through the events of that night, making sense of
the guard's words. I was there when Felix told his guards he was
leaving, and he didn't say anything about the Palace. All he said
was that he was visiting—

Lune above . . .

Felix's words flood my mind, swirling with new meaning. He

didn't say he was going to the Palace—he told his guards he was going to see Fin. Hayes Finnean Vanihail.

My heart rate spikes almost painfully. I dig my nails into my palms, but they're numb.

Felix is more than an Enforcer's son; he's the Prince's friend. It shouldn't surprise me, but I hadn't expected this. Hadn't realized when I guided him into the water, singing a deadly lullaby, that I'd ever meet the eyes of anyone who would miss him.

"Sorry." The Prince looks sheepish. "I'll admit, my memory from that night is hazy." He twists to face me. "Saoirse?"

No.

I drag my feet to stand beside him. "Sir?"

"Did I introduce you to anyone named Felix the night of the party? He's tall, gray eyes . . . probably carrying something that looks like this." He tugs a dark chain from around his neck where it's tucked into the front of his shirt with a black coin dangling from it.

I recognize it. Felix was tapping it against his desk when I interrupted. "What is that?"

"A token. He always has it with him. You're sure you didn't see him that night?"

I did see him. Just not here.

Deep breath. "I didn't see anyone who looked like that at the party, sir."

I taste something rancid and rotting. It takes me a tick to place the errant emotion—disappointment. The Prince's. He doesn't say anything as he dismisses the guard, and his expression doesn't change, but I taste it all the same.

As a rule, I don't ask about my marks, but Felix Fleming is forever branded in my memory now. As are details about him I never cared to know. Like that he was friends with the Prince.

It's that fact that makes my stomach twist. Their friendship bothers me more than it should.

"What was that about, sir?" I ask.

"You remember how I told you an Enforcer's son went missing? It was my friend Felix. His dad is panicking."

"But not you?"

"I . . ." His hand absently grabs at the black coin around his neck. "I'm sure he's fine. Flem's always been the sensible one. Too boring to get in any real trouble."

He smiles, but it doesn't match his eyes. Or the fear I sense on my tongue.

"Do you mind if I ask what that token is for?"

"We've known each other since we were kids. We found this in the Palace. It's childish, but . . ." He holds it up, showing me the smooth side where it's been cleanly sliced. "We had it cut down the middle. Flem has the heads; I have tails. Because he's the brains and I'm the . . . well, ass."

"You're close." I mean it as a question, but it comes out as a statement.

Hayes answers anyway. "Best friends." He traces a thumb over the surface of the black coin. "He's like the brother I wanted."

His expression is wistful in a way that tightens my chest. I look away, squinting at the coin instead. "Is it burned?" From a distance, it looks like it's painted black, but up close, I see it's a ranis coin charred over.

"You have a good eye." Another smile that doesn't reach his eyes. "We found it like this in my dad's office, but we never asked why it was burned. My father wouldn't have been pleased to know we were poking around."

He stares at the blackened coin for a beat longer before tucking it back out of sight.

"I'm sure Mr. Fleming will turn up soon, Hayes," says Erasmus gently.

I'd forgotten he was here.

"Right." I nod in agreement, swallowing a building pressure in my throat. "I'm sure he's fine."

CHAPTER FIFTEEN

The Woman on the Rock

I wear a plain blue dress beneath my cloak. I'm in the closet across from the King's war room again, primping. After tossing my cloak in a dusty corner, I remove my *keil* bead and run a hand through my thick hair. I arrived half an hour early but, as expected, my wait is short. Something light, flaky, and sweet, like a fresh-fruit pastry, settles on my tongue—anticipation—followed by two swift knocks on the closet door.

When I open the door, Grisham's eyes widen, and the anticipation gives way to the sweet spice of lust mingled with the citrusy zing of his surprise.

"You came." He's out of breath, but not from exertion.

I pull his arms around my waist with a seductive smile. "If I remember correctly"—I turn us around and kick the door closed—"I'm the one who invited you."

"Yes, but you're so . . ." He gives up on thinking of an adjective, choosing instead to stare into my eyes and sigh.

I hum a few notes under my breath so it feels absentminded. His eyelids droop. He's completely enraptured, and I bask in his adoration like sunlight.

"Tell me about King Larster," I say.

He takes a breath. "How did you hear about his creature cull-ings? They haven't been spoken of in centuries."

"Does it matter?" When he hesitates, I pout. "You're not going to tell me?" I make to pull away, but his fingers coil around me in a panic, desperate to hold on to me.

"Wait."

I pause. Raise an eyebrow. Slowly, deliberately. "Tell me."

"I—" He breaks off again.

"I'm sorry." I feign understanding and lean closer. My cheek presses against his chest so I can better hear his heartbeat thun-dering away like horses giving chase. My fingers glide across his back. "I understand if you can't tell me. It's all right." I hum again, soothingly this time, as though to comfort him.

His stance relaxes from the combination of my touch and voice. "What's your name?" He sighs dreamily, and I know I have him, lapping from the palm of my hand like a mewling kitten.

I tuck my face into his shoulder to disguise a smirk. "Tell me about the King."

"Can I show you?"

The plan wasn't to leave this room, but he sounds desperate.

"Of course." I scoop up my cloak and gesture to the door. "Lead the way, *Grisham*."

He shudders as I say his name. Obediently, he trots from the room.

My curiosity swells as he leads me through the Palace cor-ridors. He scans each hall before turning and checks over his shoulder constantly, both to ensure that I'm still here and that we're not being followed.

He stops in a narrow hallway that leads nowhere. While the other Palace walls are a vengeful sea, the right side of this corridor is a tiled mural of vibrant colors—sunny yellows, rose reds, and sky blues. Built into the mural is a low fountain lined with navy tiles.

The gurgling water is faint, but it's enough to stir something in me. My hand shudders, eager to take a dip into the water.

Grisham appears in front of me, pulling me from my trance. "We shouldn't be here." He wrings his hands. "I shouldn't have brought you here. We should—"

I seize him by the back of his neck and drag his face to mine, smashing our lips together.

Grisham is too stunned by the sudden, graceless act to do anything other than hold still. When I pull back, a mere three ticks later, that glazed, compliant look has returned.

"Wow." He touches his fingers to his lips with a wide smile, as if we shared something passionate and life-changing as opposed to what I imagine would happen if you touched the lips of two corpses against each other.

I don't question it. I tip my head to the side. "Wasn't there something you wanted to show me?"

He's still flustered, but he extends a hand over the fountain and uses his affinity to *churn* the water.

Set against the stone tiles on the fountain floor is a wheel of the same color, with the same tile pattern. If you're not looking for it, it's hidden, but as the water turns the wheel, it becomes more visible.

My eyes follow the moving water so intently, so longingly, I don't notice a paneled door open to the right of the fountain until Grisham beckons me through.

We stand at the base of a stone spiral staircase that stretches up into oblivion, not a single window in sight. A tower.

I start as the sliding panel slams back into place, plunging the stairs into darkness.

For a count of three, we're still, until a torch bracketed to the wall flickers alight.

Grisham holds the torch in front of him, illuminating the dusty stairwell.

"Is that the only light?" I ask.

He smiles and holds out his free hand. His smile widens when I place mine in his. "This room doesn't usually receive visitors. The King prefers it stays hidden."

The light from the torch is our only guide as we twist up the stairs. There's no railing, so I clutch Grisham's arm. He doesn't complain.

I can't tell how long we've been walking or how much farther we have to go, and I can't risk Grisham's enchantment fading before we reach our destination, so I start to sing. My voice echoes, bouncing against the stones around us.

Grisham smiles. "Has anyone ever told you that you have a beautiful voice?"

"Once or twice."

The winding stairs lead to a samsam wood door with an erstwyn handle. Grisham puts a hand on the door. "You can't tell anyone I brought you here."

"Never," I say earnestly. I move past him and push open the door myself.

I'm transported.

Thoughts of the dark, cobwebbed stairwell behind me melt like snow in spring. The room is circular, wide, and bright despite the lack of windows. The walls are a rich red and covered in paintings—some portraits, some landscapes, but all beautifully somber. Above each painting is a string of tiny chaeliss lanterns, winking like stars.

I inspect the first painting to my left. A portrait.

A broad-shouldered woman sits on a forest floor, back against a pine, legs out in front of her. Her skin is dark and deep, like bronzed mahogany. Her hair is short and pulled back with a forest-green kerchief. Her eyes are brown, and her corded, muscular legs are displayed in a pair of pants cut above the knee.

I study the painting once, twice, thrice, my frown deepening with each perusal.

First oddity: the woman's clothing and the surrounding forest are bright, but her face—something in her eyes, the slant of her mouth, the crease of her brow—is undeniably sad.

Second oddity: the painting's proportions seem . . . off. The woman's back rests against a large tree, but even while sitting, her head reaches almost halfway up the trunk.

Third oddity: I can't place what kind of creature she is. She doesn't have the bright eyes of a fae or the speckled eyes of a witch, but she also looks too strong to be human.

I sense Grisham before I feel him. Arms wrap around my waist from behind. He's humming. I think it's a rendition of my song on the staircase. He has no sense of rhythm, but I doubt he can help singing it.

My first instinct: take hold of his hands where they rest against my stomach and spin around. Pin him to the wall and sing until he draws his own blade and plunges it into his gut.

Instead, I lean into his embrace and smile. "Why did you bring me here?"

"To show you this." He nods to the portrait. "Is this your first time seeing a giant?"

I frown. "This is a giant?"

Grisham's chin taps against my shoulder as he nods. "King Larster commissioned portraits of creatures as they used to be in Keirdre."

I heard him wrong. I must have. "Did you say 'in Keirdre'?"

"Yes."

I pull away.

I feel his distaste at the distance, but I ignore it, preferring to wear a hole through the floor, pacing. My thoughts trip over themselves as I try and make sense of his words. "There used to be giants in Keirdre?"

"You didn't know?" Grisham seems genuinely surprised. "But you asked about the creature cullings. I thought—"

"Never mind that." I'm still pacing. "I thought the barrier was created to contain fae, witches, and humans."

"It was. But those weren't the only creatures in Keirdre when the barrier was created. Most of them fled before the barrier went up, but not all of them. The creatures who were left, King Larster—"

"Killed them all." I finish his sentence with a hushed voice.

Grisham doesn't respond. He doesn't have to.

I walk to the next painting.

A woman stands in front of a willow tree. Scratch that—she's *part* of the tree. The top of her body is free, but where her waist should curve into her hips, it blends seamlessly into the tree trunk.

Her skin is a perfect match for the color of the bark. Her hands clutch the branches and draw them to her, holding them over her chest. Her hair is long, green, and woven, like the leaves of the willow.

"A dryad," says Grisham. "A tree nymph."

"The King killed them too?"

"Yes."

I circle the room, stopping at each painting. They don't have engravings to identify them, but when I point, Grisham dutifully provides me with a name.

I've heard of them all, but never outside the pages of Rain's books—never as creatures who once lived in Keirdre.

My whole life, I was told there were three species in Keirdre. That a few sirens must've made it through. But that was a lie. There were other creatures within the barrier. Like sirens, they weren't supposed to be here. And like sirens, the King killed them all.

This room is a hidden, twisted homage to creatures who were wiped out—washed away like stains on a shirt and forgotten.

"Why'd he do it?" I ask. "What did King Larster have to gain by—"

My steps and words falter at the largest painting.

A woman sits on a jagged rock emerging from the sea. The brushstrokes of the ocean are so delicate, I can *feel* the spray of the sea-foam as it crashes against the craggy surface.

The perched woman has long, dark hair. It's wet and tangled from the water and hangs over her shoulders. Her skin is darker than mine, her lips are curled and parted as if she's speaking, and her face is almost startlingly beautiful.

What stands out to me—what *jars* me—are her eyes. Glowing silver.

Grisham watches me stare before he says, "She's a siren."

"You don't say." I'm too stunned for the sarcasm to come through. "Why is she so much bigger than the others?"

"King Larster hates sirens. More than anything else."

I look away from the painting to frown at him. "Why?"

"They're dangerous."

My heart is pounding so loudly, I have to strain to hear him. "What do you mean?"

"King Elrian created the barrier to keep out enemies of Keirdre. But some of those enemies slipped inside."

This part is familiar. History told to me by my aunties time and time again. The Resistance, a group of enemies to the kingdom. They've been hunting for a way out of Keirdre ever since the barrier's conception, but they've always been too small and disorganized to cause real damage.

"Before the barrier, sirens protected Keirdre from invaders by the sea. They lured enemy ships to their death. When the barrier was constructed, Keirdre no longer had any enemy ships to fight, but the sirens trapped inside still thirsted for blood. So they started hunting Keirdrens. For fun."

My tongue presses against the gap behind my false tooth where my *keil* bead should be. I knew the role sirens used to play in Keirdre, but Drina never mentioned the bloodlust. Which means either Grisham is currently lying or Drina has been lying to me for years. "Surely they could control it."

"Sirens have no impulse control. They're beautiful monsters. All they can do is kill."

I flinch. I don't know why it hurts so damned much, but it does. All he's done is lay out everything I already know about myself. I kill because I need to, and when I don't need to, I kill because I *want* to. And yet, even though he's said nothing I don't already know, hearing it confirmed *hurts*.

From my first kill—the first battle I fought and lost to my instincts—I had the flicker of a hope that I could control it. That there was more to being a siren than craving the kill.

Grisham Haverly just snuffed out that hope like a chaeliss torch.

Attempting to curb my impulses is futile. At the end of the day, when all my marks are dead and gone, when I'm no longer under the Prince's employ, when my family can no longer stomach the sight of me, when Rain has outgrown me—I will have one constant in my life: the aching desire to kill.

And I'll never have peace.

I'm not sure how long I'm lost in thought, silent, but Grisham circles in front of me, blocking my view of the painting, handing me something. "I brought this for you."

I'm sinking in visions of my bleak future, but I force a coy smile. "Did you get me a present?" The smile slips when I see it's a plain white envelope.

"It's a letter," he explains. "With the King's seal. Like you requested."

"Thank you." I snatch the letter and flip it over. Same red wax Royal seal. Almost.

Same twisting, spindly branches of a samsam tree shaping into the letter "K" for Keirdre, same apple sprouting from a single branch. But on the seal in my room—on the silver envelope—there's a branch missing. It's subtle, but after all the hours I've spent staring at it, I'm certain.

Whoever sealed the silver envelope used a different stamp—a broken stamp. And if it wasn't the King's, it must've been Prince Hayes's.

CHAPTER SIXTEEN

Creatures Culled

My aunties lied to me.

There was a reason they didn't want me working in the Palace. One they refused to tell me, but now I know. Somehow, they knew about King Larster's creature cullings. And they never told me.

I press the bloodstone, and the world melts into streams of color as I Dreamweave into Drina's consciousness.

It's late, so I expect to land in another dream, but instead, I'm in her kitchen. Drina's back is to me, and she's hunched over the counter. To her right is a bundle of spiky white flowers connected to long, reedy green stalks with a gray bulb and roots sprouting like fine hairs from the end. Luneweed.

I clear my throat.

Drina spins around. "Saoirse? What are you—"

"Tell me about the King's creature cullings."

She freezes. For half an instant, a look of something close to panic crosses her face, but it's gone before I can study it. "And here I thought you wanted to explain why the hell I had to hear from Kiernynn that you're working in the Palace."

I refuse to back down. "Is that why you didn't want me working there? Because of the creatures he's slaughtered?"

"How about I get some tea—"

"I don't want tea, Drina. I want answers."

Her hand reaching for the kettle falls to her side. "It sounds like you already know the answer, love." She sucks in a heavy breath and doesn't look at me. "There used to be other creatures in Keirdre. King Larster killed them."

"Why?"

"He never wanted them here to begin with. When King Elrian constructed the barrier, he only intended for there to be fae, witches, and humans. The fae to have control, witches for their magic, and humans for a cheap source of labor. Each species had a purpose, but not all of the other creatures were gone. And the ones who were left wanted out. They worked alongside the Resistance, searching for a way through the barrier. Staging attacks on the Palace, inciting violence—trying to find a way to undo the magic that traps us here. So King Larster killed them. To wipe out the Resistance and the other creatures all at once." She gives me a pointed look. "But he missed a few."

"Me."

"Yes . . . and others." Seeing my confusion, she presses on. "You were young when you went to live with your parents, but you and Rain weren't the only children living here. Aiya and I used to run a home for orphaned creatures."

"Other sirens?" I hate how my voice cracks with hope. It's always been just me. As much as I love my family, they'll never understand how much it takes out of me to resist my instincts. How relieved I feel when I finally—*finally*—give in.

Or how much I hate myself for letting them down when I do.

"No, my love," says Drina gently. "You were the only siren. But there were other species. Those who could pass as fae with *keil* beads. Dryads, sprites . . . many of them live as you do. Hidden."

"Where are they now?"

"We had to relocate them after a series of raids in Ketzal, looking for contraband. We supplied them with *keil* beads and sent them on their way. All over Keirdre. Vanihail, Serington, Bliddon, Phydan, Idris, and Kurr Valley."

The fae sectors. "How many of us are there?"

"We don't know."

"But they lived with you?"

"Love." Drina smiles. "There were dozens of other witches in Ketzal and Krill with similar homes. There are hundreds of orphaned creatures in Keirdre."

I place a hand to the wall, fighting the sudden urge to topple over.

Hundreds.

Hundreds.

Hundreds of creatures who survived the King's cullings. Hundreds of people forced to hide. Hundreds like me.

This morning, I was a solitary one. Tonight, I'm one of many.

I know she means to terrify me—instill a healthy fear of the Royals in me. But I'm not afraid, knowing the truth.

I'm *furious.*

Drina curses under her breath. "I know that look."

"What look?" I try for mild, but even I can't deny the snarling undercurrent of my tone.

"You know what look. The King is not one of your marks."

My fingernails dig grooves into my palms. "I never said he was."

"You didn't have to. I know you. The Royals are a temptation you don't need. The Palace is dangerous. If anyone discovers what you are, they'll kill you, just like they killed countless others."

Her words: rational.

Her concern: valid.

But it's not enough to rival my steeled resolve. "I can't leave now, Auntie. You know I can't. Why didn't you just tell me?"

"There are few old enough to remember the creature cullings. But I remember the years that followed. Anyone who mentioned the cullings disappeared. Or worse. He made an example of anyone who stepped out of line, so we stayed in place and we stayed quiet."

"You still should've told me. When I told you about the Palace—"

She interrupts with a harsh laugh. "Telling you wasn't an option. I *know* you. The last thing I wanted was to give you another reason to want to work for those horrible people." Drina's midnight eyes meet mine. They're stern . . . but mostly, they're sad. "They are the cause of all that is evil in this world, love. I'm begging you—quit."

Slowly, I shake my head. "I won't."

She sighs. "I know."

For once, I'm glad I can't taste her emotions. I have no desire to confirm her disappointment in me.

CHAPTER SEVENTEEN

Monsters in Daylight

Caruston Academy is made of blue bricks so dark, they're almost black. The lawn is a brilliant green and perfectly maintained, the students walk in neat lines, and the floor tiles are an aged gold granite. I sit beneath a samsam tree in one of Caruston's courtyards. This school has always made me feel out of place. My back is stiff against the bark, my tongue won't leave my damned *keil* bead alone, and, inexplicably, my palms itch.

It's worse than usual. I've been buzzing since last night. And not from the usual rush of bending a mark to my will, but from the new knowledge of King's Larster's cullings. I can't shake the image of the siren on the rock from my mind. Can't unhear Grisham's grim assessment: she's beautiful, cruel, and deadly.

She's me.

I whisk through my previous kills like a dance. Each came with a rush of pulsing adrenaline. Euphoria.

But then I hear Grisham's voice, reminding me bloodlust is all I'll ever know. I see Mom putting herself between me and Rain, shielding her. I feel my father's fear as he flinches away from me when I teeter on the edge of my impulses. And the euphoria shrivels up, dead.

I can explain away each kill all I want—it's for the Raze, it's for Rain, the man in question is a worm—but the truth is, it doesn't matter. My instincts don't care who's at the other end of my blade. And when they sing to me, neither do I.

At least until I'm reminded that, by anyone's definition, that makes me a monster.

My fingers dig into the neat grass, caking dirt beneath my nails as I search the hordes of students, eyes peeled for Rain. She'll be passing by soon. A fact I know because I make it a point to memorize her schedule each year.

The tightness in my chest fades like background noise when I catch a glimpse of her familiar big hair. Rain weaves through the throng of students, a much-needed bright spot after last night.

I jump to my feet. "Rain!"

She perks at the sound of her name. When she sees me, her face lights up and she squares her shoulders and charges. She launches herself at me, legs twining around my waist, arms encircling my neck. "Pinecone!"

The weight on my heart lifts, the image of the siren on the rock wisps away, and I'm calm. I needed this—needed *her*. How can I be a monster when she loves me? "It's good to see you, Beansprout."

"What are you doing here?" She unlatches her legs and stands in front of me.

"I missed you."

She looks pleased, but I know she doesn't believe me. "Did something happen?"

The siren on the rock glimmers at the corner of my mind, but I look into Rain's eyes and blot her out.

"Of course not." I loop my arm through hers. "How about we take a walk?"

Arm in arm, we stroll out of the courtyard as the last of the students flee for lessons.

"I'm supposed to be in class," says Rain after a pause.

I wink. "I won't tell if you don't."

She smiles back, but she doesn't taste happy.

"What's wrong?" I ask.

"Are you sure everything's all right? Do we need more money?"

"I handled the note."

"Are you sure?" Her eyes narrow. "Is that why you're here?"

The truth: Rain's not fae, but she has her own kind of magic—the unique ability to make all my self-doubt melt away. As a sprig, she was convinced I could battle her nightmares away. I never told her that she fights off mine just by breathing.

What I tell Rain: "I wanted to see you."

Doubt flickers in her eyes and flashes on my tongue. It stings—lune above, it just about shatters me—but she's right to mistrust me, given how often I lie to her.

"I'm serious," I insist. "I've missed you."

"I missed you, too, Pinecone." She smiles, and I soak in her energy. Even doubting me, she's warm, and it soothes me.

"Good." I throw an arm around her shoulders. "You remember that bakeshop you used to drag me to? How about we go there after school? My treat."

"Er . . . maybe tomorrow?"

Rain never turns down sweets. I frown. "What's wrong?"

"Nothing. I just have plans after school today. But it's fine!" she adds quickly. "We can go tomorrow."

I eye her suspiciously. "Where are you going after school?"

"A friend's house?" It comes out as a question.

My feet stop moving. *"What?"*

"Mom and Dad said it's fine."

I almost roll my eyes. "That's because they're too lax when it comes to your safety. You're not going."

"But—"

"No," I snap. "You know you can't spend too much time with other kids."

"Then how am I supposed to make friends?"

It's a ridiculous question. "By being *you*. Anyone would be lucky to be friends with you. Just . . . not at someone's house." I move to stand in front of her, putting my hands on her shoulders. "Promise me you're not going over there. Not just today. Ever."

"Nothing's going to happen." Her tone is pleading, but the defeat in her eyes tells me she already knows my answer.

"I know that," I say. "Because you're coming to the bakeshop with me. Right?"

A few ticks pass before she reluctantly nods. "Right."

"Good." We keep walking. "I had another reason for coming here. I want to ask you something, and I need you to be honest."

"I always am."

Soft smile I don't mean. "What do they teach you about the history of sirens here?"

Her steps slow. "I don't pay attention to that."

"Which means they do teach you something."

"Nothing important," she says quickly. "Don't worry. I know you're not what they say."

My heart stutters. "What do they say?"

"That sirens are monsters. No conscience. But I know that's not true." She smiles at me. The sunshine of her smile could end a thunderstorm. The warmth of her gaze could thaw winter.

But I'm still freezing.

"What specifically do they say?"

"It doesn't matter."

"Just tell me."

She clears her throat. "There were a few sirens left inside the barrier after King Elrian's sacrifice. They were vicious. Killing Keirdrens with no remorse. They were too powerful, so King Larster commanded their capture. They were imprisoned, and those who fought back were executed." She sounds like she's reciting something.

When I don't say anything, she burrows deeper into my side. "I know it's not true."

Any other time, her loyalty would warm me, ease my fears, and make me smile, except . . .

What if they're right?

"Pinecone?"

I've stopped walking. Rain is staring at me tentatively, spelled eyes wide and earnest.

"Yes?" I say.

"I love you."

Only because you don't know me.

I close my eyes to chase the thought away, but it lingers. Still, when I open my eyes, I'm smiling, and Rain's brow clears.

"I love you more."

CHAPTER EIGHTEEN

Midnight Orders

Zensen waits outside the Prince's bedroom when I arrive for the night shift. Which is odd, because Devlyn is already here and, usually, the day shift leaves as soon as the next wave arrives.

I hold in a frown. "Is something wrong?"

Zensen motions me forward until the three of us stand in a close-huddled circle. "I wanted to alert you both." His voice is hushed. "Hayes has been . . . off today. He's spent much of the day in his room, not speaking."

My spine stiffens, but I hold my tongue.

"Thanks for letting us know, Zen," says Devlyn.

Devlyn waits until Zensen has disappeared around the corner to sigh. "I've never seen Hayes like this before. E thinks it's because Felix is still missing."

I lean against the wall opposite him, trying for casual. "Did you know him? Felix?" It's the first time I've said his name out loud, and it tastes strange.

"Not well—I haven't worked here for long—but Hayes and Felix are close. Like brothers. And Felix is a really nice guy."

My stomach turns. *Was.*

I swallow the word. It sticks in my throat.

Devlyn must mistake my anxious silence for sadness, because he says, "I'm sure he'll turn up. He's an Enforcer's son. What's the worst that could happen?"

All I see is that black coin on a chain. The Prince clutching it close, Felix tapping it on the side of his desk. I wonder if Felix's half will ever turn up or if it's forever lost to the river.

"How are you adjusting to the Palace?" Devlyn bursts into my thoughts. "I know after the other night, we didn't get off to a good start."

And now Devlyn's transitioned from thinking I'm not speaking because of Felix, to assuming I'm still mad at him for the break-in the first night.

Which is fair, because I am. But it has nothing to do with my silence.

"Is that an apology?" I say.

Devlyn opens his mouth to echo an empty "I'm sorry," but I cut him off. "Answer me this—is everyone really involved?"

"Yes. We usually rotate who sneaks in."

"Usually?" I pick out the word. "It wasn't Jeune's turn?"

"She was curious. Wanted to get to know you. She insisted on being the one to search your room." He grins. "I suppose that didn't go as planned."

I don't return his smile. Jeune's interest in me could be innocent, but given the silver envelopes, I can't assume anything is harmless.

The Prince's door flies open before Devlyn can say anything else.

"Hayes?" says Devlyn. "Is everything all right?"

"Everything's perfect." The Prince wears a too-large grin that doesn't match the muddled taste of his emotions—metallic pain, sour regret, and bitter sorrow. "It's good to see you both. I've decided I'm tired of this damned room. I want some fun."

"Oh—all right." Devlyn looks flustered. "Should I—should I find Zen? He usually handles your party guest lists."

"Don't get Zen, he'll only spoil the fun." The Prince waves him off. "I don't want a party. I want something better. To go out." His gaze shifts to me. "The three of us."

I'm not sure in what world "better" constitutes leaving the protection of the Palace for a night of debauchery. "Sir, I don't think it's safe for the Crown Prince to go wandering around pubs in the middle of the night."

"Relax." The Prince reaches into his pocket and pulls out a *keil* bead on a rope necklace. He slings it around his throat. His jaw loses definition, his cheekbones become less pronounced, and his enchanting ocean eyes dull to a less-vibrant amber.

He's still beautiful, but his eyes no longer resemble the ocean. "See?" The Prince holds out his arms. "I'm practically a different person. Still object?"

Yes. "Is this an order, sir?" I already know his answer.

"Absolutely."

I bite back a grimace. "Then I have no objection, sir."

"Don't give me that face. It won't be that bad. You might even have fun by accident." The Prince looks me up and down. "I don't mean to be rude, Saoirse, but is there any chance you own anything more befitting a pub?"

The truth—not that I'll ever tell the Prince—is I own plenty of tiny dresses, made for luring marks. I'm about to mention finding something acceptable (with every intention of changing into black pants and a black shirt) when it occurs to me I've been presented the perfect opportunity.

I don a smile some might describe as sweet. "No, sir, I don't. But maybe Jeune would lend me one?"

His eyes light with pleasant surprise. "That's an excellent idea."

"I'll ask." I turn for Jeune's room.

"Saoirse—last thing." The Prince's eyes spark with mischief. "While we're out, don't call me Your Highness or sir. It'll draw unnecessary attention, and, as you said, the goal is to keep me safe."

I fight a scowl. "Yes, sir. Is that all?"

"Actually, since you asked, one more last thing: try to have fun. A normal person's version of fun, not yours."

"Is that an order as well, sir?"

His grin turns devious. "Yes."

Devlyn—lightbrain that he is—seems genuinely excited as he practically bounces through the hall to his room to change. I drag my feet, irritation bogging down each step.

I've managed to get my face under control by the time I rap on Jeune's door.

She raises her eyebrows when she sees me. "I thought you were with Hayes?"

"I am. He wants to go out, and I need a dress. Is there any chance—"

"Say no more." Jeune ushers me in and looks me over. "You wouldn't happen to know your measurements, would you?"

I give her a look, and she grins. "Just thought I'd check."

She turns to her wardrobe, and I look around. She's strung up ivy and blue kylith flowers over the ceiling and along the back wall to hang over her bed. Her bed is made, there are no unpacked rucksacks cluttering the floor, and her mirror hangs above her desk as mine once did.

"Take a seat. Wherever you like." Jeune opens her wardrobe and begins digging through.

I sit at her desk.

"Who's Hayes taking out with him?" Jeune's voice is muffled from the wardrobe.

"Just me and Devlyn." As I talk, I ease open her top desk drawer, silent as I dare. A few scraps of parchment.

I flip the top one over. Her handwriting is small and messy. Nothing like the writing in the blackmail note.

"Really?" says Jeune. "I figured he'd take a few friends."

I close the drawer and slide open the next. "Zensen said he's been—"

"How do you feel about blue?" Jeune ducks out of the wardrobe holding a blue-and-gold printed dress. I barely have a tick to shuffle myself in front of the desk to block the middle drawer from view.

I give her a sharp look. "Black."

She pouts. "But you'd look so good in blue."

"Black," I repeat firmly.

She mutters something under her breath but dutifully returns to her closet.

I wait a moment before opening the bottom drawer. Nothing too interesting. Scattered cosmetic bottles and jars and a small, wooden jewelry box. I slide off the lid and peek inside.

Four gold-etched *keil* beads sit on the navy satin lining.

My stomach drops.

It proves nothing. Plenty of women use *keil* beads for non-nefarious reasons, but given the silver envelope and Jeune's fascination with me, I can't afford to write her off as a suspect. There were hundreds of people in the arena for graduation. Any of them could have slipped something in Rain's bag. A smart person, as I suspect Jeune is, wouldn't leave a chance of being recognized. A smart person would disguise themselves.

I close the third drawer just as Jeune exits her wardrobe, grinning. Before I can say anything, she's in front of me, thrusting a dress into my hands. "This one. It's perfect."

It's black, which I appreciate, and as I tug it on, it hugs every curve of my body. It's off the shoulder with straps that band the sides of my arms and sweep down to meet in a plunging neckline. The hem is short. In the front, it stops at my mid-thigh, but the thickness of my thighs and width of my hips means it cups my ass in the back.

Jeune's eyebrows shoot up as she looks me over.

"If I had a body like yours, I'd burn anything loose," she says. "I might not even bother with clothes at all. Want me to do your makeup?"

"I don't paint my face."

"What about your hair?"

My hair is still coiled in a tight braid and twisted into a knot. "No."

"How long has it been braided? I bet you have an amazing curl pattern."

I shake my head. "I'm wearing the dress. That's enough."

She huffs. "What about shoes?"

I know she'll object, but I put my boots back on—the ones with the soles barely attached that Carrik hates.

As expected, she looks horrified. "What about—"

"No," I say, lacing them up. "Nothing with a heel."

"Saoirse, can't you *try*? For me?"

"I'll *try* not to kick your ass too badly on tomorrow's run." Boots on, I head for the door.

Jeune follows with a scoff. "Sorkova?"

"Yes?"

"Try to have fun."

I hate how sincere she sounds. "Why does everyone keep saying that?"

She just laughs and disappears back into her room.

I tug the bottom of the dress before knocking on the Prince's door.

I expect spelled-amber eyes—I can handle amber eyes—but when the wooden barrier is tugged open, I'm lost at sea.

It takes me two ticks to look away. It takes him longer.

The only thing I've changed about my appearance is Jeune's dress, but I guess the knowledge that the body lurking beneath the guard's uniform looks like mine is mind-boggling.

I lose track of time as the Prince stands in his doorway, staring at me, open-mouthed. He tastes spicy like cinnamon—lust. Burning and sweet. I'm familiar with the taste, but never while wearing this face that isn't mine.

"Sir?" I prompt after a pause. "Are you ready to go?"

"Um . . . yes." He drags his gaze up the curves of my hips to meet my eyes. "Where's—er—" His fascination with the shape of my body stops him from remembering Devlyn's name. "The other one?"

"Here, Hayes." Devlyn hurries down the hall, adjusting his maroon dashiki. "Whoa." He grins at me. "You scrub up good, Sorkova."

"Thanks," I mutter.

The Prince touches the rune on his chaeliss stone, snuffing the lanterns in his room. He loops the *keil* bead back around his neck, and his overwhelmingly handsome features melt into slightly less handsome features. "You ready? I have the perfect pub in mind."

Without waiting for a response, he marches down the hall to leave the Palace, Devlyn lapping at his heels.

With a sigh, I follow, mentally preparing for what I'm sure will be a long night.

CHAPTER NINETEEN

Dancing in Moonlight

I killed a fae behind this pub once. He wore black and carried a vial of ground penn seed to slip into the drinks of women who rejected him. I wore red and carried a dagger strapped to my thigh.

It's how I satisfied my cravings before the Raze. It was easy. Wear a tiny dress and wait for an unwanted hand to creep up my leg, an unsolicited finger to slip beneath the strap of my dress, or unbidden lips to press against exposed skin.

My price for unwanted physical advances is steep. If warned, I doubt they'd be willing to pay, but I figure as long as they don't ask, neither will I.

I sit at a high table with Devlyn. He's eager, taking everything in like a child on their first trip into Vanihail. Not that there's much to see. It's dim, the floor is a permanently stained wood, the clientele ranges from drunk to drunker, and the walls are coated with withered newspaper clippings.

Devlyn grins as the Prince returns, balancing three glasses, brow knitted as he weaves toward us, struggling not to spill.

He sets the glasses in the middle of the table with a series of *clink*s and a self-satisfied smile. He claims a drink and motions for us to do the same.

Devlyn grabs his. "What is it?"

"Whiskey. Straight."

"I'm not thirsty," I say.

The Prince looks like he's going to object, but he surprises me. He shoots Devlyn a grin and, without a word, they crash their glasses against each other and gulp down their drinks.

Devlyn slams his empty glass on the table. "That was great, Hayes."

"Have another." The Prince nudges my glass toward Devlyn as he stands. "Drink. I'll get the next round." He heads back to the bar.

As soon as he's gone, Devlyn looks at me. "Would it kill you to be a bit more fun?"

"It might."

"Lune above, how do you manage to make going to a pub with a Prince boring?"

I don't answer.

He downs the drink the Prince left for him, and his eyes stray to my cleavage. "You look good tonight. I bet if you loosened up—"

"What?" I cut in sharply. "I might fall into bed with you?"

His eyes take on a sly quality. "Or Hayes. He seems to like you."

"I have higher goals than bedding a Prince."

He shrugs. "You don't have to sleep with him, but you could at least be nice to him. His best friend is missing."

He doesn't mean that to hurt me, but my body tenses with the knowledge that the Prince's pain is my fault.

Devlyn's expecting an answer, but I have none, so I avert my eyes and ignore him. The Prince returns before Devlyn can call me out on my silence. He sets down two wineglasses while looking at me with a grin scorching enough to reduce steel to molten ooze. He slaps a few ranis coins on the table. "Buy whatever else you want, Dev." The words are aimed at Devlyn, but he doesn't tear his eyes from me. "Care to dance?"

"There's no music." And no dance floor. And no way in hell I'm dancing with him.

"There's an earth fae at the bar with a fiddle. I bet he'd play for a few ranis."

"I'm not dancing with you."

He takes a beat to pout before perking up. "Are you competitive?"

I don't verbally respond, but a curious quirk of my brow is all he needs to continue.

"How about a game? You ask me something about you and see if I can answer. Then I'll ask you something about me. First person who answers wrong loses. If you win, I'll take you off the night shift for the next two weeks. If I win, you dance with me. *Once.* You in?"

Mentally, I weigh the odds of winning his game. As a prince, his entire life is public information. I already know he's conducted a background check on me, but I'm still at an advantage.

"Well . . . ?" the Prince prompts.

"I'm in," I say finally. "But you go first."

"Excellent." He sits on the stool next to me and grabs a glass of wine. "What is . . . my middle name?"

"Finnean," I say. "Where did I go to school?"

"You went to Rynsen's Academy in Serington for two years before you moved to Vanihail, where you attended Strassmore School for another two years. Then you joined the Barracks."

Serington is the sector of mixed affinities. The perfect home for my father, a water fae, and my mother, an earth fae. When they took in Rain and me, we lived there for two years. When we realized what I am, we moved to Vanihail.

"My next question . . . Hmm . . ." A hint of a smirk plays at the corners of the Prince's lips, and he takes a leisurely sip of wine. "What's my brother's name?"

Is this a trick question? I frown. "You don't have a brother."

His smirk broadens. "You're wrong."

He hops from the stool and gulps down the rest of the wine before extending a hand to me. "I believe this means you owe me a dance?"

I'm still reeling from his answer. Without thinking, I place my hand in his and let him pull me to an open space in the pub.

My confused trance snaps like a twig when I feel his hands on my waist.

My hands swoop over his and shove them away with a glare.

He laughs. "It's dancing, Saoirse. You have to let me touch you."

I take hold of his hands again. I say nothing as I place them back on my waist but stay where I am, an arm's length away.

The Prince cackles. "You win. I won't move any closer without your permission."

"You don't have it."

"Noted." He laughs again. "Dancing requires reciprocity, you know."

"Meaning?"

"Meaning you can't just stand there with your hands by your sides."

"Where should I put them?"

He carefully takes my wrists and positions my hands around his neck. With the distance between us, they don't quite loop, leaving my fingers resting awkwardly on his shoulders.

"This would be easier if you let me move closer," he says.

"No."

"Fine." He sulks like a child before brightening in the same breath. "Hey!" He shouts over his shoulder at an earth fae sitting at the bar.

At the Prince's call, he procures a fiddle, as promised, and begins to play.

It's upbeat—not swaying music—but the Prince rocks me in place, swaying to the rhythm.

The entire pub brightens at the music. I should've expected this. I've never met a fae who doesn't love to dance.

A few blinks later, the pub tables are shoved back, clearing out an impromptu space on the sticky floor. Fae whirl around in time to the music, some with partners, some alone.

Bum, bum. Bum, bum.

Two fae use a wooden table for a makeshift drumbeat.

The Prince grins. He tries to guide me to the middle of the dance floor, but I plant my feet. "You already asked the earth fae to play," I accuse.

He stops pulling me. "Yes."

My eyes narrow. "You were planning on asking me about your brother when you suggested the game."

"Yes."

A spinning couple jostles against me, pushing me closer to the Prince.

My head knocks into his chest, and he tightens his grip on my waist to steady me. For an instant, I catch a whiff of his scent—sweet like honey and heady like wine. Like in the corridor outside his room, my tongue burns with the cinnamon of his lust.

I don't mean to look up, but I do and, for an instant, I'm

frozen, trapped in the heat of his gaze. Lune above, even disguised, his eyes are captivating.

The cinnamon burns more intensely.

Quickly, I push back to my original distance. My arms are stretched, putting as much space between us as possible, but it feels closer than it did before. Hotter too. Like I'm standing over a fire, ticks away from burning into nothingness.

"Sorry," he says, not looking sorry at all.

To change the subject, I say, "How do you have a brother I've never heard of?"

His smile slips. "I was wondering when you were going to ask about that. His name was Finnean."

His use of past tense doesn't slip my notice. "Was?"

"He was killed."

"Oh." I'm floored. How has no one ever mentioned the Prince's dead brother? "I'm sorry." I say the words, but I haven't decided if I mean them yet. Haven't decided if he's earned them yet.

"Don't be. It was before I was born. I never met him." His words are clipped.

"Why have I never heard of him?"

"Finnean's death broke my parents' hearts. They erased anything that reminded them of him. Outside of the Palace, anyway. From where I stand, Finnean's still here. The perfect ghost child."

Bitterness surrounds him like a fog and sits on my tongue, rancid. His hand curls around the blackened coin at his throat. Felix's coin.

The motion is so natural. Like something he's done a thousand times without thinking.

We're swaying out of tune to upbeat fiddle music, surrounded by dancing fae, but with the coin around his neck and the taste of his grief flooding my senses, I see what he's been masking. Hayes is drowning. Drinking and drowning.

"I'm sorry about Felix."

It takes me a tick to realize I've said it out loud.

The Prince's eyes snap to mine, and his hand falls away from the coin. "He's fine. I'm sure he is." The hand settles back on my waist.

I nod, but he keeps going. "My father had a meeting yesterday. About Flem. He thinks I don't know. He didn't tell me about it. Flem is my best friend, and my father won't tell me what's happening."

"Ask him. Maybe he'll let you help."

He laughs without humor. "You clearly don't know my father. He doesn't want me to know how little effort he's putting into finding Flem."

My eyes narrow. "Why do you think that?"

"My father assumes Flem is like me. Reckless and foolish. He thinks Flem is off being a lightbrain, so he doesn't want to invest time into finding him. But he has to pretend because he has to at least put on airs that he respects Enforcer Fleming."

The Prince smiles softly. "But he's wrong. Flem isn't like me. He's like you. Dependable. Smart. Hard-working . . . the kind of person you spend two minutes with and you already know you should be more like him. He's also honest." The smile extends to his eyes, faint but unmistakable. "The way you are sometimes. Blunt. Tells me exactly what I need to hear."

His gaze is steady, and my stomach is suddenly anything but, so I duck my head, watching our feet instead.

The Prince chuckles. "You finally learned to look down."

"What?"

"When we met. Do you remember?"

I look up, but focus on his chin to avoid his eyes. "Remember what?"

"You lied to me."

I will myself to stay still. "What are you—"

"You said the reason you initially rejected the job offer was because you didn't feel worthy. But you don't have a reverent bone in your body. The entire time we spoke, you made eye contact with me. No fear. No remorse. No one's ever done that before."

Looking away hadn't occurred to me. "I apologize if I insulted you, Your Highness."

He shakes his head. "None of that 'Your Highness' nonsense while we're here. And don't mistake my meaning—you're a brilliant soldier and exceedingly disciplined, but I knew from the moment I met you that as much as you bow and toss around titles, you don't hold the Crown in high esteem. And you don't like me." Flash of a perfect smile that's so sudden, it disarms me. "That's why I wanted to take you out with me."

"Because I don't like you?"

"Because I thought your hostility would be a distraction." The smile wanes. "But instead, you remind me of him."

We sway a bit longer, neither of us speaking. I hadn't thought the Prince was capable of silence, much less the peaceful kind, but here we are, swaying to fiddles and table drums. And for a moment or two, I'm not an ikatus and he's not a spoiled Prince. We're just two people, caught in a moment of quiet among the noise.

When the music fades and the fiddler transitions to the next song, it snaps the Prince from his reverie. His expression melts into a teasing smile. If I couldn't still taste the citrus peel of his rancor, I might even believe it. He drums his fingertips against my back to snag my attention. "Tell me about yourself, Saoirse. Why did you and your family move from Serington?"

I give him a look. "The game is over, Your Highness."

Amusement swirls in his eyes. "Hayes."

"The game is over." I have to look over his shoulder to say it: "Hayes."

"Hmm . . . would it change anything if I said I was really, really sad about my missing friend?"

My lips twitch in amusement despite themselves.

His eyes light up. "I saw that."

"I have no idea what you're talking about."

"Don't worry, Saoirse." He sounds smug. "I won't tell anyone you have a sense of humor." His voice drops to a whisper. "Your secret's safe with me."

CHAPTER TWENTY
Spoiled Rotten

The path Jeune picks for our next run winds through Vanihail's sector center. The shops we pass are cute, and Haraya Hall, with its large erstwyn double doors, is always beautiful, but I prefer the seclusion of our usual route through the trees. Still, I let it go. I have questions. I'd prefer Jeune be pleasant, amiable, and unsuspecting when the time comes to ask them.

Jeune is already panting as she struggles to keep up with me. "How are you not the least bit groggy after a night out?" she asks.

"I didn't drink."

"Truly?" She sounds a bit faint, so I slow, letting her catch up. She scowls. "I saw that."

"Saw what?"

"You don't have to slow down for me."

"If I didn't, I'd be running alone."

She laughs. It, too, is out of breath. "Are you always this cocky?"

"Not cocky, just honest."

Her laugh deepens, and I have to fight one of my own. She's infectious, but there's a purpose to this run. All my time with

Jeune has a purpose. She's amusing, sometimes genuine, but she was also at the Ranking. And she snuck into my room. And she has *keil* beads.

I go through the list of her offenses, pulling me back on task.

There's a bakery coming up on our right. It's not open yet, but the windows are wide and clear. Perfect.

My movements are a carefully choreographed dance. My pace slows as we pass the bakery. I stare, making a show of examining my reflection in the window. Hesitantly, I trace my fingertips over the spelled burn on my cheek.

Jeune stops, looking from me to the bakery window and back. "You all right?"

"I'm fine." I turn away and shake my head in feigned embarrassment. "It's nothing. Sometimes I forget it's there, and then I catch my reflection and—" Again, I shake my head. "Never mind. It's silly. We should keep running."

I make as if to run, but, as expected, Jeune catches my arm. "It's not silly. We can—we can talk, you know. If you want. Or you can, and I'll listen."

I pretend to think about it before sighing. "You wouldn't get it. Anytime Laa'el sees me, she tries to sell me *keil* beads. I bet you don't have to deal with that."

"Laa'el tries to sell *keil* beads to anyone with a pulse. Don't take it personally. It has nothing to do with the way you look. Because you're beautiful."

She's being sincere in that way I hate. I grit my teeth, refusing to let it deter me. "So Laa'el tries to sell them to you too?"

"All the time," Jeune assures me.

"But you've never been tempted? *Ever?*"

Her eyes narrow. Not in suspicion but because she's carefully weighing her next words. "I haven't. But that doesn't mean there's anything wrong with using them. Or anything wrong with the way you look now."

I'm surprised how disappointed I am. Against all odds, I hoped she'd tell the truth. Or, I guess I should say, I hoped the truth would be less sordid and more vain. I'd rather her be self-indulgent than a blackmailer.

I swallow my surprise. Smother the tiny, flickering hope that my suspicions were wrong.

People have a way of living down to my expectations.

Turning from the shop window, I start to run again.

Jeune matches my pace. "Are you all right?"

"Of course." I smirk, keeping my eyes vacant. "I just got tired of waiting for you to catch your breath."

She rolls her eyes with a laugh. "I swear, you're the most arrogant person I know."

"Speaking of arrogant," I begin. It's not the smoothest of transitions, but it'll do. "The Prince seems to have a lot of . . . idle time." I try and sound casual. "He must have responsibilities?"

She grins. "I knew it."

"Knew what?"

"Did something happen yesterday?"

"Between me and—" We're getting off course. "You didn't answer my question."

"Then we're even. You never answer mine."

"How about a race?" I suggest. "I win, you answer my question. You win, I answer yours."

"We both know you'd win."

"Then let's save time and you answer my question."

Her emotions hover between amused and irritated. She must settle on amused because with a smile, she says, "Hayes and his father aren't on good terms."

"That means he doesn't have responsibilities?"

"He has very *few* responsibilities," Jeune corrects.

I nod, absorbing this. "I suppose he does all of this fictional work in the war room."

"He has an office."

"Really? I've never seen it."

"Like I said. He has very little work." Jeune grins. "And don't think I didn't notice you evaded my question about last night. Did something happen with you and Hayes?"

I don't want to remember the feel of his hands on my waist, the heat of his proximity, or the silent, stolen moments where I forgot I was in a crowded pub.

The Prince has a way of drowning the outside world in the steadying ocean of his gaze.

But all I say is, "I didn't answer because it's absurd. Nothing happened. I have no interest in a spoiled Prince."

When I return to my room, I'm greeted by a flash of silver on my pillow.

I slam my door behind me.

I'm tempted to rule out Jeune as a suspect—we were just together, and she didn't leave my side the entire time—but I'm not foolish. Getting a message delivered is easy. Especially considering how simple it is to pick the damned locks in this place.

I tear open the letter.

It's time to put your new knowledge to the test. Ask Prince Hayes about Szeiryna. I want to know where it is. Report to the sentencing at Haraya Hall in eleven days. I'll be waiting to hear what you've learned.

I'm sure I don't need to reiterate the consequences if you fail to comply.

I lose track of how many times I read the letter, each attempt bringing more confusion.

I've never heard of Szeiryna, but assuming it's like my last task, I figure it has something to do with a hidden piece of Keirdren history.

My eyes skim the letter again. Someone's going through a lot of trouble to unbury Royal secrets. Why? I have no idea, but given my blackmailer's methods, I can't imagine their end goal is good.

Not that it matters. Their endgame isn't my problem. My only concern is Rain.

The Prince *loves* to overshare. Loosening his tongue shouldn't be a problem. And anything he doesn't willingly divulge won't take more than a discreet hum to convince him to spill.

The trouble: his guards.

He's surrounded by them at all times. The Prince might be easy to manipulate, but his guards will be harder to beguile. Which means if I want the freedom to hum answers from the hapless Prince, I'll have to get him alone.

CHAPTER TWENTY-ONE

Hook, Line, Sinker

Pinecone,
I haven't learned anything interesting in school for
lunes. Can't I drop out and join the Ranks instead? We
could work together! Wouldn't that be fun?
I love you!
—Beansprout

B,
If that was a joke, it wasn't funny.
How was school today? Make any new friends?
P

P,
Of course it was a joke. And it was hilarious.
School was boring. Why do you always ask me about school
and never tell me about your day? How's the Prince?

Saoirse,
Rain let me borrow her freya candle. I'm going
to assume until I hear from you that you're
slowly going insane.

Some news from the Barracks: they've brought
in the next wave of Deltas.
Carrik

B,
I already told you, all I do is work the night shift. My
most interesting daily task is staring at a door. I'd rather
hear about you.

Carrik,
They've already started the next cycle of Deltas? Have
you seen them? Who's the best?
Saoirse

P,
Today I went to school. Yesterday I went to school.
Tomorrow, I'll do the same. I live a very exciting life.

Saoirse,
You are aware these are eight-year-olds, right?
There is no "best" yet. They can't all be
prodigies like me.
Carrik

In the time I'm not writing to Rain and Carrik or running with
Jeune, I plot.

Getting the Prince all to myself is—apparently—a more difficult task than I anticipated.

For someone who claims to shun rules and propriety, the
Prince is constantly surrounded by guards.

So I spend my days plotting. Studying him.

What I learn: He's loud. His voice carries, and his laugh comes with its own echo.

He hardly takes anything seriously.

He's lonely. Most of his "friends" are the children of wealthy Vanihailian water fae who frequent the Palace. They spend time together—talking, eating, playing parlor games—but his laugh is softer when he's around them. And his eyes are less bright.

He's funny. Funnier than I'll ever admit.

He's curious. Watches me intently. Listens to me when I talk. Asks too many questions.

He's otherworldly beautiful.

And he has the strangest need to be liked. Not just by the water fae he calls "friends" but by everyone. Guards included.

It irks him that I don't like him almost as much as it intrigues him. I hate the way he watches me. The way it, at times, feels like he sees right through me. Still, I intend to use his burning curiosity to fan the flames of my own.

A week after the arrival of the third silver envelope, I've made little progress in separating the Prince from the rest of his guards.

There's tension this morning as I report to the war room for the morning briefing. As if the entire Palace is holding its breath.

Zensen stands at the head of the table as always, but he's coiled tighter than usual, and there's the barest hint of stubble on his chin. I've never seen him not clean-shaven.

The instant we're all here, he says, "Last night, we were attacked. A group of Palace guards went to a nearby pub, where they were killed. All of them." His voice is stoic, but his eyes are hard. "We're not sure who's behind this attack, but the nature of their deaths resembles killings committed by the Resistance."

"The Resistance?" Devlyn echoes. "But that's—they've been wiped out for centuries."

"There were always rumors they were still here," says Jeune.

The Resistance hasn't had a large-scale attack in years. The last one was half a century ago. A failed kidnapping involving a Royal carriage. The story muddled over time, but from what I heard, a few Resistance members tried to kidnap Queen Ikenna and were swiftly executed by her Royal guards. Killing multiple Palace guards is a feat I didn't realize they were capable of.

"I don't believe in listening to childish rumors." Erasmus looks at Zensen. "Tell us: Is this the Resistance?"

"Nothing is confirmed," says Zensen. "I am relaying what I have been told. But this is a direct attack on the Palace and Royal family. One we cannot take lightly."

There are only two reasons to kill Palace guards: to send a message or to gain access to the Palace.

"Do we know if someone broke into the Palace?" I ask.

"It's unclear. Until we know more, we must all be on alert. His Majesty has requested the remaining Palace guards stay in the Palace until we know if this is an isolated event. We cannot afford to lose more guards. Especially with Hayes's birthday in the near future."

Like the other guards, my mind whirs. Except I don't give a sheep's skull about the safety of the Palace or its guards—my every thought is drenched in Rain.

The timing of this attack isn't a coincidence. It can't be. Hundreds of years and the Resistance is nothing more than a few scattered, poorly executed attempts, yet right as I move into the Palace, right as I start receiving threats from an unknown source, they're back?

I don't believe in coincidence.

It fits. I suspected my blackmailer was someone with an agenda against the Royals. The Resistance has aimed all their previous attacks at either killing the Royal family or forcing witches to use their magic to try to break the barrier. Until now, I had no reason to suspect they would target someone like me.

If the Resistance managed a strike against Palace guards, they had a motive. And I can't think of a better motive than gaining access to the Palace.

Is the Resistance blackmailing me? I'm not sure. But I don't take chances when it comes to Rain.

The instant the briefing ends, I return to my room to scrawl a note to Rain.

> *B,*
> *How are you? Is everything all right? I love you!*
> *—P*

I feed the letter into the freya candle and wait. Intuitively, I know she might not see it until after school, but that doesn't stop me from sitting next to the freya candle and staring into the flame, willing it to turn blue with a reply that never comes.

I'm standing with Devlyn outside the Prince's door in silence—impatient on my end, bored on his—when a messenger runs at us, out of breath. "Is His Highness here?"

Devlyn and I exchange looks.

"What's this about?" Devlyn's stance is confrontational. Suspicious.

"I'm delivering an urgent message to His Highness."

"Really?" I say. "Where is it?"

"I'm under strict orders to leave the message in His Highness's office. It's regarding the Enforcer's son who went missing."

Felix. A trickle of sweat slides down my back, but I feel cold.

Devlyn looks wary. "What do you think?" he asks me.

I don't take my eyes off the messenger. "We'll tell him ourselves," I say slowly.

"Thanks for the message," Devlyn adds.

The messenger nods in acknowledgment and darts back down the hall.

I'm buzzing. My heart pounds loudly in my ears, but somehow I maintain my calm.

Devlyn tugs a hand down his face, looking drained. "Hayes isn't going to like this."

He knocks on the Prince's door anyway.

The door opens, and the Prince pokes out his head. His hair is scruffy, he hasn't shaved in a few days, and his half-lidded ocean eyes suggest he was sleeping. Or trying to. "Something wrong?"

"Sorry to disturb you," says Devlyn. "But a messenger came. A letter was delivered to your office."

The Prince sighs. "I'll check tomorrow."

He starts to close the door.

"It's about Felix," I say quickly.

It swings shut.

Devlyn and I frown at each other.

I'm contemplating knocking again when the door flies open and the Prince is striding down the hall, a silver key clutched in his hand.

Devlyn and I trot after him.

"Do you think my father is updating me on Felix?" The Prince's steps get faster as he speaks. "Maybe they've found him!"

"Er—maybe." Devlyn doesn't sound like he means it.

I take note of our path through the Palace corridors to the

Prince's office. When we get to the office door, I step in front of him before he can burst in. "Sir, I don't think that's a good idea."

His eyes are frantic. "What are you talking about? I—"

"Sir," I say gently. "A messenger told you to come here in the middle of the night. The day after an attack on Palace guards. You don't think that's suspicious?"

He hesitates, and I lower my voice further. "Please. Wait here with Devlyn. I'll go in, make sure it's safe, and then you come in. All right?" I hold out my hand for the key.

After a heavy pause, he begrudgingly shoves the key into my awaiting palm.

I slip into the office and find the chaeliss stone. I press the rune, and the office floods with light. It's smaller than I imagined. With cold gray walls and sparse furniture.

I hurry behind the desk and scan the surface. A wooden object catches my eye—a stamp. I flip it over, studying its design. Keirdre's crest, just like the one used to seal the silver envelopes. And, like the seal on the silver envelopes, there's a branch missing.

The office door slams open.

"Is everything—" Devlyn stops when he sees me at the desk, holding the stamp.

I slam it down and force a smile despite my hammering heart. "I was just coming to get you. It's clear in here."

Devlyn's eyes narrow. Even as the Prince brushes past him, he doesn't lower his suspicious glare. "What were you doing?"

"The letter." I snatch the white envelope sitting on his desk. "It's on the desk. I wanted to make sure there wasn't anything here that could hurt His Highness."

Devlyn doesn't believe me. It's clear in his eyes, and I taste something like rotten eggs—suspicion.

But the Prince either doesn't notice or doesn't care. He rips the envelope from my fingers and tears it open.

I step away from him, casting my eyes to the floor. I don't want to watch his face as he realizes the letter inside—the one I had delivered to his office earlier tonight—is blank.

It doesn't matter that I'm not looking. I can taste his anguish. It's smoky, bitter, salty, mixed with something rancid like rotting fruit—disappointment.

I watch the floor. The blank parchment floats to the wood-paneled surface as he drops it.

Still, I don't look up.

Something rattles—his desk chair.

There's a pause.

Without warning, the Prince cries out furiously.

I look up to see him sweep an arm over his desk, knocking all of its contents to the floor.

"Hayes!" Devlyn is at his side. "Are you—"

"Please don't ask if I'm all right." Hayes buries his face in his hands. "I'm not. Who the hell sent that?"

"We'll look into it tomorrow," Devlyn assures him. "It seems like *someone* wanted you to come here." He shoots me a glare sharp as splintered glass.

I tense with the accusation in his tone, but the Prince doesn't notice.

"I'm going out of my mind, and my sodding father won't tell me what's going on." The Prince's voice is muffled from his hands. "Felix has been missing for more than a week. How have they not found him?" By the end, he's shouting, a vein is bulging in his forehead, and his hands are clenched into fists.

As furious as he looks, all I sense is his smoky heartbreak and rotting disappointment. Not a trace of anger.

My stomach turns with guilt. As Devlyn comforts him, I crouch, sifting through the scattered desk items on the floor. It's a good distraction from the grieving Prince and an excuse to find the stamp again.

"I'm sorry." Hayes opens his eyes and sees me. "You don't have to do that, Saoirse."

"I don't mind." My right hand brushes the stamp. I want to pocket it, but Devlyn has one eye locked on me as he soothes the Prince.

"Seriously." The Prince is on his knees in front of me, scooping everything—including the stamp—and slamming it back on the desk. "It's my mess. I'll clean it up."

"You don't want me to get—"

"No," he says thickly. "I did this. It's my fault."

He's not talking about the desk anymore.

"Your Highness—" I start to say.

He shakes his head. "Flem shouldn't have been out that night. *I* threw the party. His guards say that's where he was going. Whatever happened to him, it's on me."

It's a punch in the gut. "Your Highness, you can't think like that. This is *not* your fault. Besides—" I try and swallow my nerves—my guilt—but instead I nearly choke on his anguish. I say it anyway: "He could still turn up."

I lie constantly, to just about everyone. But this one—this one *hurts*.

I push to my feet and hold out a hand. "Come on."

He looks at my hand and back at the mess on the floor. "I have to—"

"No," I say firmly. "You don't. I'm going to pick this up, and you're going to calm down."

He hesitates before taking my outstretched hand. I pull him to his feet and motion him to his desk chair. "Don't blame yourself for this. It's not your fault."

It's mine.

I drop to the floor and set the last few fallen pens back on the desk.

Again, Hayes is drowning. His emotions taste as they did at the pub, but this time, there's no alcohol for him to dive into. No distractions.

After a week of studying the Prince, I know how he reacts to pain—he ignores it. Shoves it to the back of his mind and skirts around it, focusing his attention on something else. Alcohol, parties, dancing . . .

Or me. He told me as much when we danced at the pub. He's fascinated by me. And he uses that fascination as a distraction.

Taking advantage of his pain seems cruel, but the blackmail note under my mattress gives me no alternatives.

"Your Highness." I set the final pen back in its place. "Any chance I can have tomorrow night free from the night shift?"

"You're a novice guard," Devlyn speaks up. "You can't—"

"It's fine." The Prince studies me. The grief in his eyes gives way to interest. Just as I knew it would. "You can work the morning shift, Saoirse. You've done it before."

"What?" The Prince was clearly speaking to me, but it's Devlyn who responds.

"Jeune didn't tell you?" The Prince shrugs. "They switched shifts last week."

"We're not allowed to switch," says Devlyn.

The Prince ignores him and focuses on me. "Why do you want the night off?"

For this to work, I need him as curious about my whereabouts as possible, so I say, "I'd prefer to keep the details of my personal life private, sir."

Conflicting emotions battle for dominance in his eyes—confusion cloudy enough to blot out the sun and curiosity hot enough to scorch a tundra. "You're not going to tell me?"

"Are you ordering me to, sir?"

He falters but—as expected—shakes his head. "Of course not."

But I taste his disappointment. Not the sad, grief-stricken disappointment from earlier but the kind that burns with fascination.

And just like that, my trap is set.

CHAPTER TWENTY-TWO

Words Unspoken,
Song Unsung

The night shift starts at midnight. I wait until the wax of my freya candle burns to a nub and watch as it slowly grows with the early minutes of morning.

I don my darkest cloak, pulling up the hood as if to obscure my appearance. When I leave my room, I stop to look both ways and, as I traverse the halls, I slip through the shadows.

The object of this game is to make my deception look authentic. As if I don't want to be seen.

The chaeliss lanterns in the training room ignite with a hiss as I enter.

I discard my cloak and cross the room to the weapons' shelf to select a crossbow, ears perked, waiting for footsteps. If I've played this game right—and I'm certain I have—I won't be alone tonight.

I prop the crossbow on my shoulder, hiding a smirk as the door creaks open behind me.

"Fancy meeting you here."

I play my role. My spine stiffens in feigned surprise before I turn to see the Prince.

Laa'el and Devlyn stand at his sides. Laa'el watches a space on the wall behind me blankly, but Devlyn's gaze on my face is shrewd and assessing.

"Your Highness." I bow.

He chuckles. "Are you ever going to stop doing that?"

"No, sir."

He gestures around the training room. "These are your plans? I admit, I was hoping for something more tawdry."

"Sorry to disappoint, Your Highness."

"I'm not disappointed. Just confused. I assumed you had secret matters to attend to."

There's a question in his tone, but he doesn't explicitly ask, so I don't answer. "Did you follow me, sir?"

"Yes." He sounds unabashed.

"Why?"

"You intrigue me," he says simply. "And I was curious about your plans. But *this* is hardly cause for secrecy."

"Sir, if you must know, my other plans fell through."

The bright light of intrigue is back and sweeter than ever, like a fire-roasted tomato. "What other plans?"

I've been able to manipulate men since I was a child. All it takes is a song. This new arena of manipulation isn't quite as thrilling as watching the expression drain from a mark's eyes, but it comes with its own kind of rush—the sweet satisfaction of outsmarting a Prince.

It's a play, and I'm the star actress. My lips part timidly, as if to speak. But before I get a word out, my gaze drifts over his shoulders—first one, then the other—to each of his guards.

I purse my lips and look away.

For my final act, I swallow, donning a pinched mask of embarrassment.

His eyes are dancing. The smoky flavor of his curiosity invades my mouth, and I have to conceal a grin.

"El, Dev." The Prince doesn't look away from me. "Leave us."

Laa'el blinks. "Hayes, we can't—"

"Saoirse won't let anything happen to me. You can wait outside my room, but you're not needed here."

"Perhaps we can wait outside the training room?" Devlyn suggests. "I don't feel comfortable leaving you with . . ." His sentence trails, but his eyes on me make his meaning clear.

"No." The Prince is firm. "I'll see you later."

Laa'el and Devlyn look at each other. Their reluctance is plain to see, but they obey and leave the training room.

The Prince's blue, blue eyes twinkle with good humor. "Lune above, I thought they'd never leave."

"Your Highness—"

"What was it you were saying before? About your other plans?"

I turn my back to him. "I wasn't saying anything, sir. I was preparing for target practice."

"No . . ." He sidles up beside me. We're not touching, but the air between us hums like a melody. "You were telling me what your plans were."

As always, he's warm. It radiates off him, enveloping me like a too-tight blanket. "I'm certain I wasn't."

His eyes narrow.

I place the crossbow on my shoulder. "Why are you so interested in me, sir?" It's a genuine question. I wear none of the usual trappings. Not my siren's face or a revealing dress. And still, his fascination persists.

"Because you don't tell me anything."

"How about a trade?"

He brightens. Leans in closer.

He's a puppet, *my* puppet.

At least, that's what I'm trying to convince myself. He bends to my will, same as any other mark. Except—

"I'm listening . . . ," he murmurs.

—except lune above, his voice is smooth like velvet, the heat of his nearness sends my skin flushing, and his eyes are as tempting as the ocean I've spent my life trying to resist.

I inhale. The breath is shaky, as if even the air is weak-kneed at his presence. As a distraction, I aim my crossbow. "You answer a question for me, and I'll answer one for you." I pull the trigger, and the bolt sails to the bull's-eye. I allow my eyes to meet his. "The catch: you can't ask what my plans were tonight."

His curiosity sets me ablaze. He plucks a bolt from my quiver and holds it out to me. *"Deal."*

It shouldn't be possible for a single word to be so heavy. But the way he says it—breathes it out like a sigh—sends a shiver up my spine.

"Excellent." I snatch the bolt and load it. My movements are jerkier than usual, but I don't think he notices. "I'll go first—have you ever heard of something called Szeiryna?"

The humor flees his face, and the interest on my tongue is replaced by something more repugnant—fear. Ice-cold. "Where did you hear that?"

I pivot to face him. "I wasn't expecting that reaction."

"Saoirse . . ." There's nothing playful in his eyes. "This isn't a game. Drop it. For your own safety."

"What does this have to do with my safety?"

He runs a hand down his face. His expression borders

desperate as he steps closer, encroaching on my space. "Forget about it. *Please.*"

In my time here, I've worked to build a tolerance for the Prince and the pull of his beauty. But when he's this intense— this *raw*—it's as if I'm seeing him for the first time.

Still, I didn't orchestrate tonight only for the Prince to refuse to answer.

Control. I need to be in control. I replay my actions: I made him follow me, I convinced him to clear the room, I convinced him to trade information. *I* am in control.

I step closer to him.

His nearness usually rattles me, but now—as I watch his eyes follow me and his throat bob with nerves—I'm flooded with the rush of my own victory.

The cinnamon lust is back. My presence affects him. It made sense to me when I was wearing a skintight dress, but I'm back in my guard's uniform and he's just as affected.

I'm unfamiliar with enticing marks when I look like a soldier, but I'm *very* familiar with using a man's desire to my advantage.

"Please?" We're completely alone, so I soften my voice, preparing it to carry the gentle lull of a song.

He wavers, expression flickering. Finally, "Depends." Mirroring my movements, he moves toward me. "What were your plans tonight?"

My eyes narrow. "You said you wouldn't ask."

"That was before I knew what you wanted to know."

"That hardly seems fair. Are you ordering me to tell you?"

He frowns. "You know I'm not."

"Then tell me. What's Szeiryna?"

His jaw tightens. "You ask a lot of questions for someone who never answers any of them."

"Please?" Another step forward. We're chest to chest. Closer than I've ever voluntarily allowed myself to be to him. For some reason, he wants me. And as long as he wants me—and as long as I *don't* feel the same—I'm in control.

Still, every part of me is alive with the knowledge of his closeness. Our hearts flutter the same shallow rhythm, and our eyes bore into each other's, unwavering. I feel light-headed, but I press on. "Please, Hayes, I—"

I'm about to insert a lilt into my voice—*just* enough of a tune to loosen his tongue—but my mouth fills with the taste of orange, and a smile brightens his face. "Did you just call me Hayes?"

I blink.

I did?

I'd planned every aspect of this night to the smallest detail—saying his name wasn't on the agenda.

I blame the distance—or lack thereof. Being this close to him is messing with my mind. I slipped, but it doesn't matter. It *can't* matter because becoming too casual with the Prince I still have every intention of using for information can only end badly.

I force a smile. "Tell me about Szeiryna?"

"Fine," he says after a pause. "Put that away." He nods to the crossbow. "I need to show you something."

I hesitate for half a moment before returning the crossbow to the rack. The Prince starts for the training room doors, and I follow. "Where are we going?"

"The library," he tells me over his shoulder.

I fight a frown but refrain from asking any more questions as we go down the hall.

He holds open the double doors to the library, and I step in.

My footsteps echo in the maze of floor-to-ceiling bookshelves. They're arranged in twists and turns like bends in a river. The curves create cozy alcoves with plush furniture for reading in solitude.

The Prince leads me to the right, and my steps falter. Mounted to the wall is a portrait of a man. He's only shown from the waist up, but I can tell he's tall. He has a regal, distinguished air about him and a proud set to his chin. Almost arrogant. The deep ochre of his skin is blemish-free, and his hair is close-cropped and coiled neatly.

What really draws my attention are his eyes. Blue like the ocean.

"Is he . . . ?" I leave the question hanging.

"My brother," the Prince confirms.

I run a hand over the portrait's golden frame. "He looks like you."

The Prince scowls at the painting. "Just the eyes. Do you think he's better-looking than me?"

He's not. Of course he's not. I don't think there's a person in Keirdre, dead or alive, more beautiful than Hayes. "I think you have a lot of animosity for someone you've never met," I say instead.

His lips tighten. "You have a sister. You love her, don't you?"

"More than anything."

"And your parents? They love you both equally?"

"Of course."

"You say of course," he mutters, "but I've been losing a war against my brother for my parents' affection my whole life—and he's been dead since before I was born. If they could, they'd replace me with him in a heartbeat. Finnean was trained by our father on how to be King by the time he could walk. I turn eighteen in a few weeks and my father has never so much as hinted he expects me to take the throne someday. I'll live forever and

I'll never be King. Finnean lived seventeen years and my father all but handed him the kingdom. It's impossible not to hate him."

I can't imagine hating Rain. I can't imagine her hating me. And, as alone as I feel—alone as I *am*—I can't imagine not being loved.

Wherever the Prince turns, he's drowning in a sea of people. Guards, advisers, and nameless fae who attend his parties and drink his wine. But aside from Felix, no friends.

Part of me wants to fixate on that. How the Prince is in constant competition for his parents' attention with a boy who no longer exists. How those who spend time with him are either employees or familial obligations. How the exception to that rule is glassy-eyed at the bottom of a river.

But a larger part of me can't see past the creatures in the portraits, the woman on the rocks, and Rain. Countless lives lost or ruined at the hands of a power-hungry King, and all his son cares about is how lonely he feels in his Royal Dollhouse.

I inhale. It's easier to breathe when I'm not aching with sympathy for the Prince. "What does your brother have to do with Szeiryna?"

"Because of how he died. He was lured to his death by a siren."

Three ticks of excruciating silence.

My legs tense, fighting an urge to run, and my heartbeat pounds faster, louder. Somehow, I manage not to move.

"A siren?" I sound small.

"There used to be sirens in Keirdre. After the barrier."

"I know," I say. "There was a few inside the barrier when King Elrian—"

"No." The Prince shakes his head. "There weren't a few. There was an entire sector. And to answer your question, that sector was called Szeiryna. My father burned it to the ground."

I wait for him to crack a smile. Flash that perfect, knee-weakening grin and reveal he's joking. But his face remains grim.

The force of this new knowledge threatens to knock me over, but I anchor myself to the floor with shaky legs. I don't have time to process this. Not yet. The note didn't ask me to find out what Szeiryna is—it demanded I uncover *where* it is.

"But how is that possible?" I ask. "If it burned down, the remains would still be somewhere in the kingdom."

"You're too curious for your own good," says the Prince. "Knowledge isn't always power. Sometimes it's dangerous. And in this case—"

"I'll be careful," I cut in. "Just tell me. *Please.*"

Our gazes clash. Conflicting emotions stir in his eyes. He's close to giving in; he just needs a nudge.

I open my mouth to plead again—this time with a hint of a song—but he drops his head and groans. "I need you to swear you won't repeat what I say. Can you do that?"

No. I've already promised this secret to another.

I nod anyway. "I promise."

"Szeiryna's remains are no longer in Keirdre." He swallows. "Because my father moved the barrier."

I stop breathing. "That's—that's impossible. The barrier can't move. King Elrian—"

"That story is a lie. King Elrian didn't create the barrier; my father did. And he tied his *own* life to it. And my mother's. And when I was born, mine. Our life forces are linked to the barrier. Each of us provides an added layer of protection. As long as the members of the Royal family live, so does the barrier. As long as the barrier lives, so does the Royal family. But that doesn't mean we're invulnerable."

I grew up breathing the story of King Elrian's sacrifice. But apparently, the barrier wasn't created by a benevolent King to keep us safe from the outside world. It was created by a merciless King determined to trap us in.

"Why would he lie about that?"

"If King Elrian gave his life to create the barrier, then it's as permanent as death. But since my father linked our own lives to the barrier—"

"It's only as permanent as you are," I realize aloud.

"Exactly." The Prince nods. "Which is why the three of us are never together in public. It would be a security risk if something were to happen to all of us at once."

This is the earth-shattering information my blackmailers wanted: confirmation that the barrier can move.

No—more than that. They wanted to know *how* it can move and, more importantly, how it can come down.

My suspicions were right. Whoever is blackmailing me is part of the group that's spent years searching for a way out of Keirdre. The same group rumored to have murdered Palace guards just last week. The Resistance.

I must be silent for too long, because the Prince ducks his head to catch my eyes. "Saoirse." He breathes my name like a prayer. "I know this is a lot. But I need you to understand how serious this is."

Oh, I understand. More than he does. He's told me a Royal secret and sworn me to silence. A vow I have every intention of breaking.

"I understand."

"Good. I don't know what I'd do if something happened to you."

I've spent the past week dodging guilt like targeted blows—guilt about killing Felix, guilt about manipulating the Prince, guilt about convincing him to tell me things he shouldn't—but now, he's standing too close and his eyes are too blue and perhaps the most disturbing new development: he's answered all my questions and I didn't even need to sing.

I'd assumed his curiosity and questions had a hidden agenda, but after tonight . . . I think he honestly, *genuinely* wants to know me.

Which is frankly more terrifying than if he had told me he's hunting sirens to appease his father.

"What's going on in that head of yours?" he says in bemusement. "You always look like you're thinking, but you never look confused."

He's wrong. I *am* confused. I expected his curiosity, I even accepted his occasional bouts of lust, but his earnest *kindness* has taken me completely by surprise. People don't usually surprise me, but the Prince has made it a habit.

The library doors open, and footsteps barrel toward us before I can think of an answer I don't have.

A man speeds around the corner. He wears a messenger uniform with a pendant pinned to his front. "Your Highness." He bows. "I'm a messenger for His Majesty. I come bearing news: Felix Fleming has been found."

I suck in a breath.

"Finally." The Prince tastes of sugary relief as his shoulders ease and his lips slip into an easy smile. "Where was he? Is he all right?"

My body freezes over like frosted glass, and I fear the whole room can see right through me.

The messenger clears his throat. "He—he's dead, sir. Found washed up against the barrier at the end of the Greysn."

Four beats of silence.

And then the Prince steps back.

It's a single step. His right foot moves just a hair away from the left, but I see it. And it shatters me.

"Dead?" the Prince echoes hollowly.

I taste something cold. It's dry like sand, smoky like ash, and salty like tears. Grief. Heavy and dark. Hayes's.

"Yes, sir. Drowned," says the messenger. "I've been instructed to urge you to come to the King's war room. There's an emergency meeting convening now."

Hayes's legs are shaking.

Unthinkingly, I step forward, catching his arm. Steadying him.

"A meeting?" Hayes still sounds empty. "They suspect foul play?"

"I'm sorry, Your Highness. I've told you all I know."

"Thank you," Hayes mumbles absently. "You're dismissed."

With a final bow, the messenger leaves.

The instant he's gone, whatever temporary bindings were holding Hayes together snap. His shoulders shudder and his knees give out.

My hand on his arm keeps him upright, but just barely. He hangs on my arm, shuddering from emotion.

I've known about Felix's death for almost two weeks. I've known that he and Hayes were close for nearly the same amount of time. But now—with a mouth full of Hayes's grief and shoulders heavy from my own lies—it's catching up to me.

He releases my arm and buries his face in his hands.

A pause.

Then, he screams.

One long, sustained scream, muffled by his hands. Startled, I reach toward him—to do what, I'm not sure—but he peels his face from his hands and, even though his anguish envelops me in an icy chill, he's not crying.

"I'm sorry, Your Highness," I say softly. It's a two-part apology. First, for my hand in his friend's death.

Second, for what I plan to do next.

I prod at my *keil* bead with my tongue, preparing myself. "If there's an investigation, who will lead it?"

"My father has investigators."

"Hmm," I say.

"What?"

He's easy—too easy—to manipulate. An hour ago, it made me feel powerful. Now, I feel drained. "Nothing, just . . . why not you? Your father wouldn't be able to shut you out of the investigation if you were leading it."

"Me?" Hayes blinks. "My father wouldn't like that."

"So?" I read his face like a recipe. In it, I see exactly what I need to say to get what I want. "Your guards are trained for deduction. What's the harm in you lending a hand?" I pause. "For your friend?"

Something clicks in his eyes. "You may have a point."

I open my mouth—preparing to ask him if I can escort him to the King's war room, with a hint of a song—when he says, "Saoirse, will you come with me?"

"I— What?"

"Will you come to the meeting with me? You're right—if something happened to Felix, I want my team leading the investigation. And by team, I mean you."

"*Me?*" I don't know why I object. I should be blurting out "yes," but I don't know how to grapple with the fact that he offered me exactly what I want on a sodding silver platter and I didn't sing. I didn't even *ask*.

"You're smart. And I trust you."

You shouldn't.

It's cruel, too cruel, to take advantage of him like this, but my alternative is to stay oblivious during the search and let the King and his investigators find me. Felix's killer and a siren, packaged as one.

So, rather than answer, I motion Hayes out of the library and toward the war room, following as if I don't know the way. Another lie to pile onto my back.

The Palace walls are storming again. The flashes of lightning are more frequent, the churning of the ocean more intense.

Hayes stops outside the war room doors. "My father takes this room seriously. You're going to walk behind me, stand behind my chair, and look at the floor—never look up and don't speak. My father's in a foul mood, and when he's in the war room, anything can set him off. Promise me you'll be careful."

His expression is stern, but the flavor of his sorrow hasn't faded from my mouth. My hand twitches, yearning to reach for him. To soothe a wound I created.

I curl my hand into a fist at my side. "I will."

"*Promise* me." His urgency is palpable.

"I promise, sir."

"Hayes," he corrects.

I don't have it in me to argue. "I promise. Hayes."

CHAPTER TWENTY-THREE

A Beautiful Woman

The King's war room makes the Prince's seem like a child's play area. It's ovular, large enough to echo, and surrounded by raised stone benches. The long wooden table in the center of the room is surrounded by frantic men standing behind the dozens of chairs, squabbling.

Only one person sits.

King Larster Vanihail is tall, even while seated. He has graying coils of hair that make him look dignified, not old. His beard is thick, coarse, and streaked with silver, and his eyes are a hardened violet. He has the look of someone who used to be handsome but has weathered, more from bitterness than time.

Hayes halts in front of me. He's still several paces away from his father, but their eyes meet across the distance, and tension crackles between them like an open flame.

"I see my son has finally decided to join us." The King doesn't yell, but when he speaks, all else falls still.

"Good to see you, Father," says Hayes. He glances at me. "*Bow*," he mouths.

My insides snarl at me. This is the man who killed my kind and slaughtered thousands. And I have to bow to him as if I owe him a shred of respect. My first instinct: sing.

With a few notes, I can destroy him as he so callously destroys everything.

Seeing him so soon after learning the extent of his treachery burns me, but Hayes is standing next to me, fresh from the knowledge that his best friend is dead. If he can keep it together, I sure as hell can.

Control. I'm in control.

I sink into a bow.

I taste the King's putrid disapproval. "Where's Zensen?"

"Occupied," says Hayes stiffly.

"And you thought it appropriate to bring a child to this meeting?"

"She and I are the same age."

"As I said. A child."

Hayes stands firm. "Is there a problem, Father?"

The King's nostrils flare. "Not as long as she understands the rules."

"She does."

"Stand, girl." Directed at me.

I straighten.

The King looks me up and down. I stand still, feet apart, hands clasped behind my back, eyes studying the shiny black marble of the floor.

"What's your name, girl?"

Girl. I hate the way he spits it out like cud.

"Saoirse Sorkova, Your Majesty."

"Where are you from, Saoirse Sorkova?"

My fingernails draw blood from my palms. "Vanihail, Your Majesty."

"What do your parents do?"

"They are millers, Your Majesty."

"What did you do to your face?"

My eyes narrow a smidge. "I burned it. Sir."

Something like surprise alights in his eyes at my somewhat brazen answer.

Hayes's fear turns acrid, and I nearly cough from the intensity.

The King is about to ask another question—maybe to challenge me—but Hayes interrupts. "Isn't this an emergency? Why are you interrogating her? If you distrust my judgment, say so. Otherwise, let's continue the meeting."

For six heartbeats, the two Vanihails—King and Prince, father and son—glare at each other.

Finally, "Fine. We have business to attend to."

Hayes walks stiffly around the table and takes his place behind a chair to the King's left. I stand as I was told, behind his chair, against the wall.

From my new position, I spot a face I recognize. Grisham Haverly.

I shouldn't be surprised. He's a King's investigator, after all, but I'd forgotten to expect him.

"Why have we convened?" asks Hayes.

"To discuss our next course of action," says the King. "Enforcer Fleming wants this sorted as quickly as possible."

For a moment, Hayes bows his head and again, I taste his grief. "You think it's murder?"

"I *know* it's murder."

"Isn't it more likely he fell in the river and couldn't swim? Most fire fae can't."

"My investigators have reason to believe this is Spektryl's kill," says the King.

"The Raze?" says Hayes incredulously. "Isn't that why he had guards?"

"Y-Your Highness?" a familiar voice stutters.

I swallow a groan.

"What?" the King snarls. "You dare speak out of turn, Haverly?"

Grisham grips the back of his chair to steady himself. The wood rattles against the floor. "I—I apologize, Your Majesty. But I have information that may be of use."

The King still looks surly but nods, giving Grisham permission to speak.

"At our last meeting, Your Majesty, we discussed Felix Fleming's disappearance. Afterward, I was approached by a beautiful woman. She asked about our investigation."

I want to run. Sprint out of the room, dive out a window, burrow through a hole in the floor—whatever it takes to escape the accusation.

I don't move.

The King rises, darkness rolling over his face like a storm. "What did you tell her?"

"N-nothing, Your Majesty."

Liar.

"I—I only thought to mention it, sir, because of another killing. By Spektryl. There was a murder before Felix Fleming. An earth fae named Brogan Nash. He was killed outside a pub in Vanihail. It was rumored to be Spektryl's kill, but the bartender swears he saw the earth fae leave with a beautiful woman."

If the wall weren't here to steady my spine, I think I'd fall over.

The King chuckles, not in good humor. "Vanihail is full of beautiful women."

Grisham swallows again. "B-but, Your Majesty, I don't think Spektryl killed Brogan Nash."

Stony silence.

"You think this woman killed the Nash boy and Felix?" says Hayes. "And then what? Came to the Palace to ask about it?"

"I don't know. All I know is that this woman at the pub led Nash to the alley where he died. If she didn't kill him herself, she was bait."

"That doesn't mean the killer wasn't Spektryl," says Hayes.

"If this woman *was* bait, then it couldn't be Spektryl, Your Highness. The Raze doesn't employ women. Which leads me to believe this woman is either the killer we're looking for or she works for another assassin. One not associated with the Raze."

"You think there's a lady assassin running around using Spektryl's name?" asks the King doubtfully.

"I'm saying there have been two murders recently believed to be the work of Spektryl yet associated with a beautiful woman who cannot be Spektryl. All I suggest, Your Majesty, is that we consider the possibility these two deaths are related and investigate the murder of Brogan Nash as well as Felix Fleming."

"I'll send a team to look into Brogan Nash's death," says the King. "If there's no connection to Fleming's murder, we'll hand the investigation back to locals and—"

"Father," Hayes interrupts boldly. "I'd like to lead a team of my own to investigate."

"No." There's not a hairsbreadth of space in the King's response for argument.

Still, Hayes's chin juts. "Why not?"

The table shrinks at his challenging words, and the King's jaw tightens. "Because I said so."

"That answer's not good enough, Father. Felix was a friend. A damned good one. My guards are just as qualified as your investigators. All Deltas are trained in investigation. Why not put my guards to use for something other than acting nursemaid to me? Lune above, you pay them enough that they should have other responsibilities."

The King's gaze flickers to me. "I heard about this one. She's a runt. How is an ikatus supposed to—"

"Father." Hayes's tone is frigid and biting. "She's more than qualified. In fact, I'd like her to personally assist in the investigation. And Laa'el."

"The *witch*? Why not bring a sodding human while you're at it?"

"I'm taking them," says Hayes. "I'll keep this council apprised of the investigation. If we require more help, I'll ask."

"If you think you're qualified to track down a Raze assassin, you're duller than I thought. We've been hunting Spektryl for years, and we still don't know who he is."

"Then it can't hurt to have fresh eyes on it."

Long silence.

"Fine," the King concedes. "You have until your birthday to give me a solid lead."

"That's only two weeks from now!"

The King smirks. "Take it or leave it."

"Fine." Hayes spits the word with venom.

"Excellent. And when you request assistance—"

"We'll be fine."

"*I'll* be there to clean up your mess." The King finishes as though Hayes hasn't spoken. He rises with a smug grin. "As always." Without another word, he and his team sweep from the room. His violet eyes meet mine as he leaves.

I expect him to move on—for his eyes to glide over me like

skates on ice in the winter—but he maintains eye contact until he passes.

It's not until the door slams behind him that I remember I was the one supposed to look away.

"Are you all right?" asks Hayes. "I'm sorry—my father can be . . . well, you saw."

"I'm fine," I say.

He searches my expression for a sign of unease before sighing. "Of course you are. I shouldn't be surprised. You're you. Unflappable."

"Why did you request Laa'el? I would've thought you'd want Zensen."

"I'll update the rest of the team tomorrow, but for tonight, I need someone with Laa'el's expertise. What time is it?"

"Probably two past midnight."

"Perfect." He starts for the door. "We can fetch Laa'el and be off. The best pubs are open until at least four after."

"You want to go to a pub now?" I question as I follow.

"Someone murdered my best friend. I want to know who and I want to know yesterday." His energy builds the faster he walks. By the time we reach his corridor, he's at a near sprint.

He raises a hand to knock on Laa'el's door, but it glides open on its own before his knuckles make contact.

Laa'el wears a powder-yellow robe and fluffy white slippers. Despite the late hour and obvious pajamas, she doesn't look like she was sleeping. "Hello, Hayes."

"We're investigating the death of an earth fae at a pub," says Hayes. "I was hoping you'd accompany us."

Laa'el looks at me. "You're bringing this one?"

"Yes. How soon can you be ready?"

She reaches into her robe pocket and pulls out a necklace—a dark river stone on a chain with a rune etched in blue on the front. She slips it around her neck, and the rune glows so brightly, I have to close my eyes to shield them.

When the light dims, Laa'el stands as she was, but she now wears a yellow dress the same color as her robe, and her silvery curls are tucked beneath a cloak the color of midnight.

She steps out of her room and closes the door. "Ready."

Hayes grins. "Excellent."

CHAPTER TWENTY-FOUR

A Face Like Hers

The stench of the River's Edge Pub is exactly as I remember. Fresh beer, stale sweat, and desperation.

A little over two weeks ago, I traipsed through this pub in a tiny black dress with a vial of poison. Now I stand at Hayes's side, and the pub crowd parts for him as they once did for me.

Hayes slides onto a barstool, waving to get the bartender's attention. The bartender, polishing a grimy glass with a ratty dishcloth, swoops on us. "Hello, what can I—" The glass crashes to the floor when he sees the pendant on Hayes's chest. "Y-Your Highness. It's an honor." He bows.

"No need to bow," says Hayes. "I just have a few questions. Do you know anyone named Brogan Nash? He was found dead behind this pub a few weeks ago."

The bartender tosses the dishcloth over his shoulder. "Er— let me find the pub owner for you, Your Highness. I'll be right back." He drops into another bow and ducks through a door behind the bar to the back.

Laa'el keeps her hood up and rests her back against the bar. She attracts uneasy stares. Witches are only allowed in Vanihail as soldiers, and even then, they're rare. Many fae have never seen one in the flesh.

I take a seat two down from Hayes. He slides over a stool, closer now, and leans into my ear.

"Can I get you a drink?" His lips turn up in a grin, but his eyes remain vacant. "I'm buying."

"I don't drink on the job, sir."

"Not even a glass of wine?"

I must make an involuntary face at the thought of fae wine, because he raises his eyebrows. "You hate the wine too?"

"Too?" I echo. "You drink it all the time."

"I only drink it socially because I've never met another fae who can't stand the swill." His tone is light, but his death grip on the coin around his throat is anything but. "It's far too sweet. Like honey. If I wanted honey, I'd drink, well—honey."

He laughs, but my tongue is slashed with a wave of his mood—it's sour like rotting lemon and cold enough to freeze my teeth.

I don't return his laugh or crack a smile. "Are you all right?" I don't mean to say it out loud. But the words are out, and I can't take them back.

Hayes's fake laugh dies. He strokes the burned coin and doesn't look at me. "I'm fine."

I should let it go. But I can't help myself. "Hayes . . ."

He sighs. "I've had two weeks to think about where I thought Felix was. Maybe it's ridiculous, but I never considered that he wasn't all right. I never considered any other outcome. And now—" He takes a breath and glances at me. "Sorry. I shouldn't have—"

"You don't have to apologize to me. For anything."

The door behind the bar opens, and an old water fae hobbles to us. "Your Highness, I apologize for the wait."

"It's all right." Hayes transitions smoothly from somber to

charming. All traces of grief evaporate from his face like morning dew, but it lingers on my tongue. His stance has changed. With me, he was relaxed, back curved, lips turned down, eyes tired. Now, he's rigid, smiling, and his eyes are empty. "What's your name?"

"Silas, sir."

"Well, Silas, I wanted to ask you about Brogan Nash."

"I remember him, sir. You tend to remember the ones who wind up dead behind your pub."

"Do you remember seeing him with anyone that night?"

Silas's eyes light knowingly. "This about that girl he was with?"

I will my body to stay still even as my heart threatens to sprint away.

"Yes. Her. Did you see her?"

Silas grins. "She was hard to miss, sir. She's the kind of lady who draws the eye."

"She was pretty?"

Silas snorts before apparently remembering he's talking to the Crown Prince of Keirdre and attempts to disguise it as a cough. "'Pretty' isn't the word, sir. She was perfect. You couldn't look away if you wanted to. And if you saw her, trust me, sir, you didn't want to. Every eye went straight to her—and she went straight to Brogan. Which was strange."

"Why?"

Silas runs his tongue along his top lip, looking embarrassed. "I've seen quite a few lovely ladies in this bar, Your Highness, and I've seen them leave with lucky men. These women . . . they either leave with someone who pays for their company or someone charming and—" He breaks off. "Let's just say, someone who looks like her doesn't end up with someone who looks like him unless . . ." He trails off.

"Unless someone paid her to." Hayes finishes what he doesn't say.

"Exactly, sir."

"Do you remember what she looks like?"

"I'd sooner forget my own name than a face like hers."

Hayes gives Laa'el a loaded look. With a nod, she shrugs off her hood and turns.

Silas tenses. I realize now that she stood facing away from the bar to keep him at ease.

Hayes smiles gently at Silas. "You mind helping my friend draw her?"

"Of course . . ." Silas's voice is wary, and his unease sours like spoiled cheese as he takes in Laa'el's speckled eyes and vibrant silver curls. Unmistakably features of a witch. "You want me to describe her?" he asks.

"Not exactly." Hayes waves for the bartender. "Can I get a pen and some parchment, please?"

"Of course, Your Highness."

The bartender disappears through the door behind the bar again.

I frown at Hayes. "What is Laa'el doing?"

"She's drawing our mystery girl."

Every part of my body freezes. My heart stops thumping, my eyes stop blinking, and my chest stops rising and falling.

"How?" My voice is steady.

"By looking into his mind."

My tongue is heavy with questions. Witches are powerful, but they can't read minds. The bartender is back before I can ask anything.

He hands Hayes an ink pen and a sheet of parchment, which Hayes gives to Laa'el.

"Close your eyes and picture her," Laa'el instructs Silas. "You're going to send me the image with your mind."

Silas stumbles back. "Y-you're going to read my mind? I don't want a sodding witch poking around—"

"Relax." The word is soothing, but Laa'el's eyes flare—displeased with his reaction—only for a tick before the flash of anger folds in on itself. "No one can read minds without permission. You are going to send me exactly what you want me to see. Nothing more and nothing less."

Silas looks like he'd rather choke on his own vomit than go near Laa'el, but one glance at the Prince has him edging toward her.

Laa'el picks up the pen in her left hand and sets the fingertips of her right hand against Silas's forehead. "Close your eyes and picture the girl. Do you see her?"

"Yes . . ." Silas's voice trembles.

"Good . . . good. Now, keep that image—sharp as you can—and picture it floating through the air, drifting, drifting . . ." Her voice is a soft lull as her hand moves across the page, sketching.

In the back of my mind, I see that Laa'el is drawing with her left hand—the same hand as the writer of the silver envelope. But I can't focus on that. I can't focus on anything other than near-paralyzing fear.

Drina is powerful, but I'm not sure even her runes will protect me from what's to come. Surreptitiously, I twist on the stool, angling my feet to the side, ready to bolt at a tick's notice. I plot my escape: out the back door, down the alley, and straight home. Gather my family and leave.

Laa'el's eyes shift rapidly behind her lids, as if she's skimming a newspaper with her eyes closed. Her brow knits, and a single line of sweat trickles down the side of her face.

Most witches have a firm grasp of physical magic, usually in the form of moving objects with their minds. Rune magic is more advanced but still largely accessible. Mental magic is far rarer and far more complex.

When Laa'el opens her eyes, there's a flush to her cheeks and a sheen to her forehead, but the once-empty parchment has an image.

The girl Laa'el drew is stunning. And she's me.

I suck in a breath, waiting for the inevitable gasp of recognition.

It never comes.

"Wow." Hayes's voice is hushed. "She's beautiful."

I'm surprised how much his reaction stings. I didn't want him to recognize me, but the fact that he didn't bothers me.

"We'll post this image everywhere," says Hayes. "After we confirm with Grisham Haverly that this is the girl who approached him."

These are reasonable steps. If I actually wanted Hayes to find the girl in the sketch, I'd support this plan. But at the moment, all I can think—

Lune above, my parents are going to kill me.

CHAPTER TWENTY-FIVE

Harsh Truths

Laa'el and I sit to the left and right of Hayes in the war room.

It's satisfying. Seats normally reserved for the rigid Zensen and crotchety Erasmus are now for us—a seventeen-year-old novice guard and a witch.

Laa'el and Hayes are reading a list that the King's investigators compiled of all of Spektryl's kills from the past year. There's no official way for investigators to confirm a kill is Spektryl's, but their assessments have always been eerily accurate. I lean over the parchment as well, but I don't read it. I can't focus.

The events of the past few weeks are a flickering dust storm, yet I sift through them, searching for the exact moment everything imploded.

Unfortunately, it leads me to a few harsh truths I'm incapable of dealing with.

First: I know when my life became a tangled web of complications—the moment I snatched that silver envelope from Rain.

Second: I know when my life became a tangled web of complications—when a member of the Raze offered me a job and I said yes.

Third harsh truth: I know when my life became so damned

complicated—when I came, screaming and flailing, into the world. A siren.

I haven't had a tick of peace since.

"Interesting." Laa'el breaks into my thoughts, one finger poised over a name near the end of the list. "I didn't realize Spektryl killed Okkler."

"Who's Okkler?" I ask the question, but I already know the answer.

Okkler was a warlock from Krill—the tiny, lesser-known witch sector in the countryside. He was my first kill for the Raze.

"Okkler used to be a member of my guard," says Hayes.

A bell rings in the recesses of my mind. An alarm.

I thought steering this investigation away from me would be simple. After all, I only started killing for the Raze six lunes ago, meaning more than half the names on this list have no connection to me. But I can't overlook the fact that two names had personal relationships with Hayes. I don't believe in coincidence.

"Are you all right?" Hayes is watching me.

"I'm fine." My voice sounds faded, like a garment washed one too many times. My eyes shift to Laa'el. I need a moment. A moment with Hayes. A moment to voice my thoughts without her listening. But first . . .

I snatch a pen and scratch on a slip of parchment.

"O-c-k-l-e-r-r," I write out. "What else do we know about him?"

Laa'el frowns. "You spelled it wrong."

"What?" I fake confusion. "Oh. Sorry." I try again. O-c-l-e-r.

Brow creased in irritation, Laa'el grabs the pen and jots down the correct spelling. "*That's* how you spell it," she says.

"Oh. Sorry." I mask my disappointment—her handwriting isn't a match for the silver envelope. "Where did you take the sketch of the mystery girl?"

"I sent it to the print room."

"Would you mind fetching a copy?"

"Why?"

"It'll help me think." As I speak, I slide a hand surreptitiously under the table and nudge Hayes's wrist.

Immediately, his eyes are on me. I try to convey with my expression what I can't say out loud: *We need to talk. Privately.*

Laa'el still looks irritated. "Get it yourself."

"El, please?" Hayes cuts in on my behalf.

The glare she sends me could scorch ice, but she doesn't say anything as she stalks from the room.

As soon as the door slams behind her, Hayes is on my side of the table, brow creased. "Why did you want her to leave?"

It's funny. This night started with a scheme to get him alone but, turns out, all I had to do was ask.

"Was Okkler rich?" I ask. It's a hope. A last-ditch, vain hope, but a hope nonetheless.

Hayes looks more confused, but he doesn't push me to answer his question first. "No. Why?"

"From a powerful family?" I suggest.

"No. Saoirse, what's going on?"

I think Okkler was killed for his relation to you.

I don't say it yet. I need to tread lightly. "Don't you think he's a strange target for the Raze? They usually kill wealthy, influential fae—not poor warlocks."

He picks up on the pointedness of my tone. "You think someone's trying to kill *me*?"

"Why else kill a Prince's guard?"

"I appreciate the concern, but Okkler was killed nearly six lunes ago. Don't you think if someone wanted me dead, they'd have killed me by now?"

"I don't know. Who did you hire to replace Okkler?"

"I didn't hire anyone after him until you."

It's possible someone killed Okkler to open a vacancy in Hayes's guard. The same someone who sent the blackmail note that made me want to work here in the first place.

"Did someone suggest you choose your next guard from the graduating Deltas?"

"No. That idea was all mine. Everyone thought it was absurd. I don't think anyone's trying to use Okkler's death to kill me."

Maybe I should drop it. Okkler was one of my kills—the last thing I want is for Hayes to trace anything back to me—but it's a hunch.

To Hayes, Okkler is one name on a long list, but to me, he's the first. That has to mean something.

"Are you sure there are no other guards of yours on that list? Or—" I think about Felix, the son of an Enforcer. "Maybe family members of a guard?"

"Nothing."

"What about your parents' guards?"

Hayes's eyes twitch like he wants to roll them, but he gives the list another look. "No, I—" The words die. "Wait. I recognize this name. Henley."

Temisen Henley. My third kill for the Raze. "You know him?"

"My father had a guard with that surname. I can't remember his first name, but he quit a few lunes back—his father died, and he had to take over the family farm."

"Farm?" I repeat. "The Raze killed a *farmer*? Not exactly rich and powerful. You don't think it's strange that two of the Raze's atypical kills were involved in your protection?"

I've captured his curiosity now. "Lune above . . . you think . . ." He doesn't finish the sentence, but I feel its intention all the same.

"Anyone on here related to your mother's guards?" I ask.

"No."

"Are you sure? Your mother didn't replace someone recently?"

"She did. But it wasn't Spektryl. It was suicide."

At that, I tense, bracing for what I know he's about to say.

"He was a water fae," says Hayes. "Feris Carp."

I remember him. I remember getting the vellum scripted with his name from my Employer. I remember knocking on his door in the middle of the night. I remember admiring the sword displayed above his mantel. I remember dancing with him in his living room when he asked. I remember sparking up a song.

And I remember telling him to fall on that sword he admired so much. He listened.

Something inside me shatters like glass.

Not because I remember Feris—and I do.

Not because I now know the Raze is plotting against the Royal family—and they are.

But because they used me to do it.

CHAPTER TWENTY-SIX

Not Enough

When I open the door for the morning briefing, I pause. Hayes stands at the head of the war room table instead of Zensen.

"Good morning." Hayes nods to each of us as we take our seats, shuffled down to make room for Zensen. "I know I'm not usually at these meetings, but last night, they found Felix. He's dead. Killed."

My mouth floods with the room's shock and, overpowering the rest, Hayes's grief.

Even though I sense his heartbreak, his face is calm. "We've been called to conduct an investigation." He looks at me. "Saoirse is my lead investigator on this."

This is a surprise to me, but before I can say anything, Erasmus speaks up. "Can a novice guard be a lead investigator?"

Hayes nods. "Good point. Saoirse, I'm promoting you to junior guard."

Devlyn flares with something bitter like citrus peel, sour like curdled milk, and briny like pickled fish. Betrayal. Erasmus, meanwhile, scowls and folds his arms like a child, oozing his usual rotting disdain.

"She's only been here a few weeks," Devlyn objects.

"I trust her." Hayes speaks firmly. "We have two deaths to investigate, and I have no use for a novice guard."

"Two?" says Jeune. "Who's the second?"

"Brogan Nash."

Jeune frowns. "I thought he was killed by Spektryl."

"We don't think it was Spektryl," says Hayes. "There was a woman who led Nash into the alley where he was killed. That same woman approached the King's investigator, Grisham Haverly, asking about Felix's disappearance."

"Who is she?" asks Jeune.

"We're not sure. She might work for the Raze, but the Raze doesn't hire women, so perhaps not. Regardless, we're tasked with finding her. When we do, we'll either learn she's a murderer or she'll lead us to who is."

"Should be easy enough," says Devlyn. "Find the only person in Keirdre who hates delicious baked goods."

The rest of the guards chuckle, but I frown. "Baked goods?"

"You know. The Nash family." Devlyn gives me a look.

"I take it that's meant to mean something."

"You've never heard of the Nash family?" says Jeune incredulously. "They run the most successful bakeries in Keirdre. How do you not know who they are?"

"I doubt he was murdered for baking," I say flatly.

"Is this woman the only connection between these two victims?" asks Jeune.

"We don't know," says Hayes. "But if there are more connections, we have to find them. And we only have until my birthday."

"Two weeks to find a Raze assassin?" says Devlyn.

"For now, we're just looking for the woman. We'll focus on the Raze later." Hayes tosses something on the table. "This is what she looks like. Be on your guard. She managed to get into the Palace once already."

I look at what he's cast on the table. It's a copy of Laa'el's sketch from last night.

"Wow," Devlyn breathes. "She's beautiful."

"It shouldn't take long to find her," says Hayes. "This image is all around Keirdre."

My head jerks up. "Already?"

"It went out with the newspaper this morning. And we have posters in every sector. If she's out there, we'll find her."

I feel sick.

Hayes frowns. "Are you all right?"

"Fine," I say.

If you disregard the fact that my parents will see my face on a wanted poster and fly into a panic. I have an urge to sprint home and warn them, but I'm working the morning shift, and there's no way I can switch again.

I take a breath. It's fine. Everything is fine. Everyone in this room is staring at the sketch, and not a single one of them can see it's me.

"Haverly thinks this woman is going to try and sneak back into the Palace," says Hayes. "If you see her, apprehend her. Whatever it takes. And be advised, Wren Fleming has stepped down as Serington's Enforcer. Tomorrow, there's a meeting with all of Keirdre's Enforcers at dinner. Zen and Saoirse will accompany me."

Devlyn and Erasmus glare at me, Devlyn in jealousy, Erasmus in disapproval. Neither of them says anything.

Zensen stands. "Remember: next week, we have a meeting with the Royal guards to review protection for Hayes's birthday celebration. We will have a party rehearsal to ensure adherence to the rules. Attendance is *mandatory*."

I clear my throat. "Zensen, if his party is on a ship, I can't attend."

"Why not?"

"I can't be near water. It makes me sick."

I pick up a hint of rotten eggs—suspicion—but he nods. "You can patrol the beach during the rehearsal."

"I'm supposed to patrol the beach," Jeune objects.

"You *both* can. As long as you stay in different sections. If there are no other questions, everyone's dismissed."

Erasmus and I are supposed to escort Hayes from the war room to the dining hall for the morning shift, but as soon as we leave the war room, Erasmus pulls Hayes to walk ahead of me. Hayes glances back at me, but Erasmus speeds up, far enough that there's a clear distance but close enough that there's no way to misinterpret his pointedness.

It's as expected as it is childish.

I'm not offended. I'm not even irritated. I've never liked Erasmus, and I could use a break from Hayes.

"Saoirse!" Jeune falls into step next to me. "I'll walk you to the dining hall." She glares at the back of Erasmus's head. "He's an ass. Don't let it get to you."

"I don't."

"Right. I don't know how I forgot. Nothing gets to you."

There's something in her tone I can't place, but I don't have the energy to decipher her meaning.

"Did something happen between you and Devlyn?" she asks.

I frown. "What do you mean?"

"He mentioned you were acting weird in Hayes's office."

Dammit. I should've known he wouldn't forget the situation with the stamp.

"What did he say?" I ask.

"He just asked if I noticed you being odd, and I said no." She eyes me. "Did something happen?"

"No. I think he's just bitter. Because of the promotion."

She doesn't believe me, but she also doesn't push. The rest of our walk to the dining hall is silent, and I float through the morning shift like a phantom. Hayes notices—he notices everything I do—but he doesn't comment.

At the end of my shift—four past midday exactly—I barely take a moment to greet the evening shift before charging back to my room, climbing out the window, and sprinting home.

Mom is pacing. Which is a bad sign. Mom is usually still. Calm and composed like a frozen lake. A pacing Mom is a terrifying one.

Dad stands in a corner, glaring at the floor of my room as if it's offended him.

They're both silent. Which is more chilling than if they'd just start screaming.

"Dad—" I try.

"Don't." He holds up a hand, quieting me.

It would be easier to stomach their reactions if they were angry. But for all of the pacing and silence, the only thing I sense from either of them is burn-your-throat whiskey: fear.

"You're going to have to say something." I finally burst.

Dad glowers at me. "What would you like me to say, Saoirse? Your face is everywhere. The entire kingdom is searching for you."

"They won't find me. My *keil* beads—"

"Don't talk to me about those damned beads! You rely too heavily on magic. Y'ddrina didn't protect you from being the most wanted person in Keirdre."

"Auntie Drina is the only reason I've survived this long. This wasn't her fault."

"Then whose fault was it?"

Mine.

But I don't say that. "The Prince is a better investigator than I gave him credit for. But you don't need to worry. The Prince doesn't recognize the assassin as me. Nobody does."

"Sweetie . . ." My mom comes to stand in front of me. "I love you, but you're drowning. You can't evade the Prince while working for him. All it takes is one person to figure it out."

"They won't—"

"You don't know that!"

I jump, startled by the fissure in my mother's composure.

Pepper-spiced anger sneaks into her terror. She grips my shoulders and stares into my eyes. "This is dangerous. I'm begging you: come home. Drop this. You're a gifted soldier. You can find another job. You don't need to work in a Palace of Royals who hate you for a Prince who hunts you."

"I can't."

"Why not?" my father snaps.

That damned envelope. The creature cullings. The plot against the Royals. The Raze using me like a toy . . .

All reasons I can't quit and all things I can't say.

I take a breath. "Were you ever going to tell me the truth about Y'ddrina?" It's true that this is a contributing factor to my need to stay at the Palace, but like all my truths, it's encircled in a lie.

Surprise, like a fleshy, rotting pear, from my parents.

"She *told* you?" says Mom.

"Why didn't you? There are hundreds of creatures in hiding and you didn't think to mention it?"

"There's nothing you can do about that," says my father.

"What if I could find more? At the Palace, I have access. I can learn what happened. *Why* it happened."

"Why does that matter?"

I almost flinch.

It's only scratching the surface of my problems, but the fact that he doesn't understand why this is important to me *hurts*.

When I don't say anything, Dad tries again, firmer this time. *"Why?"*

"Because hiding isn't enough for me." The words shoot out like a geyser, and once I start, I can't stop. "Pretending isn't enough. From the moment I knew what I was, I was alone. More than alone, I had to hide everything that makes me feel like me."

"You're not alone, Pinecone," says Mom gently. "You have us. You have Rain. Surely—"

"I can't talk about this with Rain," I say fiercely. "Ever."

"Why not?"

Because she's better than me, in every sense of the word.

Because if you split her open, you'd find good—and I can't handle her knowing I'm not the same.

Because she owns my heart, and I think she'd give it back if she knew how dark it really is.

I must be silent for too long, because I taste cold, gingery sorrow as my mom collapses on my bed, face buried in her hands. "I'm sorry, Pinecone. We thought we could make you happy. We tried to give you a good life—" She breaks off with a hiccup.

The sight of her tears extinguishes my anger. This isn't my parents' fault. My list of crimes might be endless, but their only fault in all of this is loving me.

The bed creaks as I sit next to her. "You did, Mom," I say softly. "You and Dad and Rain are a great life. You love me; I know that. I *need* that. But sometimes, being loved isn't enough. Sometimes, you need to be understood."

I rest my head on her shoulder and rub circles into her back as she cries.

There's a dip on the other side of the bed as Dad sits and wraps his arms around her.

We three sit, hugging in stillness for a stretch of time that feels like the good kind of eternity.

When Mom's cries subside, we continue to hold one another. I don't remember the last time I was this open with my parents. This honest. Even with a thousand secrets weighing down my mind, in this moment—this stolen, perfect moment—I'm weightless.

"How's Rain?" I breach the comfortable silence. "She hasn't replied to my most recent letter yet."

"She's good," says Mom quickly.

The stale bread on my tongue gives her away, and our moment fractures like a dropped mirror. She's hiding something.

I pull back from the hug. "What's wrong? Is she all right?"

"She's fine."

Again, Mom's words are too quick.

"You're a horrible liar. What happened?" My voice jumps a few pitches. "Did someone hurt her?"

"It's nothing. There was an incident at school."

My eyes flash silver of their own accord. "Did they find out—"

"No." She rushes to assuage my biggest fear. "She's fine."

My eyes dim to honey. "Then what happened?"

"She was getting teased by some kids at school. They called her a 'runt.' We took it up to the school."

I nod along. Good. Exactly as they should have.

"The parent of the main instigator was a little . . . vicious."

I stop nodding. "What does that mean?"

"He says his son can say whatever he wants. And that it's the school's fault for accepting a child from a cursed family in the first place."

"*What?*" I say. "How is Rain cursed?"

"Trellis thinks that since you and Rain are both ikatus, this whole family is cursed."

"He mentioned me? By name?" The first part of his sentence hits me belatedly. "Wait—did you say Trellis? As in, Trellis Ruster?"

The Rusters are Vanihailian water fae known for being wealthy, connected, and absolute assholes.

Trellis is the lead asshole; his wife, Vencinia, is a more demure asshole; he has an asshole daughter, Symetta; and now, he apparently has another asshole kid who enjoys terrorizing other children for fun.

My anger scalds me.

"It's fine, Pinecone." Mom tries to cool me down. "She's fine."

I don't believe her. I know how sensitive Rain is.

"Saoirse?" Trepidation threads her words like a needle.

"I'm fine."

I'm *furious*. The fury thrashes like the sea in a storm. It sings to me. Calls me to act.

I shake off the feeling and shove away from my parents to march to the door. "I need to get back to the Palace. Maybe go for a run. I'll see you both later."

"Saoirse—"

I slam the door behind me.

CHAPTER TWENTY-SEVEN

Tempted and Shattered

My sheets are the ocean, my bedcovers are the wind, tossing and turning. Each time I try to lie still, the water rages and I shift, until I'm so tangled in my bed, I'm drowning.

My mind is a battleground. Thoughts roar, demanding to be heard. They fight with blades of steel and echoing screams. The loudest repeats one name, over and over.

Trellis Ruster.

I've never hated someone as much as I hate him.

My memories of living with my aunties in Ketzal are scattered and few, but what I do remember, more vividly than anything, is clutching a tiny bundle to my chest and refusing to let go.

The sky cried the night someone left my sister on Auntie Drina's doorstep.

It was by happenstance that Aiya thought to step outside that night and spot the tiny creature, soaking wet and half frozen to death.

I remember sitting in front of the fireplace as Aiya walked inside, holding a leaking pile of blankets.

When the blankets moved, I took interest.

A little brown face stared at me with big brown eyes.

She blinked. Just the once, slowly and carefully, like she was assessing me.

And that was it. With a slip of her eyelids, my heart was hers.

I was dutiful and attentive as my aunties nursed her back to health.

I remember holding her. A teensy finger banding around my own like a ring. My heart fluttering like pages in the wind in response.

Time passed. I remember teaching her to braid, laughing at how her hands were too small to contain her big hair. I remember shrieking with laughter as we played on the riverbank.

The call of the water dulled when she was near.

We have no blood in common, no shared parentage, and we are completely different species, but from the moment I met her, she was my sister. Mine to care for, mine to love, and mine to protect. From all threats.

Like Trellis Ruster.

I'm spiraling, headed fast for the edge of my self-control.

I throw off my bedcovers and disentangle my legs from the ocean of sheets.

Boots. No socks. No time.

I need air—need to *think*.

I'm still dressed in my pajamas—loose-fitting pants and a long-sleeve shirt—as I unlatch my window.

Climbing down is easy. The castle walls are calm with the King's sleep, and as I descend, my scrambling arms and legs send ripples across the glossy surface. My room overlooks a green field. It's within the Palace gates but outside the confines of the Palace structure. It's perfect for pacing and ranting and fuming in the dead of the night, shielded from prying eyes.

The night air does little to cool my rage, but it helps me grapple with control.

I'm in control. Complete control.

I walk the length of the field, letting my thoughts mimic my feet and wander.

Trellis Ruster. As if Rain's life isn't hard enough.

All children are cruel, but fae children are a special kind of torture. They hide behind lofty expectations and judgmental stares. They use their affinities like toys and hurl insults like stones.

I near the far edge of the field, lost in the labyrinth of my thoughts.

I inhale deeply.

The air smells sweet. Refreshing, even. Almost like . . .

Dammit.

I twist on my heels and sprint for the Palace.

Rain. I smell it in the air—*feel* it hovering overhead—waiting to cascade over the field and the Palace and me.

The air grows heavy with humidity.

The pull of the water vapor is tenuous. Nothing compared to—

A drop of water lashes against my forehead, punishing me for daring to think it weak.

I push my feet harder.

I'm fast. Always have been. But not even I can outrun the rain.

Another drop. More vicious.

There's a crack of lightning, a rumble of thunder, and the downpour ricochets from the sky, drenching me. Drowning me.

I stop running.

The water is tempting. *Too* tempting.

Unable to resist, I throw out my arms and toss back my head. Lune above if it isn't invigorating. The night is cold, but standing in the rain, I'm wrapped in a blanket huddled over crackling flames.

Lightning crashes, illuminating the Keirdren skyline. The trees bend, cowering from the wind, while the Palace remains, still and resolute, watching it all.

As the image flickers away with the lightning, everything shifts into startlingly clear focus.

Kill.

Trellis Ruster is an abomination. His entire family is a mass of rotten cow cud, and he claims *we* are cursed.

Kill.

The rain pelting my ears sings it to me. Its voice is soothing, gentle, and undeniably cruel.

There's another pull inside me—reason. Telling me to flee for the safety of the indoors. Telling me to dry off. If I do, the pull to kill will evaporate like rain after a storm.

The problem: the Siren Song that lives within me doesn't want to see reason. *I* don't want to see reason.

I teeter on the precipice of logic and instinct. Right and wrong.

In the end, neither side wins. As long as I'm standing in the rain, the water wins.

My feet move before I give them clear instruction. They guide me away from the Palace, over the gate, and toward the Jeune River.

The Rusters live on the bank of the river in a house so massive, it's practically a Vanihailian landmark. My legs follow the riverbank upstream.

Removing my *keil* bead, I tuck it into the pouch around my neck.

Water thrashes from the sky, but I want to be submerged.

I close my eyes and drift forward until I feel the rushing river against my legs. Against my torso. And finally, *finally* flowing overhead, flowing around me.

My destination is upstream, against the current. The strongest water fae can't battle a river this swift, but I know the water's secret: it doesn't want to fight me. It's as eager to submit to me as I am to it.

I *push* the water against itself and it carries me, counter to the current, toward the Rusters.

The large house is only a couple hundred paces from the riverbank. I fly out of the water and explode onto the bank.

Their house is two stories of handcrafted brick with windows dotting the back of the house, each dark with curtains drawn. One window on the second floor—a glass set of double doors— opens onto a white stone balcony.

I think about knocking, but that's too polite. More than Trellis Ruster deserves and more than the punishing rain is willing to give.

My fingers find stable ridges in the rough brick and mortar. I start to climb.

I toss my leg over the balcony and stand outside the glass doors. The curtains on the other side of the window are pulled together, veiling me from the inside, but even through the storm, I hear the mingled snores of Trellis and Vencinia Ruster.

I run a palm over the glass and close my eyes. I *feel* each drop of water in my mind. I focus on the feel of each of them and *clench*.

Tension rushes out of me like an exhalation, and the rainwater on the glass freezes into a sheet of ice.

I see a flash of silver winking back at me in the icy reflection— my eyes—as I send my fist flying through the ice.

The door shatters. Ice crystals and shards of glass erupt in a fine mist.

I step through the wreckage and enter the room.

It doesn't surprise me that Trellis and Vencinia have a bed large enough that neither of them ever has to touch the other, even by accident.

They bolt upright and stare as I cross the creaking wooden floor to them. They're shaking.

Their terror is sharp and acidic. Panic never tasted so damned sweet.

Vencinia opens her mouth. She has time only for a brief, startled shriek before I send a wall of water crashing in from outside. It wraps around Vencinia's throat, squeezing like a hand.

Her shriek cuts short—sliced through like a dull blade.

"Make one noise," I say calmly, "and I'll kill you."

Tears pour down her cheeks, but she obediently keeps her wobbling lips pressed together.

Water shifts behind me—Trellis, attempting a counterattack. With an impatient flick of my wrist, the rising water crashes to the floor.

"Don't bother." I near Trellis's side of the bed.

"Wh-who are you?" He backs up but stops when he brushes against his wife.

I hear their heartbeats. The two overlapping sounds sputter in a frantic rhythm.

I come closer.

All they can see of me is glowing silver eyes. The rest of me, ensconced in black attire and cloudy nightfall, is hidden.

A chaeliss stone sits on the bedside table. My hand darts for it, and Trellis flinches as if I'm about to strike him.

I don't comment, but I smirk at his expense.

I press my thumb to the large rune in the middle. The chae-liss lanterns flicker to life, bathing the room in firelight.

Trellis's eyes find me. I'm soaked to the bone, I'm wearing my nightclothes, and my braid is sloppy from sleep, but when he sees me, his trembling extinguishes like a wet torch and all I taste is sweet, spicy lust.

"Hi." I smile. It feels feral, but he doesn't seem to notice. I lean forward, open my mouth, and let my anger pour out in a song. Low, so his wife can't hear over the storm. It's vengeful, smooth, and ominous, like darkening thunderclouds.

Trellis's vibrant blue eyes empty of all expression.

I pull away—slightly—and he follows. Slides to the edge of his bed, legs dangling over, body bent, trying to get closer to me.

From over his shoulder, Vencinia follows her husband's move-ments. "Trellis? What are you—"

"I thought I told you to shut up!" My eyes flash dangerously.

The water around her throat tightens. Not enough to choke her but enough to remind her it's there.

My silver gaze flicks back to Trellis. The bastard is still staring at me with eyes wide, glassy, and innocent, like a newborn lamb.

I brought no poison with me, I have no blade, and taking him to the nearby river is risky so soon after another, similar drowning.

Kill.

The water demands it and I intend to deliver, but first, I have a loose end to contend with.

The ring of water drops from Vencinia, soaking her bed-covers. She releases a shuddering breath, and her hands fly to her neck, feeling for damage.

"Go," I say coldly. "Now. Come back and I'll kill you. Tell anyone you saw me here and I'll return for you."

She doesn't move. She glances at Trellis, who's still staring at me, transfixed even as I threaten his wife. "Wh-what are you going—"

"I don't like to repeat myself. *Go.*"

She hesitates only a tick longer before sprinting from the room.

Kill.

The water is impatient, and my soul is restless with its discontent.

I meet Trellis's eyes and smile, that same monstrous smile as before. A song flows, louder this time, without an audience.

I slink closer to the bed. My song fades into a question to which I already know the answer: "Do you know Rain Sorkova?"

A sober Trellis Ruster would be surprised at such a random question, but Trellis Ruster is mind-numbingly drunk on me. "Yes." He's hoarse. "She's a runt."

I almost snap, but I bridle it. For now.

"Did you tell your son the Sorkovas are cursed?" I ask.

"Yes," he whispers.

"Why?"

"They have two runts in one family."

He says it like it means something. Like it justifies anything.

My eyes glow brighter.

Kill.

I sing a few more notes. Press myself closer, my face so near his that our breaths mingle.

He tries to lean in—to steal a brush of my lips against his— but I jerk back. "Don't move, Trellis."

He obeys, holding his breath in rapt attention.

I raise my arms, and the pouring rain rushes forward, eager

to meet me. It forms a sphere of water, hovering just above my open palms.

"Please." He's breathless. I realize he hasn't breathed since I told him not to move. "You know my name—what's yours?"

I smile. The sphere of water drifts closer to his head. "If you're good," I say, "maybe I'll tell you."

I stop the water. It's suspended in front of his face—brushing the tip of his nose.

My fingers dig through the leather pouch around my neck for my *keil* bead. I click it into place behind my tooth.

The transformation washes over me like freshly fallen rain. I'm me again. The me he knows, anyway. My lips stretch into a wide smirk as I say, "My name is Saoirse Sorkova."

I have the sick satisfaction of watching the shock set across his face.

He tries to run, but I *push* the sphere of water forward.

It consumes his head.

Through the glassy water, his eyes widen with panic.

I feel a tug as he tries to expel the water using his own affinity. I'm stronger than him on my own, but with the merciless rain, Siren Song in my heart, and fury in my veins, he stands no match.

Our battle is brief and vicious. My victory is inevitable.

We all have instincts. Mine is to kill. His is to breathe.

He holds on for as long as he can, resisting the urge, fighting the instinct, holding his breath.

I see the moment he gives in—the instant his body gives up the fight. Something indiscernible shifts in his eyes, and he inhales. I *feel* the water from my sphere flood his lungs. His eyelids slide shut, and his body slumps forward.

I spin around, facing the open balcony doors as he tumbles forward, splashing onto the rain-soaked floor, still littered with splintered ice and shattered glass.

I leave the house the way I came—through the wreckage.

CHAPTER TWENTY-EIGHT
What Lurks Behind

I don't regret it.

I don't regret that Trellis Ruster is dead. I don't regret that I'm the one who killed him.

My only regret is ever knowing him. Because if I didn't, killing him wouldn't have violated one of my rules: never kill someone I know.

I made my rules after my first kill, when I made the mistake of telling my father.

He looked at me like I was a stranger. A monster. It hurt like hell, but I could handle a look.

And then I tasted the rot of his horror—of his *terror*—and I was a falling crystal glass. My stomach dropped as I tumbled, and my heart shattered as I crash-landed in shambles.

I made my first rule then: no more killing.

For one year, I honored that rule.

At first, I used the water to resist my urges. I hid behind *keil* beads, avoided my abilities, refused to touch water near anyone else, and I stopped singing.

Every few lunes, my instincts would scream, louder and louder, until they were impossible to ignore and I'd give in and take a swim. It was *just* enough to sate my thirst and keep my other instincts at bay.

It took a year for the water to change its tune. It didn't just call me to swim; it screamed at me to hunt. To kill. What was once peaceful solace became my sweetest temptation.

Wykland Railsen crumbled my feeble resistance.

He was an earth fae Mom knew from Kurr Valley. He was in Vanihail for business, staying with my family for a few nights. On his last night in town, I came home to visit.

I didn't mean to kill him.

I don't even remember doing it. I have no recollection of creeping down the hall from my bedroom to Wykland's. Of singing him a soothing lullaby from our house to the Jeune River.

But it happened.

The next morning, I woke at the bottom of the river, and Wykland was gone.

I obliterated my first rule.

Worse, I learned that if I want to stay in control, I *need* the kill.

I sobbed for days. The realization broke my heart. I'm not sure I ever put it back together.

From the ashes of that first rule, two more were born: one, never kill someone I know, and two, only kill assholes.

My marks for the Raze were perfect. I didn't know them and, until Felix, I assumed they were all assholes. Why else would assassins want them dead?

Trellis Ruster satisfied only one of my usual requirements. I feel no remorse for killing him, but when I deviate from my rules, I feel like a sprig after my first kill again, tasting my father's fear of what I am and falling in darkness.

I try and push Trellis from my mind as I sneak from the Palace yet again. The last silver envelope told me to go to the sentencing at Haraya Hall, and despite my gnawing self-hatred, I won't risk not complying with my blackmailer's demands.

In the aftermath of last night's storm, Vanihail feels more chaotic. The path to Haraya is scattered with destruction. The harsh winds wreaked havoc on the crops in Kurr Valley, toppled massive trees on the main roads out of Vanihail, and, most notably, left the Greysn River blocked with debris.

With the blockage upstream near the barrier, the flow of fresh, drinkable water into Keirdre is stalled.

The only people out right now are humans scuttling around to clear the damage and fae headed to the sentencing at Haraya.

After the Palace, Haraya Hall is the second-largest structure in Vanihail. It's made from thick gray stones, massive stained glass windows, and erstwyn double doors that are wide open for the sentencing. There are sentencings every day in Sinu, but once a lune, there's a massive one here, overseen by Vanihail's Enforcer, Anarin Arkin. Attendance is optional, but judging by the number of fae coursing through the double doors like a current, it's a well-attended event.

I keep my hood up as I enter the hall. There's a wooden stage in the middle of the sentencing chamber surrounded by raised benches. Fae file in, and the room fills with the taste of fresh berries—excitement—while my stomach fills with dread.

The back wall of Haraya has a huge, circular stained glass window with hands on the inside and outside, creating a double-sided clock.

The hands move, closer and closer to ten. With each tick, the sweet anticipation of the room builds until it's so intense, my mouth feels dry.

When the clock strikes ten, a hush falls over the crowd, and Haraya blinks into darkness.

A few startled gasps.

The torches flicker to life. Anarin Arkin stands onstage. As always, she wears navy and gold for Keirdre, but she's not in uniform. She wears a long black dress, a navy headscarf, and heavy-looking golden jewelry.

She's radiant, but my eyes skirt past her.

Sitting behind her is a human. He's small, drenched in sweat, and shivering from something other than cold. He looks barely older than me. Skin and bone with sunken-in brown eyes.

"Aris Milner." Anarin's voice shatters the stillness that's fallen over the hall. She's addressing the human, but this is a show for Vanihailians, so she doesn't look away from her enraptured audience. "You're charged with being in possession of *lairic* beads." Anarin paces across the stage, and the eyes of the fae track her movements, drinking in her authority like a cordial. "Do you deny it?"

Aris mumbles in reply, too quiet to hear.

Anarin's expression darkens. "Speak up."

"I don't deny it." His voice strains from the effort and still, I barely hear him.

"Are you aware humans are forbidden from using magic?"

The crowd leans forward, hanging on Anarin's every word.

I poke my tongue against my *keil* bead. A sense of foreboding twists my stomach into a knot.

"Yes," Aris shouts in response.

"Were you aware that *lairic* beads are a form of magic?" asks Anarin.

"Yes."

Anarin stops moving. "Aris Milner, you have been found

guilty of practicing magic as a human. Do you know the punishment for that crime?"

His chin drops to his chest. "Yes."

The excitement of the fae surrounding me floods my mouth like rainwater in a river. I try to swallow it, but it lodges itself in my throat.

Death.

The price of humans using magic.

Anarin doesn't say it. Not yet. She hasn't finished her show.

"If you like," Anarin says, "we can make a deal."

His head jerks up, eyes wide with hope. "A deal?"

"Yes. *Lairic* beads are used for communicating. Tell me who you were communicating with and your life will be spared."

The hope drains from his eyes, and his shoulders slump.

Of course. A trap. It's all too common for human families to be split apart. One parent dragged off to work in Vanihail, another sent to a different sector. Most likely, this human has family he needs *lairic* beads to talk to. And if he loves them enough to risk death to stay in contact, he won't turn them in and risk them receiving the same fate.

He hangs his head and doesn't answer.

Anarin smirks, satisfaction evident in her violet eyes. She never expected him to give a name; she just wanted to build the tension of the moment.

"If you refuse to answer, you are sentenced to death."

I want to look away, but my eyes are peeled. Aris is so young—too young. There's someone out there he loves. Someone who will, in the near future, attempt to Dreamweave into the mind of someone who no longer exists.

Anarin circles around Aris's chair. He's bound, so he can't move. His fingers twitch against the arms of the chair in terror.

Anarin yanks a knife from a sheath at her waist. I flinch as she slices the blade down.

To my surprise, the ropes fall off Aris.

For a split tick, my shoulders ease—

She slices the dagger again, drawing it horizontally across his neck.

His mouth opens in a silent scream as blood spurts from his throat.

I see now why she cut his bindings. To make the scene more brutally dramatic.

His freed hands fly to his neck, and he tumbles from the chair, convulsing as blood gurgles in his throat.

A few twitches later, his body stills, and the tiny, shriveling human is dead.

Anarin is smiling. Not a shred of remorse. Her black dress is stained red, but she doesn't appear to notice.

The crowd roars in approval around me.

I'm frozen. Silent. *Horrified.*

Three weeks ago, I wanted to be Anarin. I wanted an assignment that would set me on track to be an Enforcer. I thought claiming the title would prove how far I could rise, ikatus and all.

Turns out, the title is a thin veil to disguise yet another monster.

I'm nauseous as I leave Haraya. Not from the blood but from the *sickness* of Anarin's sadistic spectacle.

A hand touches my elbow.

I twist around, hand flying to strike my assailant—and stop.

The man is tall and wearing a hood that hangs so low, it flops over his eyes and nose, leaving only his lips visible. A *keil* bead hangs around his neck, plainly evident. He wants me to see it. To know that the sliver of his face I'm seeing now isn't his.

My blackmailer in the flesh.

"You know who I am?" His voice is gruff. Also disguised by a *keil* bead.

I think about singing. He stands before me, in person, the author of the notes that threaten to expose my sister. But he's not working alone. If something happens to him, those he works with will punish Rain.

I hold in the song and say, "Yes."

"Good." He pulls me away from the passing flow of fae leaving Haraya and into the shadows.

My arm burns where he grips me, yearning to shove him off and scrub myself clean of his touch, but I don't put up a fight.

He stops and leans back, putting distance between us. "Tell me about the creature cullings."

I fold my arms. "There used to be other creatures in Keirdre. King Larster killed them all."

He doesn't react. "And Szeiryna?"

"It was a sector. It used to be—"

"I know *what* it is." My blackmailer sounds impatient. "Tell me *where* it is."

There's a pit in my stomach. From his reaction, it's clear Szeiryna is what he's really interested in. More specifically— what happened to the barrier.

I have to tell him. The threat in the silver envelopes means refusing isn't an option. The problem—

I promise.

Two words. So simple, but so, so heavy.

Hayes swore me to secrecy. Of course, at the time, I knew it was a promise I couldn't keep. But it feels worse now. Like a betrayal.

I must take too long, because my blackmailer says, "Do I need to remind you what happens if you refuse to answer?"

Rain.

My resistance crumbles.

Anything for you.

I steel myself. "Szeiryna is on the other side of the barrier."

He presses closer. "How is that possible?"

"The barrier isn't permanent." I hang my head. "It's tied to the Royals. As long as they live, so does the barrier."

I taste his eagerness at my words. "And if they were to die?"

He already knows the answer, but the tension in his stance dares me to refuse him.

"So would the barrier," I say.

He doesn't stick around for pleasantries. With a half nod, he walks away, leaving me in the shadow of Haraya Hall, alone with my thoughts and overwhelming guilt.

The Raze is already using me in a plot against the Royals. And now I've given the Resistance a new target as well:

Hayes.

CHAPTER TWENTY-NINE
Child's Play

The sight of roasted ham, stewed yams, collard greens, and pans of slightly charred cornbread is enough to make my empty stomach rumble in discontent. But the real torture is the *smell*.

I smell the hickory smoke drifting from the ham; the cinnamon-honeyed scent of the candied yams; the rich, fatty aroma wafting from the bacon grease the greens are cooked in; and the warm, buttery smell of the cornbread.

I haven't eaten since before last night's kill. The sensation of their scents combined makes my legs weak, but I can't enjoy any of it.

Anarin sits in the dining hall, at the table. She glanced at me when she strolled in, but I looked away before I could see the flicker of recognition.

Yesterday, I aspired to be her.

Today, she makes my stomach twist in disgust.

The table is full today. With the King, Prince, and eight of Keirdre's Enforcers.

Guards line the walls, humans serve, and the guests at the table pretend we don't exist.

Except for Hayes. He catches my eye and grins. He raises his glass of sickly-sweet wine toward me in a silent toast.

The sight of him rips me in half. I'm furious at him. And terrified for him. And I don't know how to reconcile the two.

I think of the humans left to clean up the aftermath of the storm last night. Of the water shortage and how the only ones affected will be families like mine. Of the man—boy, really—sentenced to death a few hours ago. And here Hayes sits, Crown Prince, stuffing his face, drinking wine, and smiling at me.

Cue anger.

But then I remember him confiding in me about the barrier. Making me promise to never tell. And how I traded the information away to someone who wants him dead.

Cue fear.

I look away.

This meeting is to select the next Enforcer of Serington. Each person at the table has a vote, and King Larster can reject the majority.

So far, this so-called meeting has been Enforcers bickering like children. It's expected. Fae hate witches, witches hate fae, and none of them give a sheep's skull what the humans think.

The result: endless spats over petty drivel.

The chair at the head of the table scrapes against the floor as the King stands. The instant he rises, conversation dies, and all eyes fix on him.

"Wren Fleming, Enforcer of Serington, has lost his son. He has asked to step down from his position. Before we commence this meeting, any objections to Enforcer Fleming's resignation?"

An earth fae raises his hand. "I have no objection, Your Majesty, however I must ask: What is being done in response to Felix's death? From what I understand, he was murdered. Is it true that there's an assassin running loose in Keirdre? I have children, Your Majesty. Is this woman targeting Enforcers?"

"We are not even sure if this woman is the killer," says the King.

The air fae Enforcer, Xeris, frowns. "With all due respect, Your Majesty, we've all seen posters of this woman in our sectors. Why search for a woman who isn't the killer?"

The King nods to Hayes. "Ask my son. He has Keirdre panicking over a pretty face. I have allowed him to attempt an investigation until his birthday. But as soon as my son turns eighteen and relinquishes his delusions, my own team will find the real culprit. Spektryl. A man."

The Enforcers look to Hayes expectantly.

He takes a long drink of his too-sweet wine and slams the glass on the table with a clinking rattle. "Lovely introduction, Father," he mutters. He raises his voice, addressing the room. "You all may think I'm foolish for sending the kingdom after a woman, but can anyone here tell me what Spektryl looks like?"

Silence.

"Can anyone tell me how old he is? Or even what kind of fae he is?"

More silence.

"We don't know anything about Spektryl, but we *do* know what this woman looks like. She could be our killer, but even if she's not, she can lead us to him. I wish my father luck in his hunt for a phantom, but my team and I—" He meets my eyes with a smile I can only describe as fond. "We pursue flesh and blood. Mock all you want—we'll catch our girl."

I've become accustomed to Hayes shirking formality. It's disarming—pleasantly so—to see him take control in a room of the most powerful people in Keirdre.

When I arrived at the Palace, I dismissed Hayes as childish—and maybe he is—but authority suits him. So well, I wonder why he doesn't do this more often.

"And in the meantime?" Carston, the Phydian Enforcer, challenges. "How do you propose we protect our families if the guards the Barracks assigns aren't effective?"

"Last I checked, you have daughters and sisters," says Hayes. "The Raze has only ever killed men."

"Might I remind you all that we are not here to discuss a woman," the King cuts in. He's scowling, but I get the feeling that his irritation has less to do with the conversation topic and more to do with the fact that Hayes is the one leading the conversation. "We are here to discuss the next Enforcer of Serington."

"Does anyone have any suggestions for the replacement?" Issabex, the witch Enforcer of Ketzal, asks. In a room of mostly fae, she stands out. Bright silver curls, skin darker than my father's, and amber eyes flecked with dark green. She's as beautiful as she is out of place.

Carston glowers at her. "None from you, witch. Serington is a fae sector."

Her eyes darken. "As if I'd wish to subject a witch Enforcer to a fae sector. You speak as if there is not a fae assassin running around murdering you in your own sectors."

"Even with an assassin, fae sectors are safer than witch sectors," says Carston.

"How would you know?" Issabex demands. "When was the last time you entered a witch sector for anything other than a raid?"

"We wouldn't conduct so many raids if you witches did your jobs and confiscated contraband."

Issabex rolls her eyes. "You love to scoff at enchanted objects, but I see none of you take issue with asking witches to rune chaeliss lights for your ballrooms or *keil* beads for your daughters."

"Chaeliss stones and *keil* beads aren't illegal," says Carston.

"Of course not," says Issabex. "You decide what's legal based on what's useful to you."

"Listen here, witch—"

"*Enough!*" The King slams a fist on the table with enough force, the Enforcers immediately duck their heads, chastened.

"Excuse us, Your Majesty," the eight of them murmur at once.

"Do any *fae* have a suggestion for a new Enforcer?" The King's tone remains scolding.

"Might I suggest Rienna Kasselton?" says Anarin.

My brows furrow. *Rienna?*

Xeris sneers. "Didn't she lose the Ranking to an ikatus?"

Hayes glances at me, fitting together the pieces.

Rienna is an odd choice for an Enforcer. She's barely eighteen. Enforcer positions are for life. It seems strange that such an important position would be selected so early. Before she's had a chance to earn it.

"Her training instructor says she's brilliant," says Anarin.

"Doesn't matter," says Xeris. "She lost to a runt."

"I have an alternative," says Carston. "A guard at the Vanihailian Barracks."

"He was given nursemaid's duty after graduation?" says Xeris dismissively. "Absolutely not."

"He never graduated. He was ejected at fourteen but was so talented, they didn't want to waste him. The fact that he was assigned nursemaid's duty is a testament to his aptitude."

My ears perk. I know this story—it's Carrik's.

I'm not sure what face I make, but Hayes looks over at me like he always does and tilts his head in an obvious question: How do I know Carrik?

My eyes drop to the floor before my face can give anything else away. I'm torn.

Do I want Carrik to gain the recognition he deserves? Of course.

Do I want him to spend his days treating humans the way his mother was treated? Sentencing them to death and reveling in it, the way Anarin does? Absolutely not.

I calm myself. Carrik's half-human. Fae *hate* humans. He's safe from this. He has to be.

"I remember hearing about this," says Anarin slowly. "Carrik Solwey. He was expelled when it was revealed his mother was human—"

Sounds of distaste around the table.

"A *human?*" says Xeris. "You want us to turn a human into an Enforcer? Carston, you're usually more sensible than this."

"I think it's a great idea."

All heads whip toward Hayes, jaws unhinged.

"Sir?" Xeris looks horrified. "Did you hear—he's human."

"Only half. And he was the best in his year. Don't you think we should determine qualifications based on ability?"

"Son." The King glowers at him. "He's human."

"*Half.* If he was fully human, he wouldn't have an affinity. The way I see it, we have two options: the one who ranked second behind an ikatus or the one who ranked first of them all. It's an easy choice. Do we not want the best leading our sectors?"

Silence. The contemplative kind.

My tongue plays with my *keil* bead, but I keep my face still.

"Why don't we vote?" Hayes stands. "Option A—the best—or Option B—second. Behind an ikatus."

One by one, Enforcers cast their votes. Of eight Enforcers, seven vote in favor of Carrik.

"Any objections, Your Majesty?" asks Anarin.

The King is silent.

Hope rises in my chest. The King hates humans more than anything. Surely—

The King smiles cruelly. "I have no objection."

My heart sinks.

"So long as my son takes responsibility for putting a human over a sector," the King continues. "When this ends poorly—and it will—the brunt of the blame falls solely on my son's shoulders. Are we in agreement?"

Hayes's gaze flickers to me once more before he nods. "Agreed."

"Then I have no objection."

"Excellent." Anarin nods. "We'll start preparations to groom Carrik Solwey to be the next Enforcer of Serington."

Hayes tries to catch my eye for the rest of the meeting, but I pick a spot on the wall and stare at it.

I try to trail behind him as he leaves, hinting I'm in no mood for his games, but he slows to walk beside me. He's done it more times than I care to count, but now, it sends my blood boiling.

"Saoirse?" he prods. "Is something wrong?"

"No." I'm still not looking at him.

He frowns. "I can plainly see that's not true."

I keep walking, not speaking.

"Whoa." He steps in front of me, hands on my shoulders, holding me in place.

I glare at his arms until he has the sense to release me. "Zen." He speaks to Zensen who stands, stoic as ever, behind me. "Can we have a moment?"

I don't want a moment with Hayes. I don't want to think about how mad I am. At myself for betraying him, at Hayes for the sentencing, and at *everything* for the fact that Carrik will step into the role of the monster who slaughtered a human onstage for entertainment.

Zensen disappears to wait around the corner.

"You didn't have to do that," I say.

"Talk to me. Have I done something? It looked like you know Carrik. I thought—"

It's too much. "Is that why you vouched for him? Because you wanted my approval? Because you wanted me to be *grateful*?"

"No! I vouched for him because we should have the best. Regardless of species." He smiles gently, trying to gauge my reaction. "And it wouldn't be a downside if you approved."

I don't return his smile. I keep picturing Anarin on that stage, slicing a blade across the human's throat—except her face is replaced with Carrik's. Doling out death sentences like the one his mother received. The image sends a shudder down my spine.

"Do you even know what Enforcers do?"

"I—" He frowns. "They enforce laws. Regulate their sectors."

Which is exactly what I would have said yesterday. But it doesn't make us the same; it *can't*. He's the Crown Prince. He should know better. "Have you seen a sentencing?"

"I have no idea what that is."

I almost laugh, but there's nothing funny about this. "I'm not surprised, Your Highness," I snap, unable to contain my fury. "Because you have no idea what the hell is going on in your own sodding kingdom."

And I'm not any better.

It's as horrifying as it is sobering.

I take a heavy breath. "I'm sorry, Your Highness. That was uncalled for."

"You don't need to apologize; just tell me what's wrong."

"Is that an order, sir?"

He tastes warm—hot. Cinnamon and peppercorn. He's frustrated. "Of course not."

"Then, nothing, sir. Nothing's wrong."

CHAPTER THIRTY
The Silver Puppeteer

It's the morning before the run-through for Hayes's party, and there's yet another silver envelope on my bed. Beside it, a burlap sack.

I groan as I rip open the letter.

Thank you for your cooperation at the sentencing. As a token of my appreciation, I've returned something of yours. For your next task, find what you can about Szeiryna in the Palace library.

My hand crumples the note and I open the bag.

My stomach drops.

It's a bag of ranis. The same ten thousand ranis I delivered to the Kivren Waterfront weeks ago.

I feel sick. Like I'm going to throw up.

Having the money back should make me happy. It's one less thing for my family to worry about. But this isn't a benign show of gratitude—it's a payoff.

I betrayed Hayes and set a maniacal group after the Royal family. My blackmailer is rewarding me for it.

I've never felt more powerless. I'm a clueless puppet on a string, dancing at the whim of two faceless puppeteers: the Resistance and the Raze. Two powerful groups, both using me from behind the screen of a title.

And now, thanks to me, both puppeteers have the same goal: kill the Royals. Kill *Hayes*.

A few weeks ago, I would've gladly stepped aside and allowed it to happen.

King Larster treats humans as lesser than fae. He slaughtered the sirens. Killed countless others. Queen Ikenna stood idly at his side, saying nothing. But Hayes . . . how much blame does he have in this?

The sentencing is fresh in my mind, and Hayes's ignorance burns me from the inside out. But I can't put him in the same group as his parents.

A knock at my door tugs me from my thoughts.

Shoving the note and bag under my mattress, I open the door.

Jeune grins. "I know we're not supposed to leave the Palace, but how would you feel about heading to the training room and sparring?"

Someone is blackmailing me about my sister. I suspect that person works for the Resistance. I suspect that person is Jeune.

Yet, here she stands, smiling. As if there isn't an ever-growing tower of silver envelopes buried beneath my mattress.

I fold my arms. "I spar alone."

"Oh." My tongue flashes with rancid disappointment. "We could just practice together, then?"

I should say yes. Try and glean information from her. But I'm still angry from yesterday's sentencing, reeling from this newest note, and Hayes is circling my mind.

"Sorry," I say instead. "Not today."

I close the door before she can say anything else.

Two of the King's guards join us for our morning briefing the next day. As we take our usual seats in the Prince's war room, they stand behind us, breathing down our necks.

Hayes unfurls a map of the ship. The diagram is sketched in dark ink over grid lines of measurement with a map scale hand drawn in the margins.

"The *Sea Queen*." Jeune reads the words across the top.

"It's the name of the ship," says Hayes proudly. "She was built for this party, so I got to name her."

The Royal guards, Rikkard and Brannon, walk us through the plan for Hayes's party. Hayes will board the ship with Zensen and Erasmus. They'll wait belowdecks in his office for the rest of the guests and guards to board. Each person boarding, guards included, will be searched for weapons, both for the rehearsal tomorrow and the actual party next week. The purpose of hosting a Royal function on a ship is to control what goes in and out. As such, all weapons are barred.

As Rikkard drones on, I study the numbers on the map. Each square on the grid indicates a measurement in cubits. In addition to the grid, the dimensions of the ship are handwritten alongside the diagram.

The problem: the dimensions of the ship according to the grid lines differ from the handwritten dimensions.

"These measurements are off," I say.

Rikkard rolls his eyes, dismissing me, but Hayes gives me his undivided attention. "What's wrong?"

"If you find the dimensions using the grid lines, they're different from the number recorded."

Hayes assesses. "Keen eye. But I wouldn't worry about it. We hired a different shipbuilder than who we normally use—he's less competent."

Rikkard looks at me in clear distaste. "You're the ikatus?"

"Yes."

"I assume you're on beach patrol tomorrow?"

I hate his tone. It's derisive and patronizing and were I not surrounded by witnesses, I'd be tempted to sing him a lullaby.

I swallow my irritation. "Yes."

"Good. I trust the witch will be there as well?"

Laa'el opens her mouth to give an assuredly scathing response, but Hayes cuts her off. "She'll be on the ship with everyone else. Jeune is our other guard on patrol duty."

Rikkard's eyes slide to Jeune. "You're putting a water fae on patrol duty? Wouldn't she be better served on the ship?"

"Are you questioning me?" Hayes asks, voice deadly low.

Rikkard stiffens.

"I know my father takes pleasure in using that tone with me, but you are *not* my father. I demand respect. Is that clear?"

Rikkard hangs his head and nods.

"I said—*is that clear?*"

"Yes, sir."

"Excellent." Hayes sounds colder than I've ever heard him. "If that's all, you're dismissed."

Hayes's spine straightens with his anger, and Rikkard's boldness wilts in response. "Of course, Your Highness." He manages a quick bow before hurrying from the room.

"Saoirse." Hayes calls my name before I can slip out. "A moment, please."

I pause, holding in a grimace as the others spill out of the room around me, all looking at me with varied levels of confusion. Jeune tastes of confused concern, Erasmus of confused anger, and Devlyn of confused suspicion.

Hayes rests his hands on the war room table. "I'm sorry to ask you this. But my party. I know you said the water makes you sick, but is there any way you could be on the ship? I'd feel safer with you there."

I can't. A ship surrounded by water and full of people? I know how this story ends: me luring everyone on board into the water, never to resurface. "Is this an order?" I say carefully.

"I don't know why you always ask me that."

I take a breath. "I have to decline."

Rancid disappointment. "Is this because of the other day?"

"No, sir. This has nothing to do with the Enforcer position. I told you. Water makes me sick."

"I've never heard of an ikatus who gets sick around water."

My eyes narrow. "And now you have. Am I dismissed?"

He hesitates. My tongue detects a flavor that's sweet like sugar and cold like frost. Wistfulness. Regret. "Can we talk?" His voice is soft and his eyes hold mine, ensnaring me in his gentle gaze.

I can't drown, but I imagine this is what it feels like. Tight chest, fluttering heart, constricting sense of panic combined with the increased yearning for some kind of unattainable release.

I take a breath—in through my nose, out through my teeth. "About what, sir?"

His back sags at the stiffness of my tone. "You're still mad at me."

"I'm not."

It's not fully a lie, nor is it the full truth.

I'm not as mad at him as I should be. I hate how little he knows about Keirdre. I hate that he spoke up for Carrik and now my best friend is going to be pulled into a life he'll hate.

But I'm not as angry at Hayes as I am at myself.

For agreeing to work for the Raze in the first place. For betraying Hayes's trust and giving the Resistance every reason to want him dead. For not knowing what Enforcers do until I saw Aris Milner's blood splash across the stage at Haraya Hall.

Hayes is clueless, yes, but I'm not any better. I *want* to be mad at him. It would make it easier to hate him like I'm supposed to, but how can I when I see those same traits reflected in myself?

"Saoirse . . ." Hayes steps closer, invading my thoughts and my space. "I don't want it to be like this between us. Please. Tell me how to fix it." Hesitantly, he reaches for my arm.

I flinch back. "Don't."

"Sorry." His hand drops to his side.

My heart clenches. I hate when he apologizes.

"You don't need to apologize to me," I say stiffly. "If there's nothing else, I'll take my leave, Your Highness."

I turn to walk out.

"I'm sorry," he blurts. "If I disappointed you."

Leave. I urge my feet to move forward. *Leave and don't engage.*

"You didn't," I say instead. "You couldn't, sir. I have no expectations of you."

CHAPTER THIRTY-ONE

Sweet Wine

The Palace library is empty this time of night, and I welcome the silent solitude.

I sit in an armchair big enough for three, legs tucked beneath me, books sprawled around me. So far, they've been useless, but I flip through book number thirty-eight as if I expect it to be different. All I want is *one* mention of Szeiryna, *one* sentence on dryads or ogres—any proof that the creatures in the portrait room were once flesh and blood in the Kingdom of Keirdre, and not always paint and canvas.

"Tell me, Saoirse, do you prefer reading to sleep?"

I snap the book shut and spin around.

Hayes stands leaned up against a bookshelf, eyes fixed on me. His lips curl in surprised amusement. "Did I scare you? I didn't think you were capable of being scared."

I tuck the book beneath the seat cushion, out of his line of sight. "I assumed I was alone. It's late." I avoid meeting his eyes. The sight of him still aggravates me.

"I noticed."

My eyes drift over his shoulders. "Where are your guards?"

"Waiting outside." He circles the chair to stand in front of me.

I shift my thigh so it rests over the bump in the cushion concealing the book. "You followed me. Again."

"I didn't. I checked the training room first. Then I figured you had to be here if you were still in the Palace."

"What made you think I was in the Palace?"

"I guessed. Hoped."

Something in the way he says "hoped" has me resisting a new and urgent need to swallow. "Did you want something, sir?"

His head drops to one side. "We're back to 'sir.' You weren't using it when I first walked in."

I hadn't expected him. When I'm prepared, I can handle Hayes. I can handle the smile and the voice and the laugh and the eyes, but when he surprises me—sneaks up like a night hawk stalking its prey—I forget to distance myself.

I don't tell him this. I don't tell him anything.

Realizing I have no reply, he takes a breath. "I want to talk to you. About the other day."

"I shouldn't have snapped." I sound hollow, even to myself. "I apologize if I spoke out of turn, Your Highness."

"You don't have to talk to me like that."

"Like what, sir?"

"Like I'm your superior."

I almost laugh. "You *are* my superior. Sir."

The taste of Hayes's disappointment—overripe and pungent like rotten fruit—is familiar to me. He drops to sit, not in a chair but on the low table in front of me. He's too big for it, so his knees are bunched up. "You're still angry with me."

"It shouldn't matter if I'm angry with you, sir."

"Well, it does." He rests his forearms on his thighs, leaning toward me. "Your opinion matters."

"Why?"

He studies the patterns in the library carpet. "Tell me the name of that book you hid when you saw me and I'll tell you."

When I don't reply, he quirks an amused eyebrow. "Don't tell me—it's the next in a long list of things I'll never know about the mystery that is Saoirse Sorkova?"

I purse my lips.

The scoff elevates to a chuckle. "You really don't give anything, do you?"

Keeping secrets feels natural, a dance I've known my whole life. But Hayes is the one who told me about Szeiryna. As far as he knows, he's the source of my curiosity.

Maybe it's a risk, but I pull the book from beneath the cushion and pass it to him. The movement forces me to rest my feet on the floor. Our knees are just barely brushing against each other, and I'm acutely aware of that small contact.

He holds my eyes as he takes the book. "What's the big secret about a history book?" He turns it over as if the answers are written on the back.

The scrunch of his brow is endearing in a way I didn't know brows could be. I almost smile. But then I remember he's dangerous for more reasons than I can count. I draw back. It puts a breath of space between our knees. Not much, but it makes my mind less hazy. "I'm looking for any mention of Szeiryna."

He nearly drops the book. "I thought my father burned them all."

"I figure he must've missed something."

"I thought I told you to drop this."

I go rigid. "I didn't realize that was an order."

"It wasn't. I just—" He runs a hand down his face, looking uncharacteristically exhausted. "Why are you so interested in this?"

As if I need an explanation for looking into the extinction of an entire species. Even if I wasn't being forced to search for more answers, I'd be curious. The history of Szeiryna—of sirens, of *me*—intrigues me as much as it scares me.

I fold my arms. "Why aren't you *more* interested? Your father destroyed an entire sector. Doesn't that bother you?"

"Bother me?" Hayes's eyes darken, and the sudden influx of pepper and vinegar on my tongue hints at his anger. "No, Saoirse, it doesn't 'bother' me—it *terrifies* me." He thrusts the book back to me. "My father won't like you asking questions."

"Why are you protecting him?"

He makes a noise of disbelief. "I'm protecting *you*."

My anger makes me sit up, bringing our chests closer. "I can take care of myself."

"Not against the King."

My eyes are so narrowed, I can hardly see him, but I'm so angry, I don't think I want to. "You should be careful, Your Highness—you sound just like him."

Hayes jerks with my words. "I'm *nothing* like him."

"And yet you condone his actions."

The cold, metallic sting of his hurt blends into the tang of his anger. "I don't condone anything!"

"Complacency and condoning are the same. I understand why you're trying to protect me now." My words drip acid. "You expect me to run scared because that's what *you* do. I'm not you, *sir*."

We're chest to chest, my knees trapped between his. Our breaths, heavy from our spat, mingle in the small space between us.

"I despise my father," says Hayes darkly. "I went to a sentencing today. You're right. It's horrible."

"Would you like a prize, Your Highness?"

He scoots closer. Our faces are so close, I feel each exhalation against my skin. Hear his heartbeat thundering away. "You're not listening. Yes, the sentencing was awful, but there's nothing I can do about that. My father hates me. If he has his way—and he will; he always does—I'll never ascend to the throne. What I think about the way he rules doesn't matter. I don't have the power to change a damned thing."

The audacity of him, claiming he has no power, infuriates me.

When Hayes walks into a room, he commands respect. He has to *ask* people not to bow to him. No one bows to me. If I look like a siren, they try to bed me. If I look like an ikatus, they despise me. "You have power, Your Highness. And sometimes, you choose to use it. When you demanded your father let you lead Felix's investigation. When you convinced the most powerful people in Keirdre that a half human can be an Enforcer. When you put your father's guard in his place. Just because you shun your authority doesn't mean it isn't given to you. Answer me this: Do you truly want to waste the rest of your absurdly long life throwing parties in your bedroom and drinking too-sweet wine? I hate bullies, Your Highness. Your father's a bully, and unless you do something, you're no better."

"No better?" Hayes repeats. "I *hate* him."

"Do you hate him because of his disdain for you or the people he's murdered?"

At that, he sits back. The taste of his anger recedes, replaced with the sharp sting of something sadder. Like watered-down tea gone cold. "That's what you think?" He speaks hollowly. "That I'm more upset I have a father who hates me than a father who slaughters? I'm not. Of *course* I hate him for what he's done.

But hatred isn't enough. I'm his son, and I still fear that stepping out of line will cost me my life. What's my life to him? He has eternity to sire another heir."

He drops his head into his hands, breathing deeply for several moments. When he looks up, the fight has drained. "Maybe I'm a coward," he says softly. "But I wish you weren't so brave. It's going to get you killed. The last person who went poking around Szeiryna ended up dead."

"What are you talking about?"

"You ever heard of Reyshka Harker?"

His tone is serious, but I can't help a disbelieving frown. Reyshka Harker is a story adults tell children to keep them away from the barrier. Legend has it, she kept trying to get to the other side, no matter how many times she was told she couldn't.

According to the story, the barrier consumed her.

They always use that word. "Consume." Like the barrier was a ravenous monster and she was smoked salt pork.

"It's not just a story," says Hayes. "She was real. But it didn't happen like the legend says. She found out about Szeiryna and tried to get out of the barrier to find it. In retaliation, my father had her bound, just inside the barrier, and moved it—only slightly—enough so it went *through* her. It killed her."

I feel sick. "You're making that up."

"I'm deadly serious. And I'm worried about you. If my father finds out you're asking about Szeiryna, he'll kill you. I—" His voice cracks. His hand reaches for me, and I think he's going to touch my cheek, but he drops it with a sigh. "I'm not a bad person. But sometimes, I think I care about you more than you do.

"This probably isn't enough, but I raised the price of flour. And wheat. And a few other crops that were absurdly low."

He's surprised me again. "Because I asked you to?"

Hayes rolls his eyes. "You didn't ask. You brought it to my attention. And it had nothing to do with you."

"Then why do it?"

"Because I should've done it years ago. It's one of the few things I can change that my father won't notice. But I didn't, because I didn't know about it. I'm sorry about that. I'm sorry about a lot of things. I'm sorry that I didn't know about sentencings. I'm sorry that I can't take them away—my father would notice. I'm sorry that the best I can do is tell you I'm learning. I'm paying attention now. And I'm sorry if that isn't enough for you."

There he goes again. Apologizing to me even though he owes me nothing. Being honest with me even though I give him nothing.

He presented his father's disdain as a burden, but I disagree. Growing up free of his father's influence made him who he is—*good*.

"What would you do differently if you were King?" I ask.

He looks surprised by the question. "It doesn't matter. My father will never—"

"This isn't about your father. It's about you. You say you don't have the power to change anything. Fine. But what if you did? What would you change?"

He doesn't hesitate. "Everything."

I wish he was lying. I wish I tasted something woodsy like deceit or sour like guilt. Some indication that the sincerity soaking his words is fake. Some reason to despise him the way I need to. But there's nothing.

Dammit.

"Why do you do that?" I mutter. It's meant for me, but of course he hears it anyway.

"Do what?"

I should purse my lips and refuse to answer, but I make the mistake of being honest. "Make it impossible to hate you."

A corner of his mouth lifts. "You don't have to try so hard."

Yes, I do.

I slide back in the armchair and tuck my legs under me again, fleeing his closeness. Maybe it makes me a coward, but it also makes it easier to think. To *breathe.*

My anger isn't gone, but it's no longer directed at him. "Carrik is a friend," I finally explain. "And I don't want him spending his life as an Enforcer now that I've seen what they do."

"I'm sorry. I understand that you're frustrated and maybe you resent me. But, Saoirse?" He reaches and, when I don't move away, places his hand on my knee. "*Please* don't use your frustration with me as a reason to be reckless. Looking into Szeiryna is dangerous. You're not going to find anything here. The only thing you'll do is give my father an excuse to hurt you."

My ears perk at a hidden meaning he didn't intend. He's right. Looking here is pointless. The King won't have left any mention of Szeiryna in the library where anyone could find it. But if the portrait room is any indication, he likes to keep records of his conquests. If not here, then maybe . . .

"I'll stop looking," I agree slowly.

Hayes breathes a sigh of relief.

"*But—*"

The sigh flows into a groan.

"I need your help."

He shoots me a warning look, sharp as a knife. "Saoirse—"

"I'll drop it. I promise. But first, can you get me into your father's office?"

He recoils. "What?"

"I want to know what he's capable of. To do that, I need answers. You said you've been to his office—when you and Felix found your coins. Can you get me in?"

"That's a dangerous request."

"I trust you."

And lune above, I mean it.

He wavers.

I know exactly what it'll take to tip him over the edge. Push him to agree. "Please," I say gently, *"Hayes."* It's the simplest manipulation, and I hate myself for it. But there's a letter in my room that makes it a necessity.

His eyes read mine like a book written in a language he'll never understand, and I find it impossible to look away. His emotions are written across his face in a large, easy-to-read font. He's concerned for me—scratch that, "concern" is too mild. He's *petrified.*

He passes a hand over his face. "Fine. But only after we find the mystery woman. After my party."

I'm fighting a rising tide of guilt. Guilt at my insurmountable lies when he so selflessly wants to help me. Guilt that he'll never find his lady assassin—me. And guilt that I can no longer deny that the heat in his eyes when he looks at me is more than benign curiosity.

Still, all I do is nod and say, "Deal."

CHAPTER THIRTY-TWO

Siren Song

I love the feeling of sand between my toes.

Any other day, I'd take the time to enjoy it. I'd allow myself a tick's indulgence to tip my head back, sprawl out in the warm sand, and bask in the sunlight.

Instead, I clutch my knees to my chest as I stare at the *Sea Queen* where it rocks in the waves.

I try to focus on the name of the ship etched in gold cursive into the navy-painted exterior, but it's a poor distraction. My eyes are still drawn to the water where it laps against the shore, only a dozen tantalizing paces away.

For a few breaths, I fantasize about jumping in, consequences be damned. In my mind, the water is cool and refreshing. The salt sticks to my skin and seeps through my pores. The ocean sluices over me and, for a moment, I imagine what it would be like to not be a monster.

While my mind dives below the depths, my body remains seated in the sand, dry. It's an absurd fantasy because if I were in the water—submerged with a ship of men so close by—it wouldn't end with me swimming peacefully in the blue sea. It would end with red-tinted waves and a sunken ship.

I keep watching the soothing rhythm of the water. There's a call hidden in its tranquility: *sing, lure, kill*.

Tempting . . .

Control. Get yourself under control.

I tear my eyes away.

On the ship, I can only make out shadowy figures moving on deck. None of them is Hayes.

The waves speed up, crashing against the ship more forcefully.

Sing, lure, kill.

I drag my fingers through the sand and lift them, enjoying the feeling of the fine crystals falling through my fingers as I attempt to distract myself from the ocean.

Sing, lure, kill.

My eyes slip closed, and I breathe in through my nose. Inhaling the salty air, exhaling the urge to dive into the water. Inhaling the heavy scent of seaweed washed up onshore, exhaling the urge to drag someone with me.

A shriek from the ship sends my eyes flying open.

The waves have progressed from angry to furious. They attack the ship, sending it lurching.

A silhouette steps onto the deck. I recognize his shape.

I don't know when I became so aware of him. Sometime from meeting him three weeks ago to now, I've familiarized myself with the shape of Hayes. The broadness of his shoulders, the set of his head, and the assuredness of his stance.

The water slams harder. The ship jolts to the side, eliciting another shriek from on board.

Hayes teeters from the force of the roiling sea. As he's off-balance, a wave *surges* from the depths and *grabs* him.

There's no other way to describe it.

The ocean reaches up, wraps its watery fist around the Crown Prince of Keirdre, and snatches him from the deck.

It yanks him under the surface, pulling, pulling, pulling, until his head is submerged. It happens in the blink of an eye—he doesn't even have time to call out.

I *try* not to panic. He's a water fae. He makes water bend to his will. This shouldn't be an issue.

Five ticks pass, and he doesn't resurface.

My fingers burrow deeper into the sand.

Another five ticks. He's still under.

My first instinct: save him.

Second instinct: think about possible witnesses. Think about the dangers of the water's call. Stay put and let someone else rescue him.

Another tick passes, and all I can think: but it's *Hayes*.

I set my second instinct alight.

Ripping my hands from the sand, I charge into the shallows before I can remind myself what happens when I give in to my instincts.

Knee-deep in the water, I raise my arms and dive.

Bliss. The water is cold, yes, but in a way that tingles against my arms, my legs, my *face*.

That initial moment feels like an eternity, but when the water settles, the weight of my mistake presses around me.

Sing, lure, kill.

It's the water's mantra, and it refuses to let me forget. My every sense is wrapped in a need to kill.

The ocean is worse than a lake, worse than a river. The ocean is limitless—when I'm in the sea, all the water in that vastness calls to me at once.

Like now: I *feel* life in the distance and I know it's Hayes and

I know I shouldn't, but every part of me wants to find him and drag him under.

Sing, lure, kill.

My legs slice the water as I swim to him.

He's already deeper than he should be. Whatever force dragged him under is stronger than I thought.

Hayes's ocean eyes are closed, and his body is still as it sinks through the murky water.

I swim closer.

Kill.

He would be my easiest mark. I don't have to sing; I don't have to seduce—not so much as a sodding fake smile. It would be easy, *so easy*, to wrap my arms around him and simply hold on. Pull him deeper under. Make him sink faster.

Kill.

Something in the water beneath us catches my eye. A coin, dark as night, on a necklace. Hayes's. Felix's.

The salty seawater is replaced with the memory of the taste of Hayes's grief the night he learned of Felix's death. I no longer see red—I see blue. The ocean blue of Hayes's eyes. That knee-weakening grin of his I hate because it makes me forget how to breathe.

Control.

The glow fades from my eyes, and I rub my hands over my face.

Like the wheel of a mill, my brain starts to churn. Hayes didn't fall; he was pulled by the water itself. And now he can't fight himself out. Which means a water fae pulled him under.

My hands shake against the compulsion of my instincts as I reach toward him. I know better than to touch him in my current state, so I *force* the water surrounding him to move, propelling him up. I snag the black coin as it slips through the water.

My gut tugs as I push. Whoever yanked him under is fighting like hell to keep him down. But I'm stronger.

I exhale when I feel his head break the surface of the water. *Kill.*

With a grunt, I shove aside the persistent call like an unwelcome hand on my ass and kick to the surface.

Hayes bobs in the rocking waves, head lolling, chin against his chest. His eyes remain closed and his chest is still.

"Hayes!" A voice calls his name from the ship above us. It's drifted ahead so we're out of sight, but there's no way to get Hayes back on deck without anyone seeing.

"Your Highness!" calls another voice.

"Hayes," I whisper into his ear, "if you can hear me, stay alive." *Kill. Kill. Kill.*

My eyes are glowing again. His close proximity and the water on my skin are toxic.

I shove the coin into his pocket, close my eyes, and *push*— the water and Hayes—away from me. The water curves into gentle waves, nudging Hayes along until his body washes up on the shore of the beach, a few paces from where I sat before, digging into the sand.

I sink beneath the surface and swim.

I'm dizzy from resisting the water's Siren Song as I emerge onto the beach. I press my hand to my forehead as I stumble the short distance from the water to Hayes. My head hurts. *Everything* hurts, but I don't have time for pain.

I hear approaching voices.

My eyes squeeze shut, and I *shove* the water off me.

When I open my eyes, I'm dry, and my dizziness lessens.

I crouch over Hayes. He's on his back, chest immobile. I *feel* the water flooding his lungs, same as I feel the crashing waves behind me.

The footsteps are getting louder—closer.

I collapse to my knees and rip open his shirt. I slam my hands on his chest, urging him to breathe.

The footsteps stop. "Lune above . . ." It's Jeune.

"What's happening?" This voice is female and unfamiliar. A woman with pale brown skin and brilliant green eyes stands at the edge of my periphery.

"It's Hayes," Jeune says back. "He's—"

I block everything out. The call of the sea, the squawk of the gulls, and the acid rising in my throat at the thought of Hayes not breathing again.

I pound his chest harder.

The footsteps start back up again, softer this time.

My compressions stop. I take a breath before pressing my mouth against Hayes's and breathing out, forcing air out of my lungs and into his. I breathe into his mouth once, twice, three times before I begin beating his chest again.

With my hands on his body, I *feel* once again for the seawater in his lungs and *yank* it, hard as I can, to expel it from his body.

I don't expect it to work, but two shuddering heartbeats later, he starts to cough.

Hayes sits up, leans over, and the water I pulled from his lungs spills onto the beach next to him.

My arms are around him before his eyes are fully opened.

I'm surprised—stunned, really—at how relieved I am he's alive.

He's still weak, so he falls onto his back, me on top of him.

Realizing the position we're in, I try to scramble away, but his arms hold me in place. His ocean eyes meet mine, half-lidded. "Saoirse," he slurs brazenly, "I was drowning."

"Shh—"

"I was drowning and I saw you."

I still. He doesn't—he *can't* mean—that he saw me underwater. His eyes were closed the entire time. At least, I thought they were.

Then, without another word, his eyes flutter shut and he passes out on the warm beach, stone-cold.

CHAPTER THIRTY-THREE

Temptress

It's the middle of the afternoon, the training room is empty, and I can't focus.

Fog swirls where my thoughts should be, leaving me incapable of anything other than sitting in the middle of an empty sparring ring, thinking and avoiding and loathing.

Thinking: a water fae tried to kill Hayes. Someone close enough to him to be on the ship. Someone responsible for his safety at the party, just a week away.

Avoiding: if I hadn't been there, he would've died.

I try to purge myself of this thought, but it keeps coming back, over and over.

Which cues the loathing: the thought of Hayes dying terrifies me. More than it should.

It's the job, I tell myself. *Protecting Hayes is part of the job.*

My self-loathing doubles because I'm lying. Hayes dying would terrify me with or without this job. I think I know why—but I'm avoiding that truth too.

"He's asking for you." Jeune stands in front of me, rocking on her heels. I didn't hear her enter, which brings on yet another tidal wave of self-loathing. "Saoirse," she says when I don't respond, "I said he's—"

"I heard." I hop out of the sparring ring.

Jeune and I walk side by side to Hayes's room. I'm lucid enough to be wary of her presence. Given her lack of regard for privacy, I expected to hate her. But she doesn't care that I'm an ikatus. She doesn't resent me for being faster than her. And she makes me laugh.

Had we been in the same year at the Barracks, I think we might've been friends—that's not a word I use lightly.

But she was on the beach when Hayes was dragged under, and she's a water fae. And she did *nothing* to save him.

Which means she either pulled him under or she wants him dead.

Is she responsible for the blackmail notes? Does she work for the Resistance?

I can't be sure of any of it. Which means it doesn't matter that she's one of the few people I actually enjoy spending time with. I can't trust her any more than I can trust myself.

We don't speak, but she keeps shooting me expectant looks. Waiting for me to do something.

Finally, "Don't you want to know how he is?"

Yes.

I shrug. "If he's asking for me, he's alive."

"Right, but . . ." She stops. Considers her next words. "I don't understand you."

I'm not sure how to respond, so I don't.

She keeps going. "He's completely enamored with you. You know that, right? You must know that."

My tongue toys with my *keil* bead. What the Prince may or may not feel for me is one of the many things I'm avoiding thinking about.

Trying to avoid thinking about.

Jeune appears to be having a conversation with herself, because she continues. "I know you care about him. You threw yourself at him when he woke up—"

"No, I didn't." I bite my tongue, too late.

She raises her eyebrows. For a tick, we're both silent.

"I don't understand you," she repeats.

We reach the Prince's hallway, and I'm spared having to respond—or having her look at me askance for *not* responding. Hayes's corridor is swarmed with fae.

I give Jeune a questioning look as we weave through the crowd to Hayes's bedroom door. "All these people live in the Palace?"

"They all live in Vanihail. They want to see if Hayes is all right." There's something accusing in her tone I choose not to unpack.

When we reach Hayes's door, Jeune stops me. "There are *hundreds* of people eager to see him, Saoirse. And he asked for you. Just you."

I purse my lips. "Why are you telling me this?"

She makes a noise I classify as exasperated. "You're frank—and you appear to be indifferent. Normally, I think he finds your frankness amusing, maybe even refreshing, but I think it'll shatter him if you're not careful."

Her hand rests on the erstwyn handle of Hayes's door, awaiting an answer I can't give.

When I say nothing, she sighs. "Are you?"

"Am I frank?" I know that's not what she's asking.

"Indifferent."

No. Yes. Of course not.

Her question calls for a one-word answer. Except Hayes's father killed my species and countless more, I killed his best friend, my wanted poster hangs on every wall in the kingdom,

I've done nothing but lie to him since we met, and when his heart stopped on the beach, so did mine.

I can't fit that into a single-word response and I can't tell Jeune—or Hayes—any of this.

Unwilling and unable to respond, I push past Jeune and tug the handle to the room without knocking.

Hayes lies in bed, buried beneath a mountain of silken sheets and richly embroidered bedcovers. Queen Ikenna stands to his left, facing away from him, whispering orders to a human servant. Standing at the foot of his bed are Zensen and Erasmus. Like his mother, they face away, talking to Devlyn. At the sound of the door closing, the Queen, guards, and humans look to me.

I clear my throat. "Your Highness," I say, "you asked for me?"

"Saoirse?" Hayes grunts and tries to prop himself up.

"Hayes," the Queen murmurs, "perhaps you shouldn't—"

"It's fine." Hayes is breathing heavily from the effort, looking at me without so much as a half glance at his mother. "Saoirse," he says. "You saved me."

I'm flooded with relief as I drink in the sight of him. He's looking better, in the sense that he's breathing, but he's so weak, he can barely move, and he looks exhausted.

The room watches me, waiting for my reaction.

I steel my expression, concealing my relief behind a cool mask of apathy. "The ocean saved you, Your Highness. I merely kept you breathing."

"Which is a function I require for living, if I'm not mistaken."

My eyes trace the patterns in the blue-and-gold rug beneath his bed.

"Can everyone but Saoirse clear the room, please?"

I open my mouth, an objection on my tongue, but the room's occupants rush past me before I can speak.

He's watching me. "You weren't here when I woke up." His tone is casual, but I taste his hurt. Mild but distinct.

"I was in the training room."

Pause. The hurt intensifies, mixing with thick confusion. "You were training?"

"No, just . . . thinking." And avoiding. And loathing.

I think he expects me to say something more, but I'm out of words to give.

He sighs, eyes sad. "You can talk to me. Like . . . *really* talk to me."

"The only thing I want to talk about is what happened to you."

"You saw, didn't you? How I fell?"

"You don't remember?"

He shakes his head. "I don't remember falling off the boat, I just remember struggling underwater, trying to control the waves, but I couldn't. The next thing I remember is waking up here. Except . . ." His expression turns hesitant.

"What?"

"While I was in the water, I had a dream."

His half-delirious words from the beach float back to me. "A dream?" I echo.

"I think it was a dream. It felt so real. It was about you. I was in the water, sinking, and you were swimming toward me. Coming to save me. Which I guess you did."

"I didn't save you," I remind him. "You washed ashore."

"How? I landed in the water near the ship—I shouldn't have been anywhere near the beach."

"I don't know," I say softly. "I guess it was a miracle. Or maybe whoever threw you overboard changed their mind."

"You think a person did this?"

"I saw what happened. You didn't fall—the waves grabbed you."

His brows furrow. "That would have to be a water fae."

"I know."

Hayes massages his temples, eyes closed again. When they open, he nods to the door. "Will you get the rest of my guards?"

"Of course, sir. And your mother?"

He chuckles humorlessly. "I promise you, she isn't still here."

Hayes's guards are clustered just outside his door, the sea of people stretched out behind them. And he's right. Queen Ikenna is nowhere to be seen.

"The Prince is asking for his guards," I tell them.

We form a semicircle around his bed. I stand next to Jeune. She doesn't say anything, but she darts side glances at me intermittently.

Hayes's fingers settle in his lap. "I'm promoting Saoirse from junior to senior guard. Effective immediately. From this point on, she is the only guard allowed to be in my presence alone."

I don't usually allow my face to express emotions, but I lose my jaw to the floor.

Zensen steps forward. "Hayes, I—" He clears his throat and swallows. "Have I done something wrong?"

"No," says Hayes coolly. "But she saved my life, and I trust her."

Zensen steps back, dutiful as ever, but there's heartbreak in his eyes like fractured glass, and it's on my tongue like frozen sawdust.

"She's a child," Erasmus objects. "Children can't be senior guards."

"Sir," I speak up, "I'm not sure a promotion is a good idea. I'm an ikatus. I have no affinity and—"

"And you managed to save my life just fine without one. Everyone else is dismissed."

I'm still as everyone files out.

Jeune taps me on the shoulder as she passes. It takes me until she's gone to realize it's meant to be comforting.

I wait until the door is closed to speak. "This is a mistake."

"You saved me. Call it what you want, but you saved me. I know you didn't attack me, and until I know who did, you're the only one I trust."

Each word is a knife in my throat. "You shouldn't."

"Why not?"

I don't have a good response. Not one I can tell him. "Only a water fae could have attacked you," I say. "And Jeune is the only water fae in your guard. But she was on the beach. It's too far for her affinity."

"I know. Which means the only water fae on deck were my parents' guards, Rikkard and Brannon. It could have been either one, and I can't assume they acted alone."

"You think one of your guards is involved?"

"Yes. I know it was impulsive to promote you, but you saved my life. I'm indebted to you. And I trust you. Unless you can tell me with certainty that you trust the other guards, I want you, and only you, to assist me in figuring out who's behind this."

He's right—misinformed but right. I know I'm not the one who pulled him off the ship and I can't, with that same clarity, rule out the others.

I find myself nodding despite my misgivings. "I accept the position, Your Highness."

"Good." He motions for me to come over to him.

With hesitation, I do, but when he pats a space on the bed beside him for me to sit, my eyes narrow.

Hayes smirks. "I knew you wouldn't, but wishful thinking. Do you think this attempt on my life has something to do with Spektryl?"

"The timing can't be a coincidence, but if the plan was to kill you at the rehearsal for your party, I don't see how the other killings make sense."

He looks confused. "To make it easier to get to me."

I shake my head. "If the plan was to kill you—*just* you—on a ship off the coast of Vanihail, getting rid of two of your parents' guards doesn't make sense. They only need one person to throw you overboard. And killing Felix doesn't make sense either. Killing the son of an Enforcer doesn't make killing you any easier. What happened on the ship right before you went overboard?"

"I was belowdecks, waiting on the stairs with Zen and E."

"And the only people on the ship were you, your guards, and your parents' guards?"

"Yes."

There's something I'm missing. "I don't see how Spektryl's killings made today's attempt on your life any easier. Why would Spektryl target Royal guards if *you* were the only mark? Your parents weren't even on the ship today. They won't be on the ship until—" My words come to a sudden halt as my brain catches up to my words.

Hayes frowns. "What?"

The night before graduation—a lifetime ago—I killed Brogan Nash. "Your Highness, do you enjoy Nash sweets?"

"Of course. Everyone does."

"Were the Nashes supposed to be serving food at your party?"

Understanding dawns on his face. "Yes."

I take a breath, mentally assembling pieces, shuffling and sorting into some semblance of logic. The Nash family business hadn't seemed important when Devlyn mentioned it, but Brogan might be linked to the Prince in a way I hadn't thought to consider. Perhaps they *all* are.

"You mentioned having to hire a new shipbuilder," I say. "Do you remember the name of the former?"

"Er . . . no."

"Do you have that list of all of Spektryl's victims?"

"Top desk drawer."

I dart across the room and find the list in the drawer. The parchment, only a week old, is already worn, and the creases are weak from overuse. I flatten the sheet on the bed so he can read. "Do you recognize a name?"

Hayes takes a moment before he perks. "This one. Hayliss Velkner. He was a shipbuilder in Vanihail."

My second kill.

If I had any doubt before, it blows away. "The Raze is targeting your party. I don't know the details, but they're going to try to kill you and your parents." It makes so much sense, I don't know how I didn't see it sooner. Hayes told me himself that he and his parents are never in the same room together in case something were to happen, to keep the barrier intact. Hayes's party is the only exception.

I frown. There's still a piece out of place. "Although, if the target is your party, it still doesn't explain the attempt on your life today."

"Maybe it does," says Hayes. "Maybe *you* weren't supposed to save me. Maybe someone else was."

I catch his meaning. "And then you would've promoted them."

"And I would have *trusted* them."

Save Hayes's life, get access to Hayes. Which raises the question: Who was supposed to save him?

My first thought is Jeune. She was on the beach, she was *insistent* she remain on patrol when Zensen told me I could stay on the beach as well, and she's the only water fae in Hayes's guard. Normally, I'd assume she was too far away to reach Hayes with her affinity, but by her own admission, she's better than other water fae.

"Your Highness, how long ago did you start planning this party?"

"About six lunes ago."

Exactly when I started working for the Raze.

I pass him the sheet and pen. "Do you think you can point out everyone on this list with a connection to this party?"

"Of course." He grabs the pen. "I'm just as curious as you are to learn about the Temptress's plan."

"Temptress?" I repeat.

"I want to give our mystery woman a name. Temptress seems fitting for someone so lovely and deadly. What do you think?"

There's nothing wrong with the name, but I prefer to discuss the Raze's plan in terms of Spektryl. Talking about the mystery woman—Temptress—makes that growing pit in my stomach swell with guilt.

I nod noncommittally. "I like it."

It doesn't take Hayes long to work through the list. In addition to the shipbuilder (Hayliss Velkner) and baker (Brogan Nash), Spektryl's kills—*my* kills—include someone related to a decorator and a few event planners. All connected to Hayes's party.

There's only one name from the past five lunes unaccounted for: Niklaus Serkis, a fire fae. We pore over every scrap of parchment in Hayes's room pertaining to the party, searching for any mention of the surname Serkis, and come up empty.

I sigh when we finally give up. "Sir, nearly every facet of this party is compromised. You need to cancel."

"No."

I expected him to say this, but it's still aggravating. "Your Highness, this is a matter of your safety."

"Careful, Saoirse, or I might accuse you of caring about me."

My nostrils flare. "It's my job to be concerned for your well-being, sir. Clearly, someone wants you dead. And whatever they're planning, it involves your party."

"I'm not canceling. We cancel, and we have to start this investigation all over again. We can figure this out. We just need to find the Temptress."

"Forget about the Temptress, you're missing the point—we know what the target is. If you have your party as planned, someone *will* attack you. Canceling is a necessity."

"No."

"All right," I say, "then we need to fire everyone you've hired to replace former employees."

"No."

I groan and throw up my hands. "Sir—"

"Saoirse." He cuts me off, mimicking my tone. "This plan has been in progress for lunes. It's elaborate. We cancel, they'll make new plans, only this time, they'll leave a narrower trail—we won't see it coming."

It's a fair point, but I don't care. "Someone tried to kill you today. They'll try it again."

"I have guards."

There's a determined set to his chin that tells me he won't back down.

I expected him to push back, but I didn't expect I'd be unable to change his mind.

My chest tightens with fear. Someone is actively trying to kill him. Today's attack is proof that the threat is someone close to him. And at his actual party, I won't be there to pull him from the water.

"If you won't cancel, you have to avoid everything connected to the Raze," I say. "That means no eating, no drinking, and no touching the decorations."

He gives me a wry look. "I'll try to keep my hands off the ice sculpture."

Somehow, this is still a joke to him.

"I'm serious," I snap. "Promise me you won't touch anything."

He studies the sternness of my expression. "Fine. I promise I won't eat, drink, or touch anything at my party."

I shouldn't be this relieved, but the crushing weight on my chest lightens with his words.

"We'll have to do the same for my parents," he adds.

I raise a skeptical eyebrow. "All due respect, Your Highness, but your parents can rot for all I care."

"I know it's a lot to ask, but if they die, it's easier to tear down the barrier."

I frown. "Is that a bad thing? There's a whole other world over there. Less restriction, creatures I've only read about in storybooks—"

"Exactly why we need to be careful. We don't know if the outside world is dangerous. If they mean us harm. The barrier can't come down until we know what's waiting on the other side.

Besides, do you remember when I told you how the barrier works? All our lives are tied to it. If it's destroyed by force—"

"You die." I finish his sentence.

He nods grimly. The fewer lives connected to the barrier, the weaker it is. Which means the same magic that created it might be able to undo it, killing Hayes in the process.

Great. Keeping Hayes alive means protecting the people I hate most.

Three lives hang in the balance of this party. And as much as I hate the idea of attending, there's no way to play nursemaid to all the Royals from the beach.

"I've changed my mind. I'll be there. On the ship."

Hayes's head falls to one side, confusion creasing his brow. "But water makes you sick."

"I'll be fine." After years of battling my instincts and losing, today, I fought and *won*. I was submerged in the ocean, Hayes was temptingly close, the water was screaming at me to kill . . .

And I resisted. For Hayes, I resisted.

He's still frowning. "Are you sure? Maybe you should—"

"If I said I can handle it, I can handle it."

The truth: I have no idea if I'll be able to keep my instincts at bay. No idea if my restraint from today is something I can replicate.

But the other truth—the one I can no longer avoid: Hayes Finnean Vanihail has wormed his way under my skin. And from there, he burrowed into my heart, so deep that I can't shake him.

Maybe agreeing to be on a ship full of potential marks and surrounded by water is a bad idea. But sometime from accepting this job to now, I've decided Hayes is worth the risk.

Hayes doesn't say anything, but I taste his emotions, sweet like chocolate and bright like an orange. Without warning, his hand snags mine. He gives it a quick squeeze. "Thank you." He lets it fall. "You have no idea how much this means to me."

I can't focus when he looks at me like that, so I pick a space on the wall behind him and stare at it. "Just doing my job."

Distance.

I start the mental chant. If I'm going to keep him alive, I need distance, so I take a breath, meet his eyes, and add, "Sir."

CHAPTER THIRTY-FOUR

Forfeit

Jeune opens her door when I knock. "Sorkova?" She looks surprised.

"Would you like to spar with me?" I ask.

She folds her arms. "I thought you sparred alone?"

I quirk an eyebrow, hoping it masks my true motive. "Is that a no?"

A slow grin slinks across her face. "Let me get dressed."

She's pleased the whole way to the training room. She doesn't even try to bombard me with conversation.

The training room is empty as Jeune and I climb into opposite sides of a sparring ring. She smirks. "You ready?"

I trace my tongue around my mouth, trying to *feel* her guilt. Any explanation as to why she left Hayes to die. Or—worse—why she dragged him below in the first place.

I taste nothing.

Aside from Carrik, I've never had friends. Until I met Jeune, I didn't think I wanted any.

For a moment, I think about not going through with this. Having a normal sparring match and embracing something real. *Fun.*

But then I see Rain after graduation, holding that first silver envelope. Hayes in the water.

If Jeune's behind either of them—or both—I need to know.

I fake a teasing grin. "Soon as you stop talking."

She laughs.

We don't count. One tick, we're at opposite sides of the ring. The next, we attack.

I land the first hit. My right fist strikes Jeune in the side. I don't wait for her to recover before hitting her other side.

I rear back my fist for a third strike. Jeune snatches my wrist and tugs me forward, twisting my body around.

For a breath, I'm restrained against her.

I kick back, catching her across the knee.

I use her brief distraction to pull away. Spinning around, I kick, and my foot slams into Jeune's shoulder with enough force to send her crashing to the mat.

I'm on top of her, knees on either side of her torso, hands gripping her wrists, pinning them to the mat beneath her.

Our eyes meet.

Hers still have that teasing light. For her, this is fun.

I sense the exact moment she realizes my eyes are devoid of humor. Her lips tug into a frown, and my mouth clouds with her confusion, like a too-salty stew. "Are you all right?"

What I'm thinking: *Are you the one blackmailing me?*

Did you try and kill Hayes?

What I say: "Why didn't you save Hayes?"

She tilts her head, studying me. "What are you talking about?" She tries to get up, but I keep her down.

Her frown deepens.

"I'm talking about yesterday," I say. "During the rehearsal.

You were on the beach. You had a clear view of the ship, you saw him fall overboard, but you didn't jump into the water to save him. You left him to drown."

The taste of Jeune's confusion is replaced with stale guilt, but her eyes flash with anger.

With a grunt, she brings her head up, slamming it into my nose. I jerk back and she frees herself, glaring at me. "I didn't see him fall."

Her fury is convincing, but the taste of her guilt speaks louder than words.

I jab at her again. "How could you not?"

Jeune flicks my attack away. "I got distracted—" Pause as she squats, swinging out a leg, trying to swipe mine from under me.

I jump over her leg and dive to the side.

"Just for a moment." Jeune's back on her feet, coming toward me. "Hayes was underwater until he washed up on the beach. I didn't know what was happening. I just saw people on deck panicking."

I want to trust her. We're both women used to being overlooked. We work harder than anyone else. We're competitive, maybe to a fault. And I *like* her.

At the Barracks, the other Deltas hated me for being an ikatus and showing them up. I swallowed their resentment and pushed forward. But Jeune has never minded, never resented. Looking at her now, I think I need that more than I realized.

But the rancid-walnut taste of her guilt leaves a dry feeling in my mouth. She's lying.

Jeune lashes out with both hands in rapid succession, trying to land a punch to either side. I grab her wrists and spin her around, crossing them over her waist and pinning them against her. "I don't believe you," I hiss into her ear.

She chuckles darkly, not bothering to struggle. "Of course not. Liars don't trust anyone. And I don't think you've said a single thing that's honest since you told us your damned name."

My cheeks warm in anger. "If you didn't throw Hayes overboard, what were you doing that was so important, you didn't see him fall?"

She slams a foot against my knee. It's a basic move. I should've seen it coming, but my guard is lower than it should be, so it's as effective as it is crude.

Jeune whirls away from me and glares. "You know what, Saoirse, you answer one question—one sodding question—and I'll tell you: Why did you take this job?"

I flinch. That wasn't the question I was expecting. "For the money."

"Really?" She scoffs in disbelief. "And yet I've never seen you spend a single coin. So where does the money go?"

Rain. It's all for Rain.

I jut out my chin. "You don't want to talk to me about what I spend money on."

We're not fighting anymore. Just circling each other, watching.

"What does that mean?" she says.

"I know you buy *keil* beads."

Her steps falter. "How—"

"Laa'el told me." A lie. But if I'm right and Laa'el is the one selling her the beads, she'll believe me. "What do you use them for?"

"None of your business," she snarls.

"I wasn't aware the concept of 'none of your business' was one you're familiar with. From the moment I got here, you've made everything about me your business."

"Are you *seriously* still mad about the first night? It was harmless!"

"It was an invasion of privacy. And I *know* it wasn't supposed to be you snooping through my room. You volunteered."

"How the hell would you know that?"

"Devlyn told me."

She laughs incredulously but doesn't look amused. "Then he also must've told you I was just curious."

"Why are you so interested in me?" We stop circling. Stand perfectly still, waiting.

"There aren't many women in the Palace guard. The only other is Laa'el, and she doesn't talk to me," she says. "I was curious. I thought we could be friends."

So did I.

But that window slammed shut when Hayes went overboard, Jeune did nothing, and she lied to me about why.

I fold my arms and offer her a lie in return: "I don't want to be friends."

She flinches. I taste her hurt—sharp, cold, metallic—and I feel it in my teeth.

"Clearly." Her tone is biting. She shoves out of the ring. "I don't know what the hell this is, Sorkova, but I want out. You seem like someone who's used to winning. I forfeit."

She storms out of the room, letting the heavy double doors thud behind her.

CHAPTER THIRTY-FIVE

Unquenched, Unsated

There's a reason I don't make a habit of running alongside large bodies of water. At least, not without yielding to my instincts and diving in.

But today, that's not an option. As I run on the beach with the ocean to my right, the usually simple exercise feels strenuous.

Current goal: get accustomed to the nearness of water without losing control. With Hayes's party less than a week away, I'm running out of time.

My thoughts circle to Jeune.

There's a pit where my stomach should be when I think of her. I want to be angry with her, but I just feel guilty.

I force Jeune from my mind. Focus on running. One foot after the other . . .

But then my mind drags me to Hayes. Another person I had no intention of liking. But I can't deny it to myself any more than I can act on it.

I run faster.

Even with my racing thoughts and sprinting feet, it's not enough to drown the tugging sensation within me, pulling me to the right. To the water.

At least, it started as a tug. It gets stronger with each passing moment. The longer I spend near the open water, the more forcefully it pulls.

Swim.

I push myself faster.

Swim.

And faster.

The water responds with a *yank*.

I lurch to the right, tripping over my ankle and crashing to the ground. A spray of sand whirls in my wake. It gets into my eyes, my mouth, my hair, making me cough.

Swim.

My head throbs with desires unsated as I get back to my feet, brushing sand from my pants.

I start running again.

The ache in my head intensifies, and the pull in my stomach swells.

My feet slow as I massage my temples. My head feels like dry kindling beside a lit match—ticks away from bursting into flames.

Maybe I should give in. Take a quick dip in the waves. So long as there's no one—

"What the hell?" Devlyn's unwelcome voice slices through my contemplations like a newly sharpened blade. He's running behind me. "I thought you ran with Jeune. What are you doing here?"

At the sound of his voice, the water's call shifts from a benign longing for the waves to a thirst for blood.

Kill.

I rub my forehead harder.

KILL.

The Siren Song is so loud, I can't hear Devlyn until he's at my side, jogging in place. "Did you not hear me? This is my usual running time. I want the beach to myself."

He's close—*so* close—and the water is a few paces away. Killing him would make things easier. He caught me poking around Hayes's office. He watches me too closely. With a few notes, I can pull him under the waves. His watchful stares will drown with him, the pounding in my head will subside, and the water will stop calling.

My eyes flash at the enticing thought.

"Sorkova, are you seriously ignoring me?"

I squeeze my eyes shut and rub the heels of my palms over my eyelids to hide the glowing silver from him.

Kill.

I shake my head. I *need* to be in control. If I can't resist killing one man, how will I resist an entire ship full of them for Hayes's party?

"Sorkova?" Concern colors his previously harsh tone. "Everything all right?" He places a hand on my arm.

It sizzles where it comes into contact with my skin.

Kill.

The ocean sings at me.

Hayes.

Another voice, louder than the first. Not the ocean's—*mine*.

Killing Devlyn means I can't be at Hayes's party. And if I'm not there, Hayes will be at the mercy of those trying to kill him.

I hiss at my warring instincts and double over. "Don't touch me."

Devlyn's hand jerks back. "What's wrong? Should I—"

He fades away.

The sound of his voice and the lapping waves, the smell of the sea and worn leather, the brightness of the sun and white sand, all fade into sweet, glorious nothingness.

My head is throbbing, I'm lying on my back, staring at the soft gray ceiling of my room at the Palace. It feels off. Beams of muted yellow streak the gray. Some lightbrain has opened my curtains. Something I've intentionally avoided since I closed them when I moved in.

The thought of having to get up and draw them again makes me groan.

"Hey, Sorkova. Thought you'd be happier to see me."

At the sound of his voice—lune above, how I'd missed that voice—I sit up.

"Carrik?" I search the room, grinning when I locate him sitting in my desk chair pushed to the foot of my bed.

He's tossing his mother's dagger casually from hand to hand. When he sees me eyeing him, he winks and tucks it back into the sheath on his boot. His *new* boot, I note.

"In the flesh." Carrik comes to the side of my bed, grinning. He leans over, arms extended, clearly intending a hug, but I hold up a hand, stopping him.

"One tick—" I look him over. He looks good. Polished like the shiny leather of his new black boots.

He's decked out in the colors of Keirdre, navy blue and gold, with new boots, a new holster for his sword around his waist, a new sheath for his dagger, and an official-looking haircut. He'd look almost like a new person altogether if not for that impish grin and the mischievous glint in those brilliant green eyes.

"What happened to you?" I say.

"You don't like it?"

I laugh. "Of course I like it. You look like you took a bath in ranis."

"You know the only thing I like better than getting an updated wardrobe?"

I smirk, sensing he's preparing for a joke. "No, what?"

"Getting an updated wardrobe with someone else's gold."

I laugh along with him, and he enfolds me in a tight hug, resting his chin on my head. "I've missed you, Sorkova."

"I've missed you too. I don't have anyone to spar with." I pull away, scoot over, and pat a space in my bed to give him room to sit. "What are you doing here?"

"You don't know?" he says in surprise. "I was told you cast the vote that made my new position possible."

"Lune above," I mutter, "did Hayes tell you that?"

"Hayes?" Carrik raises an eyebrow. "I didn't realize you were on a first-name basis with the Crown Prince. I guess this means you're on a first-name basis with the Prince of Keirdre *and* the Enforcer of Serington," he teases.

I roll my eyes. "Congratulations, Carrik." I force a smile. His happiness is infectious.

I want to warn him. Tell him what Enforcers *really* do. What he'll have to do. But I don't.

"Thanks, Sorkova."

"You never explained what you're doing *here*, in my chambers."

Carrik draws his eyebrows together. "You don't remember? You passed out. On the beach."

It floods back in with a rush of exhaustion and a stinging reminder that my headache is persistent. I throw my head onto my pillow with a groan.

"Saoirse." Carrik nudges his shoulder against mine, tone chiding. "What were you doing running on the beach? Water makes you sick."

"I was training," I mutter. "Trying to, anyway. The Prince—"

"I thought he was *Hayes*?"

"—is hosting a party on a ship next week. I'm supposed to guard."

"On a ship? Saoirse, you *just* passed out. Why can't you sit this one out?"

The simple answer: because if I do, Hayes will die.

The complicated answer: if Hayes dies, it will be my fault for falling so easily for the Raze's plan.

The impossible answer: if something happens to Hayes—

I don't finish the thought.

"I can't," I say.

"Why not?" he demands. "You shouldn't be on a ship, and you know it."

A knock at the door cuts off my response before I can think of one.

"Can I come in?"

It's Hayes.

I sit up, resting my back against the headboard. "Come in."

Hayes opens the door. His eyes linger on Carrik sitting next to me in the bed.

My tongue bathes in something rancid and bitter like a rotting grapefruit. Hayes's jaw tightens.

I see it. Carrik sees it.

Almost subtly, Carrik shifts away from me, putting more distance between us.

Hayes looks from Carrik to me and clears his throat. "Can I talk to you?"

"Of course, Your Highness." I turn to Carrik as he stands to leave. "How long will you be here?"

"Just today. I have to go to Phydan after this. I'm training, so I'm shadowing each of the other Enforcers. Vanihail's last on my rotation."

"I'll see you then?"

Ghost of a smirk. "Of course. Who else is going to humble you?"

"I imagine the answer to that is the same with or without you—nobody."

He tosses his head back and laughs. "Goodbye, Sorkova. Think about what I said—stay safe."

I want to give him a parting hug, but Hayes is still standing there, watching with ocean eyes that care too much, so I settle for a smile as he walks to the door. He bows to Hayes before he passes. "Your Highness."

Hayes nods stiffly, barely looking at him. He doesn't divulge his standard no-bowing policy or request that Carrik call him Hayes.

Hayes waits until Carrik is gone to speak. "I didn't realize you two were so close." His tone is glacial.

I don't owe him an explanation, but I say, "We were friends in the Barracks."

"I didn't realize you had friends."

I don't respond.

He takes a breath. "How are you feeling?"

"Fine."

"Why were you on the beach?"

"Practicing. If I'm going to be on a ship surrounded by water, I need to acclimate."

He comes closer. "Maybe this is a bad idea."

My eyes narrow. "I'm going."

"Saoirse—"

"*No.*" I don't mean to snap, but I do. "I'll be fine."

Hayes's eyes search mine. He doesn't speak for so long, I hope he's given up. Then, softly: "You scared me. When I saw you, I thought you were dead." His voice cracks. "I don't know what I'd do if something happened to you. And if it was my fault—"

"Stop." It's too much. *I* caused this. *I* killed every single person whose death makes it easier for the Raze to assassinate the Royals. *I* told the Resistance that killing the Royals would bring down the barrier. Every potential threat to Hayes's life is *my* doing.

"I'm going," I say. "This isn't a debate."

His shoulders sag. "Most days, I admire your bravery, but right now, I hate it."

"I'm not brave, Your Highness. Maybe your father can't see it yet, but you're going to be a great King someday. You're going to fix what your father broke. Which means I need to keep you alive. And I will. You said you trust me. Prove it. Trust me when I say I can handle myself." To prove my point, I sit up straighter. "Did you want something?"

He clearly has more to say, but he nods. "Your family is here."

"You sent for my parents?"

He looks at me like I've said something absurd. "Of course. They're important to you, and you—" He stops. Looks away.

His emotions taste murky. There's sadness. Fear. Worry. And, nearly overpowering the rest, longing. Not the sweet, innocent kind. The kind that's so rich, it hurts.

"Thank you," I say softly. "For bringing them."

He's still not looking at me. "I'll send them in."

Hayes leaves. A moment later, I hear a squeal, and a pouf of hair is shoved in my face as the girl who owns my heart throws her arms around me.

My parents stand at the other side of my room, watching.

"Beansprout." I smile through gritted teeth. "What are you doing here?" I meet Mom's eyes over her head with a sharp look.

Rain shouldn't be anywhere near the Palace.

"The Prince said you were sick," says Rain. "What happened?"

My attention is back on her. My arms tighten, and I inhale her familiar orange-and-tree-sap scent. "Nothing," I tell her. "I'm not getting enough sleep."

I sense neither Dad nor Mom believes me, but I don't owe them an explanation. They brought her here. After everything I've done to protect her, and they so carelessly throw her back in the line of danger?

I turn Rain around and start to braid her hair. "What are you doing here, Rain?"

She knows I'm serious when I use her name.

"I heard you were sick—"

"I don't care if I'm stone dead," I snap, unable to hold it in. "Stay away from the Palace."

She flinches at my tone and pulls away. "I just wanted to make sure you were all right," she mumbles.

"I can take care of myself," I say.

"Right." Her laugh is derisive—a tone I've never heard from her before. "You're invincible, and I'm the little runt you have to take care of."

There's that sodding word again. "*Runt.*" My fury with Trellis Ruster returns, as intense and fiery as it was in the downpour. "Don't listen to the Rusters." I try to braid her hair again, but she twists around to glare at me.

She's never glared at me before.

"It's not just the Rusters. It's everyone, it's everywhere, it's *you*."

"What?" I must've heard her wrong. "I would never—"

"You'd never say it." She cuts me off. "You'd probably never even think it, but your actions scream it: you think I'm incompetent."

"I don't think that, Beansprout."

"Really? You won't even *look* at Mom and Dad because you think they shouldn't have brought their little invalid, runt daughter to the big, scary Palace."

I glance at them. They edge closer to the bed, and I can't help a scowl.

Rain sees it, and her eyes narrow accusingly. "See?"

I steel my expression. "I'm worried about you. You shouldn't be here." Especially considering that blackmail note I can't mention with our parents here.

"I'm safer than you are," she says.

She's wrong. Yes, I've done more to incur the Royals' wrath, but I spent years training at the Barracks. I can sing men to my will. I can protect myself, and she's all but helpless. "You're twelve. You're still a kid."

She folds her arms stubbornly. "You're seventeen—*you're* still a kid. I don't *want* you to feel like you have to take care of me. I just want you to be my sister."

"I *am*. And as your sister, I want you to get a chance to enjoy being a kid."

Another harsh, bitter laugh. "What's to enjoy? You won't let me make friends."

My eyes sting. I've never seen this side of her. "Because I want you to be safe."

"Safe to do *what*?" she demands. "Sit around and wait for you to save me? You're always there when I need it. Just this once, I wanted to be here for you. You'd do anything for me, Saoirse. I know that. You joined the Barracks for me, you trained harder than anyone else for me, you took your side job for me, you took this job at the Palace for me . . . You ever think that maybe— just maybe—I'd do anything for you too?"

I shake my head. "That's different."

"How?"

I speak before thinking. "I don't need you here."

Hurt. I taste it—sharp and cold—and I see it on her face, quick as a flash of lightning.

"That's not what I meant," I say quickly. "I mean that I took those risks because they were necessary. But I'm not in danger. You should've stayed home."

Her ice-blue eyes harden. I've never experienced Rain's wrath before. Which might explain why I'm so wholly unprepared when she says, "Was I in danger when you killed Trellis Ruster?"

From the back of the room, I hear Mom gasp and Dad say, *"What?"*

I stare at my sister. "How do you—"

"I heard about it at school. Peryn Ruster's father was found dead in his home. You didn't think I'd figure it out? You think I'm a fool as well as useless?"

"Of course not!"

I have so much more to say—more to explain. I want to tell her how the thunderstorm fueled my rage. How the water pulled and pulled until I was an unraveled ball of twine. I want to tell her that I remember her soaking wet in a pile of blankets, so young and all alone, and knowing instantly I'd love her forever.

But I don't. I don't say anything.

I've never fought with Rain before. Never had her look at me like I was anything less than a heroine from the stories I used to read her—a character willing to battle droves of beasts to save her.

I didn't realize how much I needed that. As much as I like to pretend she needs me to protect her, the truth is, I've always needed her more. Whenever I feel the weight of my mistakes, she absolves me. Whenever I hate myself for letting my parents down, she loves me.

I never expected her to look at me like what I am—a monster. A selfish, violent creature who uses my love for her to justify what I am.

For Rain. It was all for Rain.

Except that's not true. I don't kill because Rain needs me to. I kill because I want to.

I didn't join the Barracks because I wanted to provide for her. I joined because I hate pretending to be an ikatus and I wanted to prove I'm not weak.

Rain watches me, waiting for a battle I don't know how to fight, but I just sit. Silent. Defenseless. She's right. There's nothing I can say to change that, and I don't have the energy or will to lie to her anymore.

She slides off my bed. "Fine. I won't visit you anymore. Goodbye, Saoirse."

I was always afraid Rain would wake up one day, see me for what I am, and hand my ugly, selfish heart back to me.

But I was wrong. She doesn't return it. She leaves with it and doesn't give me so much as a parting glance.

"Saoirse." It's Mom. "What is she talking about?" There's a quiver in her voice. I taste her fear.

I don't even think about trying to hide it. "I killed him." I sound hollow. "After you told me what he said. I don't regret it. I know that makes me a monster."

"You're not a—"

"Stop lying." Dad steps toward me, but I flinch. "Don't. Please don't be nice to me." I hug my knees to my chest and tell them the truth I've been dancing around since my first kill: "Sometimes, I wish you hated me," I whisper. "I can taste every time you're terrified to be around me. Or to let Rain near me. Or disappointed in me." My voice cracks. "I think it would be easier to swallow if you didn't love me."

I stare at my bed, not looking at them. "You should go. I don't want Rain wandering around the Palace alone."

Dad doesn't try and move closer to me, but he doesn't leave either. "You're not a monster."

"Yes, I—"

"No." He raises his voice, talking over me. "Being a monster is too easy. You don't get to claim you're a monster just so you can pretend you don't have choices. You do, and you keep choosing wrong. We love you for who you are, but we fear what you choose to do."

I don't move until I hear the door close behind them.

CHAPTER THIRTY-SIX

Penn Seed

The water has long since turned to ice, but it warms me from the inside like a bowl of hot stew.

The washroom tub is a dingy little thing, but sitting here submerged in frigid bathwater is the best I've felt in weeks. Maybe lunes.

It's well past midnight and the washroom is empty, leaving me alone with my endless thoughts. I usually bathe quickly, but tonight, I needed more. Water in solitude is my fortress. With no one near, there's no call to do anything other than *breathe*.

Try to, anyway. It's hard to relax when all I can think about is Rain. I always knew she would hate me someday. I just didn't realize that day would come so soon.

In need of a distraction, I slip deeper into the tub, forcing my mind to drift.

Thoughts of the Temptress fill the void my sister vacates. It does nothing to lift my spirits. I never asked questions about my marks—their jobs, their lives, their families—and now I have no choice.

Okkler was aggressive. He slid a hand up my blue dress and tried to kiss me. He was a fun kill. I sang him a slow, soothing tune and watched as he slammed his wandering hand in a doorjamb, over and over, like a beating drum, until he drank the *shikazhe* and his pain ended.

Hayliss Velkner was sweeter. Older. I wore red that night, and he didn't stand a chance.

I remember them all. Each drop of poison, each slice of my blade, each wisp of the current was another life taken and another paved stone on the Raze's path to killing the Royals. I figured they'd done something to deserve it. Something that would cause a group like the Raze to target them.

But I never asked because I didn't want to know. I told myself detaching from my marks was smart, to keep things uncomplicated. The reality, I now see, is more disturbing: I was *starving*. Too hungry for the kill to question the source.

Now I'm asking questions—but it's too late.

I sit up, pulling my head from the water. The cold of the room smacks me in the face as water drips from my tangled hair.

Standing, I *expel* the water from my body until I'm bone-dry and freezing enough to don my nightclothes.

I twist my hair into a braid as I head back to my room.

Something shimmers in the corner of my vision as I push open the door to my chambers.

My freya candle is burning blue.

My first thought: Rain.

I jab a hand over the flame. I'm eager as it fires off ash into a sheet of vellum—but it's blank. My Employer.

For several ticks, I stare at the empty page.

I have my misgivings, but my hand obliges before my mind is convinced.

My feet are the next to betray me. They carry me to bed, where I fish beneath the mattress for my *lairic* beads.

As I trace the bloodstone over the vellum, I'm resolved—I'm

not going to kill this mark. But time is ticking away until Hayes's party, and I need answers. My training instructor at the Barracks always stressed that the best way to solve a problem is to find a pattern. And the best way to scout out a pattern is to compile more data.

The more information, the clearer the pattern. The clearer the pattern, the more obvious the answer.

The text spreads across the vellum. There's no name this time. Just a location.

Odd.

Maybe this should give me pause, but it doesn't. My Employer is a man, and if he has something unsavory planned, all I need is a song for protection.

That's my self-justification, but it's deeper than that. He *used* me. Lied to me. Made me a pawn in a game I never asked to play. I want answers, yes, but I also want to prove to him that he was wrong to make a fool of me.

I tug a cloak over my nightclothes and slip out the window. I have no perception of passing time as I drag my feet to the location listed—what looks like a lonely cottage near a copse of samsam trees. There are no lights, but it's late, so that's to be expected.

I huddle closer to the side of the stone cottage and lean my face against a window. The glass is freezing. There's a thin layer of something light and fine coating the glass. From a distance, it looks like frost, but from up close, I see it's dust, lining the window from the inside.

An itch in my mind, nagging and persistent.

This cottage doesn't feel sleepy—it feels abandoned.

I barely have time to tense before large hands yank my arms behind my back.

I *feel* around the air—searching for moisture—but the night is dry.

Thousands of thoughts ricochet around my mind, but one stands out, bold like blood on snow: whoever this is sent a message to the Temptress—which means he absolutely cannot see the face of Saoirse Sorkova.

I shove my tongue behind my false tooth and spit out my *keil* bead just as my assailant spins me around.

There's a hood pulled over my attacker's face, obscuring his features. Still, I taste his shock at my appearance.

I figure he's seen the posters, but it doesn't matter. Reproductions of my face don't capture the magic of my beauty in person.

Three more hooded figures creep up behind him.

What the hell is this?

My lips part to sing—and a hand clamps my face. Fingers encased in salty leather force a wad of something soft into my mouth.

I throw back an elbow in a last-ditch attempt to escape, but I don't stand a chance. I'm strong, but I'm still one person against four, and my weapon of choice is lodged down my throat with a wad of balled-up fabric.

Another hand presses against my face, and a strange, sweet scent invades my nose.

Ground penn seed.

One of Aiya's specialty herbs. In small doses, it's a sleeping aid. In large quantities . . .

The world melts into a dizzying spiral, getting darker and darker until it fades to nothingness.

CHAPTER THIRTY-SEVEN

Weakness Feigned

My eyes open, but my surroundings are so dark, it makes no difference.

It's silent. I hear what I think is wind whistling outside, but aside from that, nothing.

Whatever was previously thrust into my mouth is still here, so I breathe through my nose, calming my heart and gathering my bearings.

My arms are bound behind me, secured by a cord thicker than rope. I'm sitting with my back against a wall and my legs tangled beneath me, sore from being stuck in this position.

My eyes are useless, so I try to *feel* around the room. Feeling for drafts and moisture—anything to tell me where I am.

The gag prohibits speech, so I release a muffled grunt, loud as I can, and strain to hear the effect. The grunt carries with the slightest echo. I gather I'm in a wide, dusty, mostly empty room with flat walls.

Which does nothing to elucidate where I am, why I'm here, or how to regain use of my bound arms.

Obviously, my Employer sent the message for an ambush, which means the Raze is behind this, but I can't figure out what

Right before my head is plunged into the trough, the gag is ripped free.

My head breaks the surface of the water. It's ice-cold. I breathe in deeply, taking it in through my mouth, my nose, my *skin*. Savoring it.

I feel *alive*.

And I'm livid. Questions circle the drain of my mind—who are they? If the Raze didn't hire me, who did? Where is my Employer?

My boiling rage drowns my curiosity.

I don't bother counting the ticks to see how long they keep me here. Time has no meaning. Nothing has meaning outside of the water, my rage, and the soon-to-be dead men around me.

Kill.

All I want is blood.

Kill.

My head is yanked back by my hair. "Tell me, who are you—"

A song flows out of my fury. They stop. Their hands drop from my body like stones and they stare, eyes ablaze, as I sing.

I rise. The melody swells, and the silver flash of my eyes illuminates the room.

"You." I nod to the man closest to me. "Untie me. *Now*."

"O-of course."

His fumbling fingers unknot the cord.

I flex my hands and twist my wrists as I traipse in a circle around the men, singing, plotting. I finish my circuit behind the trough, facing their blank stares.

I smile.

The water from the trough rushes into the air. It swirls, tracing patterns overhead, before I release it. The mass of water crashes over us. I stop it before it reaches the ground.

Thousands of water droplets float, suspended in midair, like a rainstorm caught frozen in time.

The men don't move.

I inhale. I *sense* the sparks of their excitement, *taste* the sweet spice of their lust, *feel* the blankness of their minds.

"Who has a blade?" I ask, sprinkling sugar into my tone.

Four hands shoot up, eager to please. Dolls. Mine.

"On my count," I say breathily, "you and you"—I point to two of the men—"are going to ram your blades into each other. And you two"—I point to the remaining men—"will do the same. Understand?"

They stare.

Kill.

I know their stillness isn't refusal, but my rage demands a response, so I sing another four notes. *"Do you understand?"*

Nods all around, but still no words. I don't think they're capable.

"Excellent." I smile again, this one dripping with malice so sweet, I lick my lips to taste it. "One . . ."

The four of them draw their swords.

"Two . . ."

They turn, blades out, facing their partners. "Three."

Their blades slash in sync with one another.

All four of them stagger. They each have a blade buried in their gut, but their eyes stay trained on me, desperately seeking my approval even as they collapse to their knees, with scattered thuds and low groans.

Blood seeps from their wounds, soaking their shirts.

One of them reaches for me. He falls forward, and the force of his body smacking the floor drives the blade deeper into his stomach. The pointed end tears through his back and his body stills.

The other three don't even notice.

I turn and march away, the taste of their collective longing lingering on my tongue as I make my way to the door. The frozen raindrops spill, soaking me and the four bodies behind me.

For five ticks, I savor the feeling. The rush of a fresh kill, the pulse of victory.

But then the sensation from the water fades like cheap dye, and the urge to kill—now sated—ebbs like the tide.

I'm no longer a siren standing over the spoils of her conquest but a girl, surrounded by the bodies of the men who kidnapped her.

The kill normally makes me feel like I've won something. But all I feel now is empty.

I lurch for the exit, too exhausted to walk straight.

The Raze tried to torture me. The people I thought I worked for. But if the Raze didn't hire me, who did? Why did my Employer lie? And if my Employer doesn't work for the Raze, how did they contact me tonight?

I'm outside now. I shiver. Even though the air is freezing, my body isn't reacting to the cold. It's reacting to the startling and terrifying realization that I didn't even *ask*.

My head is flooded with questions, but the moment I had an opportunity to demand answers, I lost control.

That is what scares me. *That* is why I can't walk straight. Not because of the kidnapping, or the attempted torture, or even the four-way murder—but the realization that I am powerless to resist my own instincts.

Grisham Haverly said it in the portrait room: sirens are monsters. We kill endlessly with no remorse.

I want Rain. I want to hug her, breathe in the scent of tree sap and oranges, and know that she loves me.

Except I let her see what I really am, and now she hates me.

My parents told me I can control this—that I'm not a monster—but they're wrong. Tonight, when it mattered, my instincts won. Just like they always have.

Just like they always will.

CHAPTER THIRTY-EIGHT

Water on Fire

I rely on my feet to guide me, first to that little cottage where they grabbed me to retrieve my fallen *keil* bead, then, from there, back to the Palace.

Tears rain down my face. I don't know when I started crying, but I can't stop.

Scaling the side of the Palace is as mindless as my trek here. My mind is foggy as I climb through my window—so foggy, I don't notice my chaeliss light is already lit until I turn to find a figure sitting on my floor.

His back rests against the foot of my bed, his chin slumps against his chest, and his eyelids droop like a wilting flower.

At the sound of the window closing, he jumps.

My teary eyes widen. "Hayes—I mean, Y-Your Highness." I duck my head, hiding my swollen red eyes.

"Saoirse." His voice is as bleary as his face. "We need to—" He breaks off, scrambling to his feet. "Did you just call me Hayes?"

I keep looking away, composing myself. Trying to.

He's in front of me, hands cresting my shoulders, ocean eyes intense. "Have you—are you all right?"

"I'm fine." I push his hands away and brush past him.

In need of something to do, I set my hands on my desk and rest my weight against them.

I fold my arms when I realize they're shaking.

"Saoirse, what's wrong?" He's behind me now, hands feather-light on my arms, sliding up and down. Calming.

I shrug him off.

"I already told you, I'm fine, Your Highness. What are you doing here?"

He doesn't answer. His arms encircle my waist like a belt. But warmer. Softer. More Hayes.

I'm a dangling thread away from coming undone. "Y-Your High—"

"Shhh . . ." Ignoring my protests, Hayes turns me around and gently guides my face into his shoulder. "It's all right if you need to cry. I promise I won't look."

I inhale, basking in his warmth despite myself. As soon as the world around me is obscured by the velvety fabric of his shirt, the floodgates open and the sobs pour out of me, unencumbered.

He's warm. *Safe.* And I realize as I burrow my face deeper into his shirt that I've memorized his scent.

He doesn't say anything. His left hand rests against my back, rubbing soothing circles, while the other stays banded around my waist.

"Hayes . . . ," I whisper, caught off guard by the intimate embrace.

"Shhh," he says again.

I normally oppose being shushed like a child, but the soft lull of his voice calms me in a way I won't admit, and I find I'd rather sob in silence than speak.

Without warning, Hayes scoops me into his arms, one arm

under the bend of my knee and the other supporting the weight of my back.

He carries me to the bed.

My face is still hiding in the folds of his clothes, but I hear two heavy thunks as he kicks off his shoes before climbing into the bed, me cradled against his chest, murmuring in my ear. "You don't have to talk. You don't have to do anything." I feel pressure on the top of my head—his lips.

The liar in me wants to shove him away and kick him out, but the truthful part—the part I'm too exhausted to deny— wants to stay right here, wrapped up in soft hands and gentle words. *His* hands, *his* words.

Tonight, I realized that fighting my instincts is futile. And for some reason, my every instinct pulls me to Hayes.

I close my eyes and allow myself to drift to sleep.

When I pry my tear-glued lids open, I'm still tucked against Hayes's chest. He has one arm around me, running his hand up and down my side absently, while his other hand rolls a *keil* bead between his forefinger and thumb. He looks puzzled.

My eyes snap open fully, and I yank away from him. "What are you doing?" My gaze jumps from his hand with the bead to the open bedside-table drawer he's obviously poked through. "Were you looking through my stuff?"

Hayes holds up his hands. "Sorry. I was looking for your chaeliss stone." His eyes sweep my face. "You use *keil* beads?"

"That's none of your business. *Sir.*" I snatch the bead and lean over him to shove it in the drawer, slamming it shut.

"You don't seem the type to use *keil* beads," he says. "You don't seem like the kind of person who cares what others think."

"I don't." It comes out as a snarl.

He holds up his hands again. "I believe you. If there's anyone who's above the opinions of others, it's you."

I tense, waiting for the inevitable question that never comes.

My lips slacken from a vicious snarl to a confused frown. "You're not going to ask me why I use the *keil* beads?"

"No."

I frown. "You're . . . not going to ask me what happened last night?"

"Not unless you want to tell me."

I stare at him in confusion for so long, he chuckles. "You're adorable when you let yourself emote."

The emotion seeps from my face, and he sighs. "I should've seen that coming." He swings his legs out of bed. "I should leave. I know when I'm not wanted."

I watch him slip on his boots. His shirt is crumpled from a night of resting against my headboard and his back must ache, but he doesn't complain.

"Thank you," I blurt before I can remind myself not to.

He freezes, halfway finished lacing up his second boot. "What did you say?"

I roll my eyes and avert my attention from his steady gaze. "I won't say it a second time."

He smiles. It's as gentle as it is sad. "You don't have to push me away. You have no idea how badly I want to be that person for you."

"What person?"

"Someone you trust."

My eyes search his. I've never had a man look at me the way he is now without a song as a preface. "Why?" I ask finally.

He steps closer and leans across my bed, slowly, slowly, waiting for me to move.

I don't.

He presses his lips to my forehead in a whisper of a kiss that tingles like rain.

My first instinct: close my eyes. Lean forward. Savor the feeling of being cared for.

I don't wait for my second instinct to set in.

"I can't tell you why." His lips tickle my skin. "You wouldn't believe me."

He pulls back to look at me and, for a tick, I'm swimming in the vibrant sea of his eyes. As much as I tried not to, I know Hayes. He's naive and easily distracted. Impulsive. Too trusting. Lonely. And funny and genuine and beautiful and *good*.

I know the shape of his smile, the taste of his happiness, the heat of his embrace, and the blue of his eyes. And I *like* him.

But everything he knows about me—everything he wants from me—is a lie. The tick passes and I scoot away. "Goodbye, Your Highness."

He hovers, eyes gentle. "I'll see you at dinner? Or should I replace—"

"No special treatment," I say. "I'm scheduled for the evening shift, so I'll see you then. Sir."

He nods but doesn't leave. "You *can* trust me, Saoirse. I trust you. Implicitly."

"You shouldn't." The words are out before I can rein them in.

"Why not?" he challenges. "Have you done something you're not proud of? So have I. So has everyone. It doesn't matter. You probably think I know nothing about you—and maybe you're right—but that doesn't mean I don't know *you*."

I want to laugh, but it's not funny. "No, you don't."

"You're stubborn and snarky and rude. You're annoyed by just about everything. You think I'm childish. You're irreverent and short-tempered and—" He crouches next to my bed, putting our eyelines on the same level. "You take my breath away."

I forget how to breathe. My brain forgets how to function. Somehow, I still manage to say, "Because I'm rude?"

He leans forward until there's a whisper of air between our foreheads. "Because I see you." His voice is soft. "You're stubborn because you're passionate. You're snarky because you're too smart for the people around you. You're rude because you don't like wasting time. You hate everything, but that means the things you do, you do with conviction. You think I'm childish because I am. And you make me want to grow up."

I feel exposed. He's laying me out bare, and I have no retort to keep him away. I'm utterly defenseless against the onslaught of his words, but I don't want to fight back.

"You're irreverent because you respect hard work." He keeps going. "You're short-tempered because you've been overlooked your whole life and you know you deserve more."

"Your Highness—" It comes out as a croak.

"Let me finish. You won't let me know you the way I want to, but you could drown me or burn me, do your absolute worst to me, but there's nothing you could do that would shake my belief in you."

He's sincere like he always is. But there's a limit to how much anyone, even Hayes, could understand or forgive.

A deadly melody in the dark of night.

A whispered order, "Two drops on your tongue."

Vacant eyes dragged downstream.

Blue, endless blue.

And so much red.

I take a breath. "You should go, Your Highness."

I've caused him so much disappointment, I should be immune to its effects, but right now, the taste burns. I tell myself it's better this way. Whatever he thinks he feels for me is a lie.

Still, part of me—scratch that, *all* of me—wants him to stay.

Instead, he smiles, eyes sad, and says, "Goodbye, Saoirse." Even though I asked him to leave, the moment he does, I feel cold.

I fall back on my bed and close my eyes.

Prince Hayes Finnean Vanihail is full of warmth and excitement and energy and he's so, so beautiful . . .

But his brother was murdered by my kind. His father swore to kill every last one of us. Even if my species wasn't meant to be long-ago extinct, Hayes himself is hunting me, the Temptress who murdered his best friend.

On all fronts, the Prince is dangerous. But as I stare at my ceiling, I'm struck with the realization that I'm not afraid of all the ways he could hurt me. Instead I'm petrified at how easy it would be for me to shatter him.

CHAPTER THIRTY-NINE

Worse Than Death

The Raze never hired me.

It's the only conclusion that makes sense.

I spend the day in my room with my thoughts. When my evening shift starts at four after midday, I'm still processing.

Do I trust the word of the men who snatched me? Of course not. But I can't deny that as much as I hate to admit I've been fooled yet again, it makes sense.

The Raze's most recent victims (*my* victims) don't fit with their usual targets. Their goals (kill the Royals) don't align with what the Raze would want. The wealthy fae who control the Raze profit from King Larster's corruption. Killing him off is the last thing they would want.

Which means my real Employer is someone else. Someone who would want to rid Keirdre of the Royal family and blame the Raze in the process.

The only answer that makes sense is the Resistance. After all, I already know they're plotting against the Royals and black-mailing me to do it.

During the evening shift, I avoid eye contact with Hayes and barely speak. He doesn't say anything, but I taste his hurt at my silence. After this morning, even if I wasn't trying to make sense of the Raze and Resistance, I'd want to stay away.

At midnight, I return to my room. My hand hovers over the doorknob—it's unlocked. Which is odd because I'm *sure* I locked it.

Carefully, I push open the door and take swift inventory. Nothing is out of place. I check under my mattress and my nightstand. My runed beads are all accounted for.

Did I forget to lock my door? I don't think I did, but if nothing was taken, what other reason would someone have to enter my room?

My fingernails dig into my palms, breaking the skin. I barely notice. It's the morning of Hayes's party and I'm out of time.

I did everything I could—snuck aboard the *Sea Queen* this morning, made final preparations for the party, came here to visit Drina—but I fear it's not enough. I sit on my aunties' sofa, a black garment bag in my lap. "This doesn't look like what I asked for."

"It's better." Aiya paces the room, inspecting her roses and larkspurs. "It's a dress. I had it made with your measurements." She taps the stem of a wilting rose and coaxes it to stand fully upright, petals fuller and brighter than before.

"So . . . not what I asked for," I clarify. I drape the bag over the back of the sofa. "Listen, I don't need a dress—"

"You do," Aiya insists. Satisfied with her flowers, she stands by Drina, who leans into her side. "You're attending a Royal function. You need a nice dress. If you'd just open it—"

"I don't need to open it," I say. "I need a way to be on a boat surrounded by water and not kill everyone on board."

Maybe I'm harsh, but I'm too anxious to feel guilty. A dress isn't going to fix everything I've ruined or keep Hayes alive.

Auntie Drina scowls. "You could at least pretend to be grateful. Aiya was excited to buy that for you."

A dress seems pointless. Dress a monster up in pretty clothes and she's still a monster. My dad said it himself—the only difference between me and a monster is control. And I have none. Which is why I'm here.

Still, I take a breath. "Thank you, Auntie," I say to Aiya. "I'm sure it's lovely. I hadn't really thought about what I was going to wear."

Aiya grins. "I figured as much."

I'm reminded of Jeune, digging through her wardrobe, hunting for a dress for me to wear that night out with Hayes and Devlyn. The memory has me meeting Aiya's eyes with a smile.

But then I remember how we left things. That Jeune hates me and is possibly plotting to kill Hayes, and my mood sours again.

I clear my throat. "Did you find anything for me?"

Drina hands me a glass vial. "This should help."

I inspect it by firelight. The glass is tinted dark green, obscuring the color of the liquid inside. "What is it?"

"What you asked for. *Xaladran*," says Drina. "It's a poison that will dull the effects of your . . . urges."

"Why have you never given me this before?"

"It's for emergencies," says Drina darkly. "*Xaladran* is incredibly dangerous. It's worse than death. And there's no antidote."

"What's worse than death?"

"Too much will strip you of your abilities. Permanently. A *very* small amount will give you what you want—it will dull the call of the water, but it will also dull your other abilities."

"For how long?"